Thunder on the St. Johns

Also by Lee Gramling:

Riders of the Suwannee
Trail from St. Augustine

Thunder on the St. Johns

A Cracker Western
by
Lee Gramling

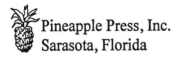
Pineapple Press, Inc.
Sarasota, Florida

Pineapple Press, Inc.
P.O. Drawer 16008
Southside Station
Sarasota, FL 34239

LIBRARY OF CONGRESS CATALOGING-IN-PUBLICATION DATA

Gramling, Lee, 1942-
    Thunder on the St. Johns / by Lee Gramling
        p.   cm.
    ISBN 1-56164-064-6 — ISBN 1-56164-080-8 (pbk.)
    1. Frontier and pioneer life—Florida—Fiction. 2. Florida-
-History—1821-1865—Fiction. 3. Family—Florida-
-Fiction.
    I. Title II. Title: Thunder on the Saint Johns.
PS3557.R2228T48   1994
813' .54—dc20   94-12984
                                                                    CIP

First Edition   10 9 8 7 6 5 4 3 2 1

Design by June Cussen
Composition by Cynthia Keenan
Printed and bound by
        Kingsport Press, Kingsport, Tennessee

Dedicated to the memory of my mother and father,
Margaret and Gene Gramling

With special thanks to
Dr. James M. Denham and
Mrs. Lillian Dillard Gibson
for their historical insights.

Central Florida, 1850

Contents

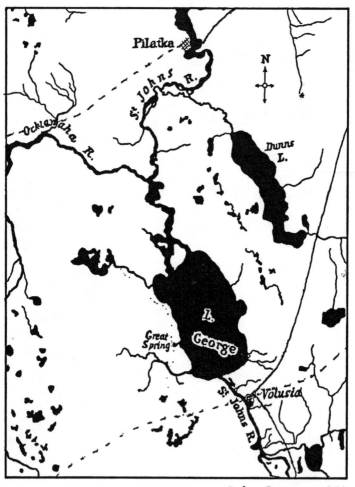

Lake George, 1850

1

Twin rows of oil lamps cast shimmering yellow daggers across the dark waters of the river as the paddle-wheeler chugged toward a bend past a deserted landing a short distance north of Savannah. Suddenly, with a puff of steam and a clank of machinery, the pilot reversed gears and steered hard for the near shore.

No sooner had the hull touched the sandy bottom than the gangway lowered and a tall man dressed in a black broadcloth suit and black hat stepped across, leading a sleek dun mare with dark mane and tail. As they reached the bank the man placed a calming hand on the mare's neck, then turned and waved to the unseen pilot. An instant later the heavy pistons throbbed and the boat began backing away once more into the current.

"Hold on there!" The voice came from a stairway leading up to the Texas deck, a short distance abaft the pilothouse. "Bring her back in again, pilot! We want us some words with that man down there!" The

9

speaker took the remaining steps two at a time and advanced to enter the wheelhouse, his fist dropping to the butt of a large revolver at his belt.

The gears ground again and the boat halted its backward motion. A second man, young and elegantly dressed, appeared from the shadows of the lower deck and stepped up on the gangway. He crossed it in two strides and leapt nimbly over the few feet of water at its far end. The man with the horse stood waiting, his feet slightly apart and his arms at his sides.

"Yes, Mr. Jordan?" He spoke calmly, but with a hint of mild impatience as they faced one another in the crisp winter air. "You had something more you wished to say to me?"

"I do. That's my horse you've got there, and I want her back."

"As we both know, Mr. Jordan, this *was* your horse. That was before you believed your three queens would beat my three treys, plus a fourth in the hole." He shrugged. "It was the luck of the cards, sir. I backed my belief with cash, you with a bill of sale for the mare . . ." He raised a hand carefully to the left breast of his jacket. ". . . which I now have in my pocket."

"Bill of sale be damned! I've raised that mare from a colt. She is three-quarters pure Arabian!"

"I believed you when you first told me that, sir. Else I would not have accepted your chit for the value you placed upon it."

"Damn you! That is my mare, and I want her returned this instant!"

"She is my mare now, Mr. Jordan. Won fairly and squarely, before witnesses."

"The witnesses are my friends. They will testify

to whatever I say. My family has been in this country for more than three generations, and is well-known all through this part of Georgia." The young man curled his lips into a taunting sneer. "If I were to claim, for example, that you cheated during the play . . ."

"*If* you were to say that, Mr. Jordan," the gambler's voice suddenly grew colder than the night, "it would be no matter for family or witnesses. It would be between the two of us." He paused, deliberately fixing the other's eyes with his own. "And would be settled on the instant." After a moment he shrugged and went on in a more conversational tone. "I half expected something of the sort. It is why I arranged with the pilot to set me ashore at this place, discreetly, in hopes of avoiding any difficulty. I still think it would be best if we parted peacefully, without further unpleasantries."

Jordan stood watching the black-clad man balefully, his mouth compressed into a taut, thin line. When nothing more was said, the latter gathered the mare's reins and turned to mount. "A good evening to you, sir . . ."

"Liar! Cheat!" The younger man's voice suddenly became shrill as he produced a wicked-looking four-barreled pepperbox from his coat pocket. "I'll see you in hell before —"

The words broke off in a scream as two .36-caliber balls from twin Navy Colts ripped without warning into Jordan's chest and throat. The man in black had drawn and fired in a single motion, from crossed leather holsters beneath his jacket. He stepped quickly to his left as the big pistols bucked in his hands. Jordan's pepperbox discharged one harmless barrel into the air, then fell to the ground from lifeless fingers.

There was a shout from the wheelhouse as the passenger who'd gone in with the pilot appeared at the rail.

"Beau! Damn it, Beau! . . ." The large pistol in his hand started to lift almost of its own accord. But it halted suddenly as his eyes focused on the man on shore, standing perfectly still in the moonlight with both Colts aimed squarely at his chest.

"Don't even give it a thought, Quinn. I'd as soon not have two damned fools' blood on my hands tonight." Quinn Jordan lowered his pistol slowly, then let it fall to the deck with a dull thud.

"Good. Now you just stand there with both hands on that rail while this young lady and I start making some tracks away from this place." He replaced his left-hand pistol in its holster and once more gathered the mare's reins.

"You won't get away with this! You're dead already, only you don't know it yet!"

Without answering, the man in black started moving slowly toward the sheltering darkness of the forest behind him. His remaining pistol was still in his hand, cocked and aimed deliberately at the speaker's breast.

"That's my brother lyin' there, and we got three more brothers at home who'll take this just as hard as me. An' five or six cousins besides. We'll all be looking for you now, mister. Lookin' for the one who shot our youngest down in cold blood!"

The man with the horse reached a narrow trail among the trees. After retreating another dozen yards he holstered his second pistol and mounted quickly.

As they cantered away to the south he could still hear Quinn Jordan shouting wildly into the night:

"There won't be no place left on this earth where you can hide! No swamp thick enough or hole deep enough or mountain high enough! We won't ever stop lookin'! Not if it takes ever one of us the rest of our days!"

The big man's voice was still railing indistinctly as they rounded a bend and the rider bent forward to let the mare line out into the frozen moonlight.

It had been almost ten o'clock when they left the river landing, and the north Georgia night was bitterly cold this time of year. Wind off the frozen marshes numbed the cheeks and pricked at the ears with icy fingers. Back among the trees, white patches of snow could be seen clinging stubbornly to lower ground where the sun seldom reached.

The man in black had not seen any other horses on board the boat, and so doubted there would be an immediate pursuit. But he had it in mind to keep riding through the night in any case, not making camp until shortly before dawn and then only in some secluded spot where detection would be less likely.

From conversations he'd heard in the salon and around the gaming tables, there was reason to believe the Jordan family was every bit as well-known and respected in this part of the country as the younger one, Beau, had suggested. That meant there would be small chance of anything resembling a fair trial with regard to the shooting, nor the question of the mare's ownership either. As far as the local folk would be concerned he was a stranger, a murderer and a horse thief, with the usual penalty for the last two being death by hanging.

His only hope at the moment was to try to make

it to some place beyond the Jordans' power and influence. Yet he had no cause to doubt Quinn's threat of a long and tenacious pursuit. A big family like that, with abundant resources and friends in high places, could keep up the chase for years if need be. How far could he run? Where on this continent could he find a refuge where no one had heard the name of Jordan, or cared?

There was the West, of course. Only a few years earlier people had begun migrating there by the thousands, lured on by tales of gold and dreams of unimagined wealth in the hills of California. But a gambler was a skeptic by nature, putting his faith not in hopes or dreams but in the odds, which, if known, could always be relied upon. San Francisco was nearly four thousand miles away, a full year's journey, and almost every foot of it shaped by risk and danger. Those were odds the man in black cared little for.

Another frontier lay closer, one he had been hearing about ever since childhood. It too was a place of danger — as much, perhaps, but no more than the far West. And the distance to this frontier was only a few hundred miles. That fact alone ought to reduce the odds against him considerably.

The mare was running well, her breath rising now in rhythmic puffs from delicately flared nostrils. Somewhere he remembered reading that the Saracens of old had preferred mares over stallions in battle for their intelligence and manageability when the going became difficult. She was a beautiful animal, certainly, and perhaps it was that as much as his own pride which had led him to refuse any compromise in the face of the Jordans' threats.

Not that she might hope for much in the way of proper care and treatment from her new master. He'd no land and no resources aside from his guns, this one suit of clothes, and the saddle he'd kept when he exchanged his last mount for a modest stake to permit entry into the next game of chance which came along. It had been that way almost as long as the black-clad man could remember and showed little sign of improving in the future. It was why until now he had managed to avoid attachments of any kind, with humans as well as horses.

The rider lowered his head and turned up his coat collar against the biting cold. If the stories he'd heard were correct, at least the weather on that Florida frontier promised to be more temperate and agreeable than any he might expect in the far West. . . .

Joshua Carpenter paused at the edge of the small clearing with his arms full of firewood, watching the figures of men and women move about in the rough square made by four canvas-covered wagons. His brother's oxen were unyoked now, and he could see Elias leading them to a place where the dry winter grass might be just a little thicker in the bend of a creek some twenty yards away.

It was a long three months since they'd left their family's place in North Carolina, and only yesterday they had finally crossed the St. Marys River into Florida. With the January frosts and the low swamps hereabouts, the land didn't look too different from that Cape Fear River country where Josh had spent the first thirteen years of his life. Not that he wasn't aware of all the territory they'd covered in between, at the steady plodding pace of six to ten miles a day. Every mile of it had been filled with trouble and danger, it seemed, with wild beasts and dense swamps, and so many creek and river crossings he'd stopped counting weeks ago when he got up to a hundred.

It would take at least another month or more of travel before they finally reached that lake country farther south, where his brother had made up his mind to stake out a homestead. With the time needed after that to find a place, file claim on it, clear the land and get a crop in, they'd be doing well to have even a one-room cabin built before winter set in the following year.

Josh smiled in spite of himself as he watched Mary Carpenter unload food and cooking utensils from the box at the back of their wagon, passing them down into the willing but sometimes clumsy hands of six-year-old Sara Jane, who was laying them on a blanket beside the rear wheels just inside the square. In the glow from the late afternoon sun he couldn't help thinking what a handsome woman his brother's wife was. At thirteen Josh was of an age to begin noticing such things.

He'd been on the trail to Florida long enough now to wonder too how many more years she'd be able to keep looking like that, with the cares and trials of frontier life weighing more heavily on her each day. Three weary months of outdoor living already, and maybe twice that long again before she'd have even a chance to set up something like real housekeeping. Clearing the land and making a crop came first, and building a home would just have to wait until that task was under way.

Not that Mary was the fragile type some men manage to get themselves saddled with. She was a worker, and game as they come. Cheerful, too, most of the time, no matter what this country or bad luck seemed to toss their way.

'Lias had moved over to Hoke County after his marriage, and Josh hadn't really known Mary before joining up for their trek to Florida. He'd come along mostly to give his parents one less mouth to feed, the times being hard as always for small farmers in the Carolina tidewater. But after some weeks on the trail he'd decided that he fully approved of his brother's choice in women. The fact was, he liked Mary a lot.

A pine lighter knot slipped from his arms and Josh stooped to pick it up. As he did he saw the Budds' two mangy dogs beginning to sniff around the Carpenters' wagon again, looking for spare food or some kind of mischief to get into. Satan, 'Lias's own black mastiff, was down on his belly behind the front wheel, growling low in his throat and explaining in dog language that maybe those two would be better off to go looking for somebody else's territory to do their nosing around in.

He saw Mary glance at the dogs, then go back to setting out things for supper. Nobody else seemed to pay them any mind. Old Levi Budd and his three grown sons had finally managed to stir themselves from the jug at the back of their first wagon, and were just now starting to unhitch their eight mules in order.to lead them to water and grass.

Josh didn't care for the Budds. He'd felt that way ever since the four rough-looking men with their two sparsely loaded wagons had overtaken the Carpenters a week ago back in Georgia. When his brother accepted their invitation to travel together on this final leg of the journey, he must have had a little trouble keeping his feelings to himself. Because 'Lias had taken him aside that night and spoken seriously to him, man to man:

"We don't got to become their bosom friends, Josh," he'd said. "And we don't got to approve of everything they do. But on the frontier we got to learn to be neighborly towards all kinds of folks. In this country everbody's got to pull together and help each other when there's the need." He put a hand on his younger brother's shoulder. "And right now, I reckon maybe it's us that's got the need for help a heap more'n the Budds do."

Josh could agree with that part at least. Ever since they'd had to leave the Rogers family behind when Mr. Rogers came down with the fever, they'd had a time of it trying to make it through those coastal lowlands with just themselves and the one wagon. The extra teams and the Budds' strong backs had made a big difference when it came time to cross a creek or a river, or to cut logs for a corduroy road through some patch of low swamp where the trail had played out.

But still Josh didn't like them. And he couldn't even explain exactly why that was.

He saw Mary stand up and poke her head around the wagon cover to catch his eye, letting him know with a wry smile and a toss of her head that she'd appreciate it if he'd stop his daydreaming long enough to bring the wood in so they could start the fire for supper. He nodded and hurried across the clearing.

'Lias had untied old Maude, their milk cow, from the back of the wagon to lead her to water and grass by this time, and he was returning when the fire was finally lit and starting to blaze up nicely. He took his hands from his pockets and held them out over the crackling flames, pausing a moment to inhale the pleasant odor of pine smoke and take a good long look around them.

"Goin' to be a cold one tonight again," he said. "I reckon."

After a minute he indicated a patch of woods nearby with a jerk of his head. "Josh, you better go cut some palmetto fans from that stand over yonder while it's still light enough to see pretty good. I'll help you tote 'em in and build a windbreak under the wagon here whilst Mary and Sara Jane are busy gettin' supper on."

He seemed to consider, then glanced over his shoulder at the wagon behind theirs and shrugged. "Might's well cut down a mess of extras too, 'long as you're about it. I expect maybe the Merriweathers could use a bit of a windbreak their ownselves."

He slipped the big Bowie knife from his belt and handed it to Josh. "You go on along now. I'll be over to help in a couple of minutes."

Josh took the knife and crossed to the palmetto brake his brother had indicated, kneeling beside it in the gathering twilight and starting to cut fans with broad back-and-forth sweeps of the sharp blade. From time to time he paused in his work to look back toward the camp where three fires could be seen now, red and yellow beacons against the growing dark of the surrounding woods.

Their cheerful glow seemed to make even the rough enclosure of the wagons take on a kind of familiar homey look. It was the only home Josh Carpenter had known for three months now, and the only one he could expect to know for many more months to come.

2 🖑

JOSH MADE GOOD PROGRESS on the palmetto fans at first, but when the knife started to dull on the tough stalks and his arm began to tire, he found himself having to do more sawing and less slashing, taking one stalk at a time and making a regular job out of it. Cutting the fans for one windbreak would have been enough of a chore after a full day of walking. Twice that many meant working up a sizable sweat here in the chill evening air.

Not that it was in him to complain or feel resentful about the extra work. It was just a part of what 'Lias had said earlier about helping out other folks whenever they'd the need.

When he sat back on his heels at last to take a rest, he wiped his sleeve across his forehead and glanced back toward their camp. 'Lias was standing beside the Merriweathers' fire now, talking to Mr. Merriweather and probably explaining how to arrange the palmetto fans so as to stop the wind and reflect the fire's warmth back under the wagon where their sleeping rolls would be laid out. It was the kind of thing that would be perfectly obvious to Josh or any of his family, who'd been raised in the country and spent much of their lives out-of-doors.

But the Merriweathers were city folks, from Charleston and later Savannah, they'd said. Until a few months ago it seemed like they'd never had to go any farther than the mercantile store or a corner grocery to get what was needed for a comfortable life. Possibly they'd had someone to send out on even those small errands.

From the looks of their wagon, they'd had enough material comforts at one time. It was so loaded down now with furniture and other fixings there wasn't even room inside for the older couple to sleep. That was why they'd had to make do with spreading their blankets on the ground underneath.

Both appeared to be in their fifties, and it was enough to make a fellow wonder why such folks would leave a home in the city at that time of their lives to start all over again in the wilds of Florida. Of course they might not have had any choice in the matter. But the past wasn't something folks asked each other about on the frontier. And the Merriweathers hadn't volunteered any explanations of their own.

At least one thing was clear. Those two older people were having themselves a regular time of it now, trying to learn enough to get by in the wilderness.

When the Carpenters and Budds had come across their camp two days ago, they'd been out of food for almost a week and had been reduced to living on roots and bark tea. Mr. Merriweather had an old Yaeger rifle, but just barely knew enough to prime and load it, let alone stalk game in the dead of winter. All he'd managed to shoot up until then was one scrawny cottontail.

So the newcomers shared what they had — most of it coming from the Carpenters' meager store — and 'Lias had killed some rabbits and squirrels the next morning to make a hot stew with a little meat in it. And when the time came to move on, they'd felt obliged to ask the Merriweathers to join them, at least until they could reach someplace in Florida where there'd be a chance for those two to make it on their own.

The shadows were growing dark among the trees now, and Josh went back to cutting palmettos with a will. Before long 'Lias joined him and they both started gathering the fans to take back to camp.

With Mr. Merriweather helping, in another half hour the men had constructed windbreaks under both wagons. They took the time to collect some leaves and pine needles too, to put under their blankets and bedrolls for the night. When they'd finished this task the welcome smell of coffee filled the clearing, and supper was finally ready.

The meal consisted of beans, bacon, and fried cornbread. They'd been forced to travel late in order to find this patch of dry ground beside the trail for a campsite, and there hadn't been time to try restocking their larder with fish or fresh meat before dark. That was something 'Lias intended to remedy tomorrow even if it meant getting a late start or perhaps camping in the same place for a second night. He hadn't consulted the Budds about it yet but expected few complaints. A glance toward their own cook-fire suggested they weren't in much better shape themselves.

Still, the supper was hot and well-seasoned with herbs and wild onions Mary found along the trail. And there was plenty of it. Everyone set to with a will, talking little in order to do full justice to the food before them. By the time the plates were empty and a fresh pot of coffee was bubbling on the coals, even Mrs. Merriweather was beginning to look a little more cheerful than she had earlier in the journey. Until now she'd scarcely left their wagon, speaking just to her husband and seeming to avoid the company of the others when they gathered of an evening or at the daily noonings.

But tonight she was seated on the log 'Lias had pulled over beside the fire for a bench, talking to Mary as if they'd known one another for years. The older lady had even found a bit of ribbon and lace somewhere in their wagon, which she'd presented to Sara Jane with proper solemnity and a warm twinkle in her eye.

She must have been a beautiful woman at one time, Josh thought. It still showed in her smile, though her face and body were pale and thin now as if she'd suffered from some serious illness. Her manners and speech were of a kind he and his family had almost no experience with, clearly marking her as one of the Quality — probably born to a big plantation or some fine brick home in the city. It made her appear as out-of-place in this swampy wilderness as a Kentucky thoroughbred hitched to the business end of a plow.

When the meal was over and everyone was finishing a second cup of coffee, Mrs. Merriweather suddenly rose and began bustling around the camp like an Irish maid, gathering up the metal dishes and utensils and fending off Mary's protests with a determined shake of her head.

"No, no, my dear. You just sit there where it's warm and be comfortable for a while. You've done so much for us already, the least I can do is try to help out with the few tasks I may be able to perform reasonably well. And it turns out washing dishes is one of them." She picked up a bar of soap from the shelf at the back of the wagon and pulled her shawl more tightly about her shoulders, making ready to start for the creek.

Elias spoke quietly from where he was sharpening his knife by the light of the fire: "Joshua, why don't you go on down there with Miz Merriweather and help keep her company for a bit? You can take some of them traps out the back of the wagon and set 'em up in the most likely places for otter or beaver. Save me the trouble of havin' to do it later on."

Josh knew his brother's suggestion had nothing to do with setting traps. As a rule 'Lias was almighty particular about how and where his string was put out, and he generally insisted on supervising that job himself. But there were creatures in these dark woods that could be a lot more dangerous than otter or beaver. They'd come across the sign of a prowling panther just the night before. This was his way of sending somebody along to look after the lady without her feelings getting hurt.

He crossed to the wagon and glanced back to see his brother's approving nod as he slid their double-barreled percussion shotgun out and settled it in the crook of his arm. Taking hold of a string of traps, he slung them over his left shoulder, then smiled at Mrs. Merriweather and led her to a sandy bank of the creek where she could wash her dishes and he'd have a good view of the forest all around.

When she was finished he asked her to wait while he ran out the traps and set them up near the water in places he thought might be the best spots. Then he returned to help the lady carry her dishes back to camp.

'Lias had gone to bring their oxen and milk cow into the enclosure in the meantime, and Mary was spreading out the ground cloths and blankets as they returned. Little Sara Jane was already asleep in her own snug bed inside the wagon.

"'Bout time for one more cup of coffee," 'Lias said as Josh stood the shotgun against the near wheel and Mrs. Merriweather started handing dishes to Mary to be replaced in their box of kitchen things. "Then I reckon we'll all of us be ready for a good night's sleep."

He dipped a gourd into the barrel on the wagon and knelt to put some cold water in the coffeepot to settle the grounds. Mr. Merriweather had just come back from seeing to their own camp and livestock.

"Be another long day tomorrow I expect," the older Carpenter went on, lifting the pot to pour for his companions. "Me, I plan to be up before first light and do a little huntin'. Might's well try the fish in that creek there, too, before we move on." He looked at his wife and grinned. "Not that I got anything against your beans an' hoecakes, honey. But God's bounty seems to be mighty evident in this Florida wilderness. And I've a mind to take advantage of whatever it is that He'd be pleased to put in our way."

Mr. Merriweather was seated on the log beside

the fire. He lowered his head to take a swallow of coffee, then looked up under his hat brim at the man across from him.

"I'd surely like to help with the gathering of food, Mr. Carpenter. Seems it's the least I should do. But the trouble is," — he hesitated, then shook his head — "I just don't have any experience at it. I'm afraid I'd only get in your way, or what's worse, maybe scare off the game while you're trying to stalk it."

'Lias hunkered down and placed both hands around his cup to warm them before glancing at the other man. "Don't you pay no mind to that right now, Mr. Merriweather. I reckon Josh and me can keep meat on the table for a while. And Mary. She's a fair hand with a fishing pole herself. In the meantime, why don't you just keep a eye on whatever it is we're doing, an' then ask questions when you come to something you don't understand? I've the feeling you're a pretty smart gent, and you'll pick things up quick enough once you set your mind to it."

"I suppose so." The older gentleman didn't sound convinced. "I do appreciate your patience and willingness to help us learn. But until we can manage to 'pick things up,' as you say —" He looked at his wife. "Well, it's only fair that we should offer to pay you something for your trouble in the meantime. We are not entirely without resources, you know. Even here."

Elias met the other man's eyes for a moment, then shook his head. "No, sir. I thank you kindly, Mr. Merriweather, but no. 'Twouldn't be decent or Christian to take money for doin' what we'd be doin' anyhow, reaching out a helpin' hand to somebody in need. It wouldn't no way be right." He paused and glanced over his shoulder toward the other campfire, where the four Budd men were squatting in a circle and now openly passing the clay jug between them.

"And if you'll pardon me saying so," 'Lias lowered his voice to just above a whisper. "It might not be too awful smart either, lettin' everbody you run into along the trail here know you've got some cash money about your wagon or your person. There's them would take that as a mighty big temptation to appropriate it for theirselves. And you need to realize too that the only law you're liable to find for quite a few miles now is going to be at the end of a Colt six-shooter or a double-barreled shotgun."

Merriweather followed the younger man's glance. Then he nodded and shrugged, a helpless expression in his eyes. "I see what you mean," he said quietly. "It seems we have a good deal more to learn about life on the frontier than simply how to procure meat for our table."

"It'll come, Mr. Merriweather." 'Lias drained his cup and rose to replace it inside the wagon. "Don't you worry. All it means is just keepin' your wits sharpened up and not ever taking nothing for granted. Appears to me that's a pretty good rule to follow 'most anytime, no matter where a fellow sets out to make his way in the world."

He turned and caught Josh's eye. "All right, boy. I reckon it's time we got ourselves into those blankets now, an' . . ."

With a suddenness that made the whole party jump, the Budds' dogs started barking and baying furiously from where they were tied now behind one of the wagons. Satan rose up from his place too, looking out beyond the circle of light and growling ominously.

"Hello the fire!" The voice came from a hardwood thicket some dozen yards beyond the enclosure. "How's for some coffee? Maybe a bite of supper if you've got it to spare?"

Without answering, 'Lias reached in the wagon and brought out his heavy hunting rifle, holding it in both hands while he turned around with his thumb on the hammer. Josh eased himself away from the fire until he could feel the stock of the shotgun where it rested upright against the wagon wheel. His fingers closed around it and he looked up to see several pistols and a rifle in the Budds' hands as well.

"You folks won't be needing all that hardware," the voice said calmly from the darkness, "unless you've got in mind to have yourselves a war. It's just me out here. And I'm friendly."

There was some movement about the Budds' campfire as old man Levi stepped forward to peer into the shadows. After a moment he spit a long stream of tobacco juice on the ground and uncocked his pistol. "All right," he called, shoving the weapon back into his belt. "Come on in and let's have a look at you." His boys were standing behind him, and Josh saw them relax as he said that. But he realized suddenly that the oldest, Jake, was not among them.

'Lias nodded and lowered the muzzle of his own rifle, then spoke softly to Satan, who had moved to his side still growling low in his throat. At his words the black mastiff quieted and sat back on his haunches, his ears pricked and alert.

The Budds' dogs kept yelping and dancing at the end of their ropes until Clyde reached down to take a smoldering stick from the fire and throw it at them. A moment later the stranger stepped into the light.

He was wearing a black broadcloth suit and a low-crowned black hat with a wide brim. His polished calf-high boots were of a matching color, and Josh thought it odd that he didn't have on any overcoat — considering the weather and how well-dressed the man appeared to be otherwise. The horse he was leading was a fine-looking animal, a sleek line-back dun that evidently had more than a trace of Arab in its heritage.

As he came near the Carpenter's wagon the man paused and looked around the camp slowly, his eyes resting on each member of the company in turn. His thumbs were hooked in his belt, and when they moved slightly to one side two pearl-handled Colt revolvers could be seen, their butts tilted forward in the black leather holsters at his waist. For a long moment no one spoke.

Mary had risen to replace the pot of beans on the coals. She hesitated when she saw the revolvers, eyeing the newcomer warily before returning to the wagon to start slicing bacon into a frying pan with a large knife. 'Lias set his rifle aside and began to rinse out a cup.

"Not much here in the way of fancy vittles," he said as the visitor finished tying his horse to the wagon tongue and stepped toward the fire. He knelt to fill the cup with coffee and handed it up to the stranger. "But you're more'n welcome to the same as what we've et."

The man in black smiled for the first time since he'd appeared from the darkness.

"I expect if it's good enough for you folks, it'll

suit the likes of me just fine." He tasted the coffee, then reached up to push his hat back from his forehead. "And a good deal better than anything else I've had to eat these past few days."

Mary brought the frying pan and set it over the coals. "Supper will be ready in a few minutes, Mr. . . ."

At first it appeared the newcomer hadn't heard. He took a swallow of coffee and set the cup down carefully before finally turning to face his hostess. When their eyes met he reached up to remove his hat and bowed formally. "The name is Ramsay, ma'am. Charles Nathan Ramsay when I first came into this world." As he replaced the hat and bent to take up his cup again, he added, "But most folks now just call me Chance."

'Lias rose and held out a hand, which the other took in a firm grip. "I'm Elias Carpenter. This here's my wife Mary and my brother Joshua. These other folks are Mr. and Mrs. Merriweather, and the gents by the next fire are the Budds — Levi, Jake, Reuben and Clyde."

Josh saw that Jake had reappeared from behind one of the wagons now, carrying a long Kentucky rifle in his hands.

The man who had introduced himself as Ramsay bowed to Mrs. Merriweather, then nodded to the others. "I'm pleased to make your acquaintance."

While the bacon sizzled and Mary placed some left-over cornbread beside the fire to warm, Ramsay finished his coffee and returned to his horse. After retethering the animal to make it easier for it to reach the dry grass nearby, he removed a blanket from his bedroll behind the saddle and laid it gently across the mare's back.

On his return he accepted a bar of soap and a towel from Mrs. Merriweather and went to the creek to wash his hands. If he was aware of the curious eyes that followed his every movement, the stranger gave no sign of it.

Yet Josh knew he was not alone in wanting to learn more about this well-dressed and well-armed visitor. There was something about the man — some vague impression of danger perhaps — which had everyone here strangely on edge. The Budds had returned to their own fire, passing around the jug again and talking among themselves in low tones. All thoughts of an early rest seemed to have been temporarily forgotten.

Apparently Chance Ramsay wasn't a man given to idle conversation, however, for when he returned he accepted a plate from Mary with only a brief word of thanks. He sat on the log and proceeded to eat his supper in silence.

3 🖋

"THAT WAS A VERY FINE MEAL, MA'AM," the newcomer said at last, setting his plate aside and reaching out to pour himself more coffee. "I can't recall when I've eaten better." He replaced the pot and held his hot cup in both hands, sipping contentedly.

A moment later Clyde Budd was standing beside him.

Clyde was the youngest of the Budd boys, perhaps seventeen or eighteen, yet big for his age, and with a reckless swaggering manner even 'Lias sometimes had a hard time ignoring. Josh knew that his brother feared no man; it simply wasn't in his nature to seek trouble when it could be avoided. And they'd faced enough difficulties on this trek to Florida without fighting among themselves. But there had been times when Clyde's hot temper and rough manner had pushed him almost to his limit.

Fortunately, the Budds kept mostly to themselves, and old man Levi in particular seemed to prefer it that way. Since he ruled his boys with an iron hand, there had been no troublesome incidents so far.

But it seemed the youngest Budd was looking for trouble now, and not trying very hard to hide it. He was standing only a few inches away from the stranger, staring down at him with his legs apart and a crooked, taunting smile on his lips. A brace of single-shot pistols were prominently displayed in his belt.

Josh glanced across the clearing and saw that old man Levi had disappeared into the woods temporarily. Reuben and Jake were standing by their fire now, talking quietly together but with frequent looks toward the Carpenters' camp which betrayed a clear interest in their brother's activities. The boy noticed also that the other Budds kept their weapons close at hand.

"Those sure are some fancy shootin' irons you've got there, mister." Clyde's eyes glinted in the firelight as he leaned forward and pointed, doing his best to make his smile seem like an innocent grin. "Right purty." He held out a dirty hand. "You mind if I hold one of them for just a minute? So's I can have me a better look at it."

Chance Ramsay took a long, slow swallow of coffee. When he spoke he did not meet the younger man's eyes.

"Yes."

"How's that?" Clyde seemed confused by the answer.

"Yes. I mind." The man in black sipped his coffee again, his face expressionless. After a moment he added, "Nobody touches my weapons but me." He shifted his weight slightly to glance up at the young man standing beside him.

"That's a pretty general rule with most men in

this country." His voice was mild. "I'm surprised you wouldn't know better than to ask."

Clyde's unshaven cheeks became flushed as he opened his mouth to speak, then closed it again abruptly. Ramsay had turned back to his earlier position on the log, looking straight ahead with his cup in his left hand. It appeared that as far as he was concerned, the conversation was over.

"You're awful high and mighty, ain't you?" the youngest Budd managed finally. A dangerous edge had crept into his voice. "Come in here wearin' them dude clothes an' bowin' to the ladies an' treatin' others like they was some kind of trash underneath your feet." He leaned forward so that his face was only inches from the other man's. "Who the hell are you, mister? What you doin' out here on this road in the middle of the night? You huntin' after somethin' or somebody?" His eyes narrowed suddenly and he turned his head to spit before straightening up. "Or runnin' away from it?"

"I've already said that my name is Ramsay. I hailed this camp in hopes of finding a warm fire with perhaps a bit of coffee and hospitality." The stranger glanced at Mary and 'Lias, smiling faintly. "Which I did, and for which I am very grateful."

His eyes and his voice grew colder as he turned back to Clyde and regarded him with a penetrating stare. "As to where I have come from, and where I shall go after I leave here, that is no one's business but my own."

"I'll be damned if it ain't! We don't know nothin' a-tall about you, mister. An' as far as anybody here can tell, you're just some kind of a high-toned thief or a God-damned killer runnin' from the law. I got me a good mind to . . ."

Clyde's hands moved toward the pistols in his belt, but as he met the visitor's eyes he seemed to change his mind. The hands lowered and he wiped them on his trousers. Levi had reappeared from behind the wagons now, and he was slowly crossing the enclosure with his other sons on either side.

Ramsay gave a slight shrug and turned his back on the man next to him. "You've a suspicious nature, boy. And a foul mouth to go with it. There are ladies present, and if I were you . . ."

"Damn it!" Clyde's face suddenly grew livid. He glanced at his approaching kin, then reached out to take hold of the seated man's shoulder. "You look at me when you're talkin' to me!"

What happened next occurred so fast Josh could not be sure of the exact sequence. It seemed that one moment Clyde's fingers were gripping the dark fabric of Ramsay's jacket, and the next the young man was lying on the ground beside the fire, gasping for breath and heaving his shoulders in an effort to recover the wind that had been knocked from him by the fall.

In the same instant Chance Ramsay rose and turned to face the remaining Budds with two Navy Colts in his hands. Their silvered barrels gleamed redly in the firelight. He stood perfectly still, but a reckless challenge had appeared in his eyes.

"I am neither a thief nor a murderer," he said evenly, "though whether or not you men believe that makes less difference to me than you may imagine. But there are limits to my patience. So if any of you feel the need to push the matter, this would be the time."

With two quick motions he reholstered both pistols. "Make your play if you want, and let's have an end to it."

Reuben, the second youngest, started to lift up his rifle but old Levi ground a heel down hard on his instep. The boy yelped in pain.

"You just stop an' think about that, Rube." The older man kept his eyes on Ramsay as he spoke. "I got a idea this gent would fill your hide with lead so fast you couldn't even begin to get ready for a shot."

"There's only one of him, Pa," Jake said in a broad stage whisper from a few yards away, "an' four of us. You reckon . . ."

"I *reckon*, boy, that the one of him is liable to turn out to be just a few more than what you're figuring on." He spat tobacco juice and shook his head. "An' this here's a damn fool business to be startin' no shootin' war over anyhow. Clyde was way out of line. I expect he'd better learn to put a leash on that tongue of his, or he's liable to find hisself pushin' up daisies afore we even reach that promised land to the south." He took a cautious step forward and looked down at his son. "Ain't that right, Clyde?"

The youngest Budd was sitting up now with his head on his chest, still having trouble breathing but appearing to be more angry than hurt.

"Damn it, Pa," he gasped. "That wasn't fair! He tricked me!" After a second he rolled over onto his hands and knees, then got to his feet with an effort. He glared at Ramsay. "If we can't shoot him, how 'bout roughin' him up just a little bit? I reckon without them big ol' horse pistols he ain't so much. I could take him easy!"

Chance Ramsay glanced at the others, then stepped back from the fire and made as if to unbuckle his gun belts. "All right son," he said, a faint smile playing about his lips. "If you're bound and determined to have yourself an education tonight, I expect I can be your teacher for one more lesson."

"Now hold on! Just hold on, the both of you!" Levi Budd reached out to take a grip on his son's belt from behind, jerking him roughly away toward the center of the clearing. "Clyde, you get your tail back over there to the wagon and stop any more of your foolishness. You already made your try onct, and you come up short. Get on over there now, an' slap some cold water on your face so's to cool yourself down a mite!"

Jake came and put an arm around Clyde's waist, leading him back to the nearest wagon with Reuben close behind. Levi approached Ramsay and spread his arms in a conciliatory gesture. "Boys!" he said sadly. "Ain't got the good sense God give to a chicken. What's a father to do?" He shook his head, then took a step closer and held out a hand.

"No hard feelin's, Mr. Ramsay? You know boys'll be boys. But I'll try and keep a tighter rein on that Clyde from now on anyhow. I reckon he's got a sight more to learn before he'll be fit to look a full-growed man in the eye."

Chance Ramsay took the offered hand. "No hard feelings, Mr. Budd. And thanks." He watched while Levi joined the others. Then he resumed his seat on the log and began to pour a fresh cup of coffee.

'Lias squatted by the fire to refill his own cup while Mary picked up the visitor's empty plate and finished putting things away for the night. Mr. and Mrs. Merriweather stood a short distance away, looking on but saying nothing.

At last Josh crawled out from under the wagon where he'd remained during the confrontation. He hesitated a moment, looking at Ramsay. Then he sat down on the log beside the man in black.

"That was some fancy move you put on Clyde," he said enthusiastically. "I admired to see somebody take the wind out of his sails for onct."

When the man didn't reply, the boy fell silent. After a short time he tried again. "I never did see anybody get two guns into play so quick!" He paused. "You generally hit what you're aimin' at? I mean whenever you pull iron so sudden like that?"

"Generally." Ramsay took a swallow of coffee. "If I have to. Fortunately, there wasn't any need for shooting tonight."

"That's true." 'Lias spoke quietly from his own place beside the fire. "And I reckon it was how fast you drawed made the difference between shootin' and not shootin' this time. Sort of got them boys to thinkin'. And after they'd done thought about it, weren't no chance for 'em to do much of anything else."

"That was the idea." Ramsay lowered his cup and glanced at the older brother. "I wasn't looking for any killing when I came here tonight, and I hoped to avoid it if there was any way possible."

"Yet you were ready enough to shoot." Mary Carpenter had returned from the wagon to stand behind her husband. "A sight readier than most, it seems to me." Her eyes were cool as she met those of their guest. "That makes me right curious myself to know the kind of a man you are, Mr. Ramsay. And how you come to be traveling this road so late at night."

The visitor looked at her, then shrugged and reached up to push his hat back from his forehead. "You ask a difficult question, ma'am. As to the kind of man I am, that is. I've thought about it often enough, but never have found an answer to satisfy myself." He paused.

"As to why I'm traveling this road so late, that's easier to explain. I found myself embarrassed for supplies temporarily and so kept riding in hopes of coming across some generous party of travelers like yourselves where I might obtain a meal." He smiled at her. "It was beyond my fondest expectations that in the process I would make the acquaintance of a lady of such surpassing beauty as well as cooking ability!" Chance Ramsay winked at 'Lias, and Mary tossed her head.

"Hmpf. Fancy words don't make a gentleman. And I've still got me a few questions that I'd like the answers to sooner or later!" She turned and climbed up inside the wagon, pulling together the blankets that covered its opening behind her with a sharp tug.

"Will you stay the night, sir?" Mrs. Merriweather spoke quietly from her place beyond the fire. "I'm afraid there's little to offer in the way of accommodations, but you are welcome to the warmth of our fires and the protection of our compound."

"Thank you, ma'am. It's kind of you to ask." Ramsay glanced quickly toward the Budds' camp, where the four men were finally starting to lay out their bedrolls for the night. He turned to 'Lias. "I would stay, but only if you think it will cause no further trouble."

The older Carpenter considered, then shook his head. "Don't expect so," he said. "We've had our disagreements with 'em too, time to time. But it don't appear in their nature to hold a grudge. Mostly they just keeps to theirselves, hoverin' round them two wagons like they was bees around a honeysuckle. Tonight was somethin' out of the ordinary, and I don't believe it would of happened a-tall if the old man had been watchin' close. Generally they don't even come round our fires of a evenin' to chew the fat." 'Lias hesitated.

"'Course I wouldn't take all them friendly words ol' Levi spoke too much to heart neither, 'f I was you. I've a idea he was just sayin' whatever he had to say so's to keep his boys out of a fight where they might come out second best."

Ramsay nodded. "I had that impression too. But when a man tries to avoid trouble for whatever reason, I expect the least I can do is meet him halfway."

He stood up to lead his horse inside the compound and unsaddle it. While the rest of the party were getting ready for the night, the man in black spent a quarter of an hour rubbing the mare down with handfuls of dry grass before he replaced the blanket on its back and then spread his ground cloth and remaining blanket near the Carpenters' fire.

Just before Josh closed his eyes, he looked over at where Chance Ramsay had made his bed and saw their guest arranging one of his gunbelts within easy reach of the saddle he was using as a pillow. The other weapon was already out of sight beneath the covers.

Now that was a careful man!

The pre-dawn air was cold and still when 'Lias Carpenter rose and began to gather his things for the hunt. Hoarfrost silvered the grass between low-burning campfires, and the motionless limbs of trees reached out ghostly fingers overhead as he arched his back to stretch the kinks from ground-stiffened muscles. Moving quietly so as not to wake the others, he gently broke the crust of ice on the water-barrel to take a drink, then replaced the dipper and stood for several minutes studying the darkened landscape outside the square of wagons. At last he took up his rifle and went to unleash Satan, moving silently off into the forest with the mastiff at his heels.

After a few minutes Chance Ramsay rose also. When he'd put on his hat and buckled his guns about him he drew on his boots, then knelt to add a few small sticks to the fire. While rubbing his hands together, he studied the ground and made note of the route the man and his dog had taken. Then he turned up his coat collar, tugged his hat brim lower against the cold, and after another moment was striding purposefully into the woods in the opposite direction.

By the time Josh opened his eyes a half hour later the shadows were fading and orange-red streaks had begun to color the eastern sky. Mary was already stirring about the fire as he climbed from his blankets and pulled on his shoes to join her.

Two shots seemed to shatter the morning stillness, echoing among the trees of the dense woods to the south. Mary and Josh looked at one another. They knew 'Lias had gone out hunting earlier. But these sounded more like the flat explosions of a pistol than the sharp cracks of a rifle.

For a time it was silent again. Then two more shots could be heard, followed several minutes later by the boom of 'Lias' rifle from farther away in the opposite direction. Everyone in camp was awake by now, going about their morning tasks. They all stopped what they were doing to watch when Chance Ramsay emerged from the trees with a bloody deerskin over his shoulder.

"Breakfast," he said, smiling cheerfully as he made his way between the wagons to the Carpenters' campfire. 'Lias' rifle spoke again in the distance while Ramsay lowered his burden at Mary's feet. The man in black turned to Josh.

"I could use a little help bringing the rest back to camp. There are a couple of fat turkeys out there, together with what's left of the deer. I hung the meat up from some tree limbs, but that wouldn't discourage a hungry predator for long."

Josh stared at the man beside him. "You got all that with only just a *pistol*?" he asked, his voice showing his disbelief.

"Yes." Ramsay shrugged, still smiling. "It's not so much the weapon, you know, as how a man's able to use it. Though Colonel Colt does make a fine firearm."

They were gone but a short time before reappearing in camp with their prizes. Soon Josh's older brother arrived also, carrying a deer of his own, together with an otter and two beavers that had been caught in the traps during the night.

This would be more than enough meat for their

immediate needs. But 'Lias decided it might be a good idea to stay here a day or two longer anyway, hunting and fishing and taking a well-earned break from the hardships of travel. They'd preserve the extra meat with salt and smoke, and could make a start at curing the hides as well. These last would be valuable items of trade once they finally reached a settlement.

While breakfast was cooking, 'Lias walked across the compound to discuss his plan with the Budds.

4 ⚡

Josh stood nearby to watch as Chance Ramsay sat on the log beside the fire and began cleaning his pistols, taking each one out of its holster in turn and removing the cylinder, then running a cloth through the barrel and wiping the parts carefully before reassembling it. The man in black checked the loads as he did so, and made sure the percussion caps were seated firmly on the nipple behind each chamber prior to reholstering the weapon.

"Those are genuine Colts, ain't they?" the boy asked after a few minutes, partly from curiosity but also in an effort to strike up a conversation with their untalkative guest. Neither he nor his brother owned a revolver, and they'd only seen a few of them in the poor tidewater country where they grew up.

"Uh-huh. Navy Model eighteen-fifty-one. The latest available." He held one up so that Josh could examine the barrel. "That engraving is of the Battle of Campeche, in the Texas War for Independence."

The boy shook his head admiringly. "They sure

are a couple of pretty shootin' irons. Clyde was right about that part last night, anyhow."

"Yes. But looks aren't everything. These are also very finely balanced and as accurate as any sidearm in the world at the moment." The man's face seemed to darken briefly as he spun the cylinder and replaced the second pistol in its holster. "Yet their purpose is to kill, like any weapon. And that," he concluded quietly, "is not always so pretty."

Mr. and Mrs. Merriweather joined the group while Ramsay got to his feet and went over to start rolling up his blankets and ground cloth.

"Will you be leaving right away, Mr. Ramsay?" the older lady asked. "It seems a shame that we have only just met, and now must part so quickly. You've surely proven your usefulness as a hunter. And if your journey should happen to take you in the same direction we are going . . ."

"I'm grateful for the thought, ma'am." The man in black bowed and touched his hat. "But I'll be on my way right after breakfast. I'm accustomed to traveling alone, and it has always seemed to suit my nature best."

She studied him for a brief moment, then shrugged. "As you wish. But I think I can speak for all of us when I say that you would be welcome." Ramsay glanced up at the others. Josh and Mr. Merriweather were both nodding their agreement. Mary seemed too busy with her cooking just then to turn around.

"My thanks again, ma'am." The visitor picked up his saddle and walked to where the mare was tethered nearby. "Perhaps we'll meet somewhere in Florida later on." When he'd completed his preparations he went to the creek to wash his face and hands. Upon his return, breakfast was ready, and 'Lias had rejoined the group around the fire.

"Them Budds ain't of a mind to stay," the other man was saying. He took a plate from Mary and reached out to remove a venison steak from its skewer over the coals. "Said somethin' about the place gettin' all fished out an' hunted out if the lot of us was to keep a-workin' it hereabouts." He squatted to fill his cup from the coffee pot. "I'd a feelin' that was only just talk, though. They'd somethin' else concernin' 'em. Don't rightly know what it could be, 'cept maybe what happened last night."

Ramsay glanced up from under his hat brim. "Well, if that's the case, they can set their minds at rest. In another hour I'll be gone, and with luck our paths will not cross again."

The older Carpenter didn't respond immediately. He cut a bite of meat and put it in his mouth, chewing thoughtfully. "I said *maybe* that was it." He shook his head. "But then again I ain't so sure. Seems to me them gents been acting kind of anxious ever since we crossed the St. Marys an' come to this here hard sand road yesterday mornin'."

He settled himself more comfortably with his back against the log and went on between bites: "Y'know, a team of oxes like ours is mighty handy in marshy ground where their hooves'll spread out and their strength'll pull a heavy wagon through the wet earth. But on a hard-packed trail they still ain't going to move any faster. Oxes is steady but slow. Them mules like the Budds got is different. They'll maybe struggle some gettin' through the swampy places. But you give 'em a good road and some wagons that ain't too heavy loaded, and they'll flat leave a team of oxes behind." He glanced at the Merriweathers.

"You folks mightn't of noticed it yet with your own two mules, because your wagon's so full of goods. But light as them Budds appear to be travelin' and with four animals to each wagon, we'd prob'ly be slowin' them boys down considerable from now on out. I got the feelin' maybe they're in some bigger hurry to get to wherever it is they're a-goin' than we are." He paused and took a swallow of coffee before reaching out to refill his cup. Josh looked across the fire at him.

"They ain't all that light loaded," he said, aware of the curious glances of Mary and the Merriweathers but paying them no mind. "You see the ruts whenever they come through that swampy place t'other side of the river? They was plumb deep for a couple wagons without nothing showin' in 'em any higher'n the tailboards. I'd a thought to remark on it at the time, only we got so busy afterwards with the crossin' an' all that I forgot."

'Lias looked at him. "You're right, now I think on it. An' that's a curious thing too, ain't it? But I reckon it don't make so much difference to what I was sayin' just now. They'd still be able to make a sight better time on a good road with their teams than we would, and it appears movin' fast may be some important to 'em." He shrugged. "Anyways, it'd explain why stayin' in this spot a couple days longer wouldn't suit their plans very much."

After a moment Josh had another idea. "You don't s'pose it could be because they've already got theirselves some place picked out down south of here?" he asked. "Some special piece of prime land they don't want nobody else gettin' to before they can?"

"Maybe," 'Lias answered. "I reckon that could be it." He looked at his companions and grinned. "But if that's the case I don't plan to worry myself a awful lot about it. From what I hear there's a passel of fine lands for homesteadin' all over this country. I expect we can still manage to find someplace to make our stand."

As soon as breakfast was over, Ramsay said his good-byes. He accepted a small sack from Mary containing part of the deer he'd shot, together with small quantities of bacon and cornbread, but declined the offer of additional supplies with a smile and a wave of his hand.

"As Mr. Carpenter says, God's bounty appears rich in this Florida land. I expect I'll make out well enough." He removed his hat and bowed to Mary. "But I will surely miss your good cooking, ma'am. It's something a man like me finds little of, traveling alone."

"My thanks for sayin' it, Mr. Ramsay. You have yourself a safe trip now."

"I'll try, ma'am."

As he turned to lead the mare out of the enclosure, Ramsay glanced back and saw that the Budds had already broken camp and were bringing their mules from the creek to hitch them to the wagons. They clearly meant to waste no time getting onto the trail.

Clyde was having some problems with his charges on this cold morning, however. He swore suddenly as the larger of the two mules he was leading brayed and kicked out with its hind legs, and was forced to side-step quickly in order to avoid the hooves. When he

whipped the reins up across the animal's face in re-
taliation, the beast lowered its head and nipped him
lightly on the leg. Without warning the youngest Budd
flew into a violent rage.

"Damn you! I'll teach you to bite me!" Picking up
a pine log at his feet, he swung it into the mule's side
with all his might. When the soft wood shattered at
the blow, he started to lay about the unlucky creature's
head and flanks with the iron trace-chains, cutting the
flesh and drawing blood.

Chance Ramsay was across the clearing in an instant. He threw a well-placed kick to the back of Clyde's
knee, saw the larger man fall, and stepped to the nearest wagon where a long leather bullwhip lay in coils
upon the seat.

Before the other man had time to rise from the
ground, Ramsay had seized the whip and without un-
rolling it, began to rain heavy blows upon Clyde's neck
and shoulders. Two, three, four, five times he struck,
forward and back, with broad roundhouse swings that
used every ounce of strength in his wiry body. A sixth
blow with the still-coiled whip knocked Clyde's hat
from his head, and he sprawled face down on the icy
ground at the gambler's feet, sobbing and crying out
for mercy.

"I don't expect the mule liked it any better than
you did," the man standing over him said contemptu-
ously. He threw the whip down at Clyde's elbow and
started to turn away. "But at least he took it without
complaining."

Suddenly the other Budd men appeared from
between the wagons. Their eyes grew hard when they
saw their youngest on the ground, and their hands

moved instinctively toward their weapons.

But once again Chance Ramsay's pistols appeared with eye-blinking suddenness. The hammers of both weapons drew back with an audible click as he turned around, and a glance at their owner's eyes left no doubt in anyone's mind that he was prepared to fire in the next instant.

There was a strained silence. Then Reuben Budd reached out carefully and stood his rifle up against the side of the nearest wagon before advancing to help Clyde to his feet. A moment later old Levi lowered his own gnarled hand away from the pistol in his belt and spat on the ground.

"That's two, mister," he said quietly. "And it's a Budd's come out the worst for it both times." He shifted his tobacco to the opposite cheek and spat again. "You reckon maybe three will be the lucky charm?"

"I'd prefer not to find out, Mr. Budd." Ramsay's voice was cold, his face revealing no trace of emotion. "I've little interest in pursuing a quarrel with you or your family. But I cannot abide to see an animal mistreated. It would have been the same to me no matter who the offender was." He took a slow step backward, and then another. The pistols in his hands remained steady and unwavering. "I am leaving now, and soon you will be on your way as well. With luck, we will not meet again."

The man in black continued his backward progress until he reached the spot where he had left his horse. Everyone watched in silence while he holstered one of his pistols to take the reins from Josh, then turned the mare so that he could face the Budds as he mounted. Swinging quickly into the saddle, he nodded to the Carpenters and the Merriweathers without taking his eyes or his remaining pistol off the men across the clearing.

"My thanks again for your hospitality," he said mildly. Before anyone could answer, Chance Ramsay had turned the mare and brought her into a fast canter, soon disappearing along the tree-lined road to the south.

Josh saw out of the corner of his eye that Levi and his sons watched until the rider was completely out of sight before returning to their preparations for the day's journey. Clyde spoke angrily to his father as they turned away, but the old man's terse reply seemed to end the conversation abruptly.

A half hour later the Budds' two wagons rolled out of the clearing as well. There was not even a backward wave to acknowledge their brief traveling companionship with the Carpenters and Merriweathers, and nothing had been said on either side about the possibility of meeting up again farther south. It appeared this was to be a permanent separation, and Josh had the impression that was the most agreeable outcome for everyone concerned.

As the sounds of the wagons faded into the distance it was almost as if a heavy weight had been lifted from the shoulders of those in camp. A kind of peace that hadn't existed earlier seemed to settle over the frozen Florida woods, and each remaining member of the party appeared to breathe a little easier now that the five men — Chance Ramsay with his two pearl-handled Colts as well as the Budds — were no longer a part of their lives.

Josh realized that he had mixed feelings about

this, for something about the black-clad visitor had attracted him even though he had been well aware of the dangerous nature of such a man, with his deadly skills and his apparent readiness to use them. The boy understood his feelings a little better, after overhearing a conversation between Mary and Mrs. Merriweather while the women were cleaning and putting away their breakfast dishes:

". . . can't believe you actually asked that man to travel with us!" his brother's wife was saying. "It's clear enough from the beating he give Clyde and those two big pistols what come so ready to his hands that he's a violent one. Prob'ly a killer. There's blood on that feller's hands, you mark my words. And will be again before much more time has passed!"

"Yes," the older woman had answered, "you may be correct in what you say. Yet all the same there was something about him which suggests to me that Chance Ramsay is a gentleman. And as your husband pointed out last night, we are traveling through a lawless and dangerous land now, a land where any man's best or worst nature could show itself suddenly and without warning." She was silent for a moment before continuing.

"Despite what some might call my breeding and education," Mrs. Merriweather smiled faintly, "I have come to think of myself as an extremely practical woman. And when there are those for whom the freedom of a new land may conspire with their baser instincts to turn them to wanton crime, to theft or murder or worse, then the only answer I can see for such violence is the swift, sure violence of justice in return. There can be no reasoning with such animals. They will only take that as a sign of weakness." The older lady had paused again, briefly.

"Think of it what you will, my dear, for some reason I felt safer when Mr. Ramsay was with us. I respect your husband, and I love my own dearly. But there are times, and places, when a man of Mr. Ramsay's particular . . . competence . . . is a great comfort to have around!"

Mary and Josh spent the morning fishing, accompanied by Mr. Merriweather, who despite his earlier protests seemed to take readily enough to the task. In a few hours the three had caught several good-sized bass together with a number of bream and were all feeling more cheerful than they had formerly. The sun's warmth was pleasant after the bitter night; the clean, crisp air in the forest was invigorating; and the day was quickly becoming one of those that made a person feel good to be alive. As they gathered their catch to return to camp, Josh even noticed Mr. Merriweather whistling a lively tune under his breath.

When they reached the wagons Mrs. Merriweather was bustling about the fire adding final touches to a meal of venison stew, rice, and hot biscuits. The smells of cooking were hearty and rich, and when Mary tasted the stew and made some complimentary remark, the older lady fairly beamed.

"All the girls in our family had to learn to cook," she said with a mild attempt at modesty, "though I've had little enough practice these past few years." As she picked up a pair of tongs and knelt to place coals on the lid of the heavy skillet containing the biscuits, she brushed a strand of hair off her forehead. "Now if these will only brown a little, I think our dinner will be ready."

'Lias had spent the morning scraping the animal hides before preparing a mixture of water and deer brains to soak them in. The curing process would take longer than the few days they'd spend here, but after stretching the pelts on racks of green willow it could be completed during the evenings or other breaks in their travels. Properly cured, the deer hides would eventually become as soft as cloth, and could then be waterproofed with smoke for use as moccasins or clothing.

While Mary and Sara Jane were getting the plates and cups from the wagon, 'Lias went to the creek to wash up. On his return he paused to glance at the fish his companions had caught.

"That's a right fair take for one mornin's fishing. Reckon I wasn't much mistook about the bounty of this land hereabouts." He grinned at Josh. "But you got your work cut out for you now, boy, don't you? Cleanin' all of them." He accepted a cup and plate from Mary and squatted near the fire. "I'll go on an' make us a smokin' rack this afternoon so's we can start to cure the bigger ones. But how about tonight we take a mess of them brim and have us a old-fashioned fish-fry? Make it a kind of a celebration, like. For finally arrivin' in these Florida lands."

The idea sounded good; it had been a long time since any of them had been able to enjoy a night of just socializing. Usually they were so tired after the day's trek that everyone fell into their blankets after supper and slept until dawn, when it was time to do it all over again.

"That's a real fine idea," Mary said. "We've enough lard, I think. And prob'ly the makings for a pudding or a cobbler of some kind for dessert." She looked at her husband. "Though it could leave us kind of short down the road a piece. . . ."

"Don't you fret, honey." 'Lias smiled. "I've the idea we'll be able to make it up before long. I got a good feelin' 'bout this country, like I said. Might run into a b'ar in his hole before the winter's out, or a wild hog or two. An' we'll have some pelts in any case to trade for what's needful. You go on an' fix whatever you want tonight. It's high time we had us a little fun an' frolic after all we been through so far!"

5

WHEN THE NOON MEAL WAS OVER, every-
one went back to work with fresh energy. 'Lias disappeared into the forest to cut branches for frames and a
drying rack, while the women rummaged through their
provisions and planned the evening's feast. Mr.
Merriweather, encouraged by his morning's success,
returned to the creek with the hope of doubling their
supply of fish singlehandedly. Josh gathered up a
couple of pans and a knife, and carried their earlier
catch a short way downstream to begin cleaning it.

He worked steadily for a time, but it was a weari-
some job, scaling and removing the entrails, throwing
the offal into the water and preserving the heads as
bait for their traps that night. After an hour he was
only half finished and decided it was time to take a
break.

Placing a towel over the fish he'd already cleaned,
he pushed the pan away with his foot and stretched
out on the sloping bank. His fingers were cold from
constantly dipping them into the icy water, and he

thrust them under his shirt to warm them.

The afternoon sun felt good on his face and the ground had soaked up some of its warmth as well. He lay for a time with his eyes closed enjoying the sunlight, the gentle smells of the forest, and the quiet sound of running water and insects in the distance.

Occasionally his eyes opened, and in time he became aware of a glittering object beside the stream some dozen yards away. It appeared to be gold in color, though perhaps that was just a reflection from the sun. Yet it was clearly man-made, of some kind of metal or glass. From his prone position on the bank, Josh couldn't quite tell what it was.

He tried to ignore it. The ground where he lay was warm, the grass was soft, and he had no desire to move for several minutes yet. It was probably a thing of no importance anyway: a cast-off button or a piece of harness, something else of the kind. He'd take a look when he rose to resume cleaning the fish. Maybe after a little nap . . .

Yet curiosity nagged at him, and he found himself raising his head several times to squint into the sunlit reflections off the water, trying to make out the shape more distinctly. Finally he stirred and with a shrug of mild annoyance, got to his feet and walked over to it. Kneeling again on the soft earth beside the stream, he reached out a hand and lifted the object from the grass.

It was a gold locket, perhaps two inches in diameter and very finely crafted. Pieces of gold chain dangled from a small ring at its top, the links at the ends broken and twisted as if they had been pulled apart by some rude force. After studying the engraved cover for a moment, Josh pressed the stud that opened it.

There was a picture inside, a miniature painting done in soft colors by an artist of considerable skill and an eye for detail. The boy remained kneeling for a long time, staring down at the locket in silent fascination. A lady's face gazed back at him with dark smiling eyes that seemed to meet his own and peer into his very soul.

It was almost as if she were alive. He had never seen such a beautiful woman, even in pictures. And he felt something stirring inside him that was unlike anything he had ever experienced before. Josh Carpenter had never known what grown-ups meant when they talked of love, but maybe the way he felt now was something like it.

Finally he managed to tear his eyes from the lady's and close the cover. He looked around trying to decide where the locket might have come from. This was near the spot where the Budds had watered their mules, but somehow Josh couldn't imagine any of those hard, cold men having an object of such beauty with him, much less knowing a woman of the sort portrayed inside.

That might be a kind of prejudice on his part, but as he thought about it Josh decided it was far more likely the locket belonged to Mr. Merriweather. The older gentleman had probably lost it while fishing in the stream that morning. Mrs. Merriweather's eyes were blue, so it could not be a painting of her in her younger days. But perhaps it was a daughter, or some other female relation.

When he'd come to this conclusion, Josh made

up his mind to return the locket at the fish fry that night. For some reason he could not explain, he wanted to keep it with him just a little while longer, to have it in his pocket and be able to open it privately and look down at least one more time into those dark, beautiful eyes.

❖   ❖   ❖

The rest of the afternoon went quickly. Josh soon finished his immediate task and returned to camp in time to help 'Lias dig a fire pit and construct a rack for smoking and drying the meats. When Mr. Merriweather appeared, proudly displaying his latest catch, the boy took him to the creek and furthered his education by showing the older gentleman how to clean and prepare the fish himself. They set a good number of bream aside for the evening meal, then placed the rest over the fire pit with the other meats to smoke.

As the winter sun disappeared below the treetops the men hurried to gather a large supply of wood for both fires. Mary and Mrs. Merriweather had concocted a fine-looking pudding of rice and raisins earlier, which now sat cooling at the back of the Carpenters' wagon. A large skillet filled with grease was put on the coals to heat while the batter for hush puppies was made, and the fish were rolled in corn meal seasoned with salt and pepper. Soon the rich, pungent smells of cooking filled the crisp evening air.

Everyone ate their fill that night and then some. When the meal was over and a fresh pot of coffee was bubbling among the embers, Mr. Merriweather produced a small flask of bourbon that he shared with 'Lias to "help ward off the cold," and before long Josh's brother got out the old harmonica he called his "French harp" and began to play songs from their Carolina homeland. Mr. Merriweather surprised his new friends by returning to their own wagon and digging out an ancient violin from among their belongings. He tuned it by the fire and was soon joining in while the others lent their voices to the impromptu songfest.

The older man played well, Josh thought, with full round tones that probably spoke of formal training sometime in the past. It wasn't quite the same as the enthusiastic but ruder fiddling he was used to, but after the gentleman had been playing awhile he swung into "Old Zip Coon" and "Rosin, the Beau," and the evening began to seem a lot like one of those old-fashioned frolics he remembered from back home.

Soon 'Lias put down his harmonica and began to dance with Mary, and after a bit Josh was persuaded to take a turn with Mrs. Merriweather. The older lady danced gracefully but with considerable spirit for a woman her age. When Mr. Merriweather took a break to refill his cup with coffee, they all sat down again laughing. 'Lias slapped his knees with both hands and looked across the fire at his companions.

"Now ain't this just fine as frog's hair! A feast an' a frolic to celebrate our arrival in the promised land! An' way past due, if'n you ask me." He added some bourbon to his coffee and took a swallow. "Friends, I've the feelin' we're all of us goin' to make our fortunes here in this Florida land. Hard work's the ticket to success and we'll have a-plenty of that. But if folks can't have some fun whilst they're about it, then all the hard work an' the strivin' ain't nearly worth the trouble!" He turned to the older man beside him.

"Mr. Merriweather, a man what plays the fiddle

like you do will never lack for friends in this new country. You mark my words. It's a talent will make you a popular feller any place you set your mind to settle down in." He grinned and took a deep breath, leaning back on the log with his hands on his knees. "I swear, another couple turns like that last one an' I think I'm just liable to . . .

"Hello the fire!"

The voice spoke sharply from outside the circle of light, then added more mildly, "You reckon you-all could stand to have a few more guests at the party? For a couple minutes, anyhow?" There was a brief pause. "We're all of us friendly."

The first man to step forward after 'Lias's acknowledgment was tall and rangy, wearing a thick mustache speckled with gray. He had two pistols in holsters strapped outside his long woolen coat and carried a percussion carbine in the crook of his elbow. The others seemed heavily armed as well when they made their appearance. There were six in all.

A tin star glinted dully in the firelight as the first man came closer to introduce himself.

"I'm Sheriff J. T. Braden from up to Ware County, Georgia. This here's my posse." Mary was putting on a fresh pot of coffee as the men approached the fire to warm themselves. Braden studied the faces of the Carpenters and Merriweathers for a moment, then asked, "You folks been camped here long?"

"Second night at this place," 'Lias answered. "Takin' a little break to do us a mite of huntin' an' fishing before moving on. Plannin' to homestead somewheres down around that lake country to the south we done heard about." He paused and met the newcomer's eyes. "You got some particular reason for askin'?"

"Uh-huh." Braden stood his carbine up against a wagon wheel and reached out his hands to warm them over the fire. "As you might figure, we ain't all out here in the cold an' the dark just to entertain ourselves. We're a-lookin' for somebody."

"Must want him kind of bad," 'Lias said quietly, "to come all the way down here from Georgia after him."

"Them. Two men, near as we can figure from the sign was left behind. And you're right, son. We want 'em bad."

"What did they do?" Mr. Merriweather had set his fiddle aside and taken out an old briar pipe. When no one answered immediately he looked up from filling it and shrugged awkwardly. "Not that it's any of my business, I suppose."

After a minute one of the men spat his wad of tobacco out into the fire, sending a shower of sparks toward the night sky. "I'll tell you what they done!" His voice had an odd, choking quality. "They done killed a entire family up there beside Long Creek! Husband, wife an' li'l eight-year-old daughter. Prettiest little thing that ever . . ." He swallowed suddenly and turned away, walking off several yards into the darkness.

"Ben there was the girl's uncle," the sheriff said. "Her momma was Ben's sister. It was him who found the bodies, little over four days ago now." He thrust his hands into his coat pockets and gazed at the fire for a long moment. "I seen 'em too, and that's somethin' I ain't never going to forget. Not in a month of Sundays." He shook his head. "Though I surely wish that I was able to."

Another man spoke up from beside the fire: "That goes for me double. I helped with the layin' out. Looked like somethin' wild Injuns might of done." He paused and glanced at the Carpenters. "Only it wasn't. White men. We found the sign plain enough, and they was spotted by a couple neighbor folks too, a hour or so afterwards. Trailed 'em good that first day. But then they lost theirselves down by the Okefenokee, and we had to backtrack an' start over again. Ain't seen hide nor hair of 'em since."

"What makes you think they come this way?" 'Lias asked. "Was it me who'd done anything like what you say, I might just stay holed up in that deep ole swamp for good, maybe never come out."

"Might be they done that," Braden agreed. "Only I don't figure it's so. They appeared to be travelin' right fast an' hard 'fore they come up on them folks they killed, movin' north to south. I figure they'd some-place special they meant to get to down thisaway, and would likely keep on a-headin' for it afterwards." He shrugged and glanced at 'Lias.

"Leastways, you can see now why it is we're so interested in crossin' paths with them gents. An' why we'd be wantin' to hear about any strangers you might of seen whilst you-all was on your way down here."

"I reckon." 'Lias was thoughtful. "But the only folks we come acrost the past couple weeks is the Merriweathers here. An' the Budds, who we traveled with for a spell. They was rough men all right, yet I'd have trouble believin' even they could of done somethin' like that. Anyhow they was with us for near 'bout a week. An' there was four of 'em: old man Levi Budd an' his three sons, together with their two wagons."

"Two wagons, huh?" Braden scratched his head. "Didn't happen to be trailin' along with a big ole white an' tan stallion by any chance?"

"Nope. Alls they had was mules. Two teams of four. No ridin' animals a-tall."

The sheriff shook his head. "Don't sound much like 'em. That horse was stole from the homestead along with some other goods, but Marth an' Jed Carter didn't own no mules." He accepted a cup of coffee from Mary.

"I reckon we'll be wantin' to have us a talk with them gents all the same though, since it appears they was in the neighborhood an' might of seen somethin'. Which way was they a-headin'?"

"South, the same as us. Only they decided to go on an' leave out this mornin' rather than wait around whilst we finished with the huntin' and such we meant to do here." Sheriff Braden nodded and sipped his coffee in silence.

"It seems to me, Sheriff," Mrs. Merriweather spoke over her shoulder as she finished handing cups to the others, "that no matter how badly you may want those murderers, you are still out of your jurisdiction here. Do you propose to consult with the Florida authorities before making an arrest and taking those men back to Georgia?"

Braden glanced up over his cup at her, then shook his head. "No, ma'am," he said calmly. "First place, there ain't no Florida law any closer to here than Jacksonville or Amelia Island over on the coast. An' in the second place . . ." He paused and looked at the others. "Well, I reckon if we can be real sure we got the men who done these here killin's, we don't have no plans to bring 'em back into Georgia a-tall. If you know what I mean."

The visitors finished their coffee without further conversation, and the sheriff handed his cup back to Mary before reaching out to pick up his carbine. "We're mighty grateful for the warmth and the hospitality, folks. But I reckon we'll be riding now. Mayhap we'll catch up to those Budd men you was tellin' us about along towards daybreak."

The posse members began filtering back through the trees to where they'd tied their horses. Braden paused at the edge of the fire's light and turned back.

"'Long as I'm askin' about strangers in the neighborhood," he said in an offhand manner, "you-all didn't happen to meet up with some gent ridin' a Arab mare by any chance? Dressed out like a dude maybe, in a black broadcloth suit, boots an' a black hat?"

'Lias opened his mouth to speak, but Mrs. Merriweather answered first:

"No, Sheriff. We haven't seen anyone at all who matches that description." She smiled at him from her place by the fire. "We'd surely remember anyone dressed and mounted as you say. He doesn't sound like your average homesteader."

"No, ma'am. And I didn't expect you'd seen him. More'n likely he's on his way to Texas by now, or maybe even Californy. But I thought I'd ask anyway. Got me a warrant for a gent like that, supposed to of kilt a man an' stole that horse a couple days back, up on the Savannah River. Folks in those parts seem to want him right bad their ownselves."

When the posse had ridden on, everyone around the fire turned to look at Mrs. Merriweather. Mary was the first to speak:

"Why in the world did you tell those men we hadn't seen anyone dressed in black with an Arabian mare? You know that description fits Mr. Ramsay to a T."

The older woman was silent for several seconds. Then she shrugged and glanced at the others. "Just a feeling, perhaps. Or maybe it was something the sheriff said earlier, about what they meant to do with those men they're hunting." She looked at Mary. "They've every intention of lynching them, you know. And accused killer or not, I still believe a man has a right to a fair trial before being compelled to meet his Maker."

'Lias stirred himself to begin putting things away for the night. "I expect you're right, ma'am. Don't hold so much with lynch law my ownself. Yet I reckon I know how those men felt. If somethin' like that was to ever happen to Mary or little Sara Jane . . ." He didn't finish the sentence, but just picked up the big skillet and carried it to the edge of the clearing where he could pour out the grease.

As Josh was rolling in his blankets by the fire a short time later, he felt something hard against his thigh and suddenly recalled the locket he'd discovered on the riverbank. It had slipped his mind until then, what with the party and the dancing and then the visit from Sheriff Braden's posse.

He took it out and placed it carefully in his shoe together with his knife and the other items from his pockets. It was too late now to ask Mr. Merriweather about it, for the older couple had already retired for the night. He made up his mind to do it first thing in the morning, over breakfast.

6 🗲

CHANCE RAMSAY COULD HEAR the gunfire clearly in the cold, still hour before dawn. His hand gripped the pistol at his side automatically as he woke, and after a long moment he raised himself up on one elbow to listen.

He guessed the shooting to be several miles from the place where he'd made a dry camp in this small hollow surrounded by oaks, hickories, and hardwood scrub. But the sound carried far in the clear morning air. For a short while the silent forest seemed to be alive with the staccato thunder of rifles, pistols and shotguns. At last it ceased, followed several minutes later by the crack of a solitary pistol shot, and another. Then there was no sound at all.

Ramsay rose, shivering in the icy darkness as he put on his hat and strapped his gunbelts around him. He sat on the blankets to pull on his boots, and a few minutes later, after rolling up his bedding, he took his saddle and strode to the small grove where he had picketed the mare.

He knew it would be plain foolishness to ride up to the scene of such recent violence, especially as he had no personal stake in the outcome. But it wasn't in him to leave a thing like that alone or forget it. There might be survivors who needed his help.

The sky was growing light when he reached the main road to the south once more, drawing rein some dozen yards to the east near a small clearing surrounded by tall pine and water oak. The acrid smell of gunpowder still clung to the ground and about the frozen branches of scrub trees as he dismounted and drew one of his pistols, advancing cautiously with his thumb on the hammer and every sense alert.

There was no movement. The virgin forest appeared as deserted and still as the first day the Creator had laid His hand upon it.

After a watchful minute, Ramsay looped the mare's reins over a low bush and stepped into the clearing. He halted suddenly and took in a sharp, involuntary breath.

Six bodies were sprawled among the tall weeds and bramble that covered the open place, crushing down the brown stalks underneath as their bright red blood mingled with the silvery carpet of hoarfrost. The ground was broken and trampled, making it appear the men had been mounted when they first entered the clearing. A dark shape at the forest's edge confirmed the fact, revealing where one horse had shared the fate of its master.

Some of the men had been shot from their saddles and died where they fell. One or two appeared to have made it to the ground and drawn their weapons before being blasted out of existence. Yet none had remained on their feet for long.

Ramsay stood and surveyed the scene grimly, his lips pressed together in a taut narrow line. He backed away then and circled the edge of the clearing looking for signs of those who had taken part in the ambush. On the side nearest the road he saw what appeared to be wagon tracks. They had been ridden over by the new arrivals and were difficult to follow. But it seemed that they led into the woods on the other side of the clearing.

After another dozen steps his attention was suddenly caught by a faint moan from one of the men on the ground. He paused, motionless. When he heard the sound again and could identify its source, he moved quickly to kneel beside the victim's crumpled body.

As he reached out to turn the man over, a tin star glimmered faintly in the early morning light, fixed to the breast of the other's long woolen overcoat.

Josh Carpenter woke at first light, half-frozen and rolling over to find that their campfire had died down to embers. 'Lias was sound asleep and snoring softly in his blankets a few yards away.

There was a vague feeling that something besides the cold had awakened Josh, some sound or other intrusion on his senses. But he could recall nothing in particular. And a second glance at his brother's peaceful form led him to suspect that it had been nothing more than some quickly forgotten dream.

He stirred and reached out from his blankets to lay several fresh sticks on the fire. When the fat pine caught and began to blaze up, Josh rose to a sitting position with his blankets still around his shoulders, and began adding more fuel until the flames climbed higher and he could feel the welcome warmth against his face.

A few minutes later 'Lias opened his eyes and rolled over, shaking his head slowly from side to side. He glanced at his younger brother.

"Reckon maybe I overslept myself a mite this mornin'," he said in a tone of mild regret. "Don't recall nothin' a-tall since first layin' my head down last evenin'. Too much dancin' and harmonica playin' too far into the night, I guess."

"Uh-huh." Josh shrugged off his blankets and stood to warm his back at the fire. "An' mebbe just a mite too much of Mr. Merriweather's Kentucky liquor whilst you was about it."

'Lias grinned sheepishly. "Mebbe." He rolled out of his blankets and stood up to join his brother. "I ain't so used to it, an' that's a fact. Ain't had nary drop since we left the Carolinas." He yawned and stretched broadly. "But I reckon onct in a long journey like this won't be the death of me. And it was like a kind of a christenin' after all."

"A christenin'?"

"A fresh beginnin', and a new hope for the future. For ever one of us." 'Lias looked around at the trees and the palmetto brakes lining the creek nearby, as if seeing them for the first time. He took in long breaths of the cold air, turning all the way around in a circle with his hands on his hips. "We're in Florida, boy. Our new home!" After another deep breath he met his brother's eyes.

"Didn't give it so much thought until last night.

And then when we was singin' and dancin' and frolickin' like real for-sure settlers, all of a sudden it struck me. We're here at last." He sat down on his blanket to pull on his boots.

"Oh, I know we still got us a heap of country to cover before we can find a fittin' place and stake out a homestead like we been talkin' about. But we're here. An' that's the very first step towards makin' ourselves a whole new life!"

Josh nodded his understanding. He hadn't considered it much himself, what it meant to be settling down and building a home in this new land. Three months could be a lifetime for a boy of thirteen, and for that long the endless trail had been his only reality. But when he heard 'Lias speak of it, carving out a new place for themselves in this country began to seem a lot more real. A thing to make plans for, to look forward to.

His brother's enthusiasm brought a sudden grin to his lips, and Josh found himself filled with renewed energy and determination. It was as if this business of completing their journey and building a home in the Florida wilderness was too important to waste even another minute now in the doing. He sat down quickly and reached for his shoes while 'Lias made his way into the woods to check on their traps.

The golden locket plunked to the ground as he shook out his right shoe, and Josh took it up to turn it thoughtfully between his fingers. Then with a glance over his shoulder, he opened the cover and looked once more into the dark, smiling eyes of the face within. The woman in the painting was beautiful, and that was simple fact. It meant something very special to a boy of Josh's limited experience with women.

He found himself wondering again who she was. He'd guessed it was some relative or a friend of Mr. or Mrs. Merriweather, and at least he'd be able to find out about that before the day got much older. But he wanted to know more. He wanted to know everything about her. Embarrassed suddenly for reasons he could not explain, Josh closed the locket and thrust it into his shirt. Then he finished tying his shoes and picked up the coffeepot from beside the fire, hurrying to the creek to refill it.

Over breakfast he again took out the gold object and showed it to the older couple. Both studied it curiously, but without recognition. Mr. Merriweather handed it back with a shrug of his shoulders.

"No, son, it's not something of ours. I've never seen the lady before." He looked at his wife. "Nor you, Jessie?" Mrs. Merriweather shook her head.

'Lias held out a hand. "You mind if I hold that a minute?" He studied the painting briefly, then passed it to Mary. "Handsome woman, sure enough. But nobody we'd know. Picture like that must of cost a pretty to have it done, fine a work as it appears to be." He was thoughtful for a moment, then asked, "You reckon maybe it belonged to that Mr. Ramsay? He 'peared like mebbe the sort who'd know a woman like that once upon a time, an' could of had the money to pay for it, too."

Josh shook his head. "I thought of that. But I can't recall Mr. Ramsay ever bein' down near to that creek bank where I found it. Unless maybe he crossed over it whilst he was out a-huntin' yesterday mornin'."

"Well if it wasn't his'n," 'Lias said, "I reckon it

could of been dropped by some others who made their camp hereabouts sometime earlier. It's a likely enough place, an' we're surely not the first who ever stayed here."

No one mentioned the possibility of the locket belonging to the Budds, and Josh realized it was probably for the same reason he'd rejected the idea the day before. Nobody could imagine those rough-and-tumble Budd men even knowing a woman like the one in the painting, much less having the money to pay an artist of the kind it would take to produce it. But it could have been theirs, he thought. All the same.

Mary closed the cover and handed it back. "You keep it for now, Josh. Maybe some day you'll come acrost whoever it belonged to. Or maybe you won't. If not then I reckon this will be something you can pass along to your children by and by, with a little bit of a story, and a mystery." She smiled. "Little mystery always seems to make a family keepsake the more special somehow."

'Lias's traps had yielded another beaver and an otter during the night. And that day Josh, Mary, and Mr. Merriweather managed another good catch of fish. After supper 'Lias shot his second deer. There was more than enough meat now for their present needs as well as for the days ahead. They used the last of their salt to preserve the excess, with plans to trade for more when they finally reached a settlement. Since there was no reason to remain here longer, they made plans to resume their journey the following day.

Over supper Mr. Merriweather took 'Lias to one side and spoke earnestly with him for a long time. When the two rejoined the others, the younger man looked thoughtfully at his wife and Josh.

"Mr. Merriweather here's made us a offer that I think maybe we'd ought to consider at least." He seemed a little embarrassed. "Much as I don't cotton to the idea of takin' money from folks for helpin' 'em when they've a need, this here would make the last leg of our trip a whole sight easier. And I guess we'd be able to repay 'em somewhat by stayin' together and helpin' out onct we get down to that lake country an' stake out our claims."

"What I have suggested," the older gentleman said when 'Lias hesitated, "is that Jessica and I use a small amount of our personal resources to pay for steamer passage for the six of us, with the wagons and live-stock, from Jacksonville up the St. Johns as far as the settlement of Enterprise. We can afford it, and you cannot. Yet after reaching that country, my wife and I would be as helpless as babes in the woods without someone to teach us and guide us in the days to come. I offer no charity, simply a reasonable trade: our fi-nances to take us farther south, against your skill and assistance when we arrive and begin to build our homes."

'Lias looked at his wife. "What you think, honey?"

"I think it sounds like a right fair trade." Josh spoke quickly from where he sat beside the fire, then paused, suddenly aware of all the adult eyes that had turned his way. "I mean," he went on, "it ain't like we'd be taking somethin' for nothin'. We'd be doin' our part accordin' to our ability, and so would Mr. and Mrs. Merriweather here. Fair value for fair value." He shrugged. "Well, anyhow, that's the way it 'pears to me."

Mary nodded. "I hold with Josh. It'll sure take some weeks off our travels and give us that much better chance to get a crop in and a house built before the next winter comes around. And if we was helpin' these folks to get theirselves started out right, then everbody'd be the better off for it." She turned to the older couple and smiled. "I reckon maybe I've already started feelin' like we was neighbors. This here'll be just one more chance to keep a-feelin' that way whenever we get down to where it is we're goin'."

'Lias held out a hand to Mr. Merriweather. "I expect that settles it then. Partners. You folks pay the passage, an' we'll do all we can to get both homesteads a-goin'. From now on we'll be like them French fellers said: One for all, an' all for one."

"That's splendid!" Merriweather took the offered hand and clapped his other on top of it. "Here's to a new life in a new land. —And for the first time since Jessie and I left Savannah, I honestly believe we might make a go of it!"

The cabin sat back against a stand of pines halfway up a low sand hill. It was a rude affair of notched logs and hand-hewn shingles. But there was smoke rising from the clay chimney as Ramsay approached, and that meant at least some hope for warmth and shelter. He had walked perhaps four miles by now, leading the mare with the wounded lawman tied across his saddle.

As they entered the raked sand yard the door opened slightly and a woman's voice called out from the darkness inside:

"Hold it up there, mister! I got me a shotgun what I ain't afeared to use, and a right suspicious nature to go along with it. 'Fore you take another step, you'd better explain to me just who you are an' what it is you got there."

"The name's Ramsay, ma'am. Chance Ramsay. And I have a wounded man with me. It appears he's some kind of lawman. He's hit hard, and he'll need good care and a bit of luck if he's going to have much hope of making it."

"Well, this ain't no hospital and I ain't no doctor. Nearest doc's some ten, twelve mile off, over Jacksonville way."

"Yes, ma'am. But I don't believe this man can make it that far. He's been badly shot up. We've been traveling for over an hour now, and the shooting happened perhaps an hour before that. You may have heard the sound of it."

"I heard." There was a long pause. "Was you any part of that?" she asked finally.

"No, ma'am. I rode up there when I heard the gunfire, and found this man and five others. The rest are all dead."

There was another long silence. Then the woman's voice said quietly, "Lordy, whatever is this world coming to?" A moment later the door opened and she appeared on the porch with her shotgun in her hands. She was a large woman, dressed in homespun with a dark shawl over her shoulders and a faded calico bonnet covering her graying hair. She looked hard at Ramsay and the man on the horse before finally standing the shotgun up against the wall and stepping forward.

"All right," she said. "Let's get him inside and find out what can be done."

As they carried the wounded man up the steps and into the cabin, she spoke again between efforts. "I'm Lucy Steed. My man's been gone to town since yesterday and I'm all by my lonesome." They maneuvered their burden through the door and onto the thin mattress covering a rope spring bed against one wall facing the fire. "Can't blame a woman alone for bein' cautious. 'Specially after all that shootin' out there before it even got light good. Sounded to me like some kind of a Injun war was startin' up again for sure!"

When they'd removed the man's long coat Ramsay took his own jacket off and set it aside before drawing a knife to begin cutting away the shirt, where dark stains indicated at least two wounds in the victim's upper body. One proved to be just below the right shoulder; the other was in his side lower down near the belt. He saw also that blood had begun soaking through one leg of the injured man's woolen trousers.

Lucy Steed poured water from a bucket by the door into a pot which she hung over the fire, then began rummaging through a trunk at the foot of the bed for lint and scraps of cloth to use as bandages.

"Reckon everbody out here's done a mite of doctorin' time to time," she said, smiling grimly, "'spite of what I told you earlier. Folks does whatever they got to do when money's scarce an' help's a long ways off." She rose to join her visitor at the side of the bed.

"Yes, ma'am." The man in black accepted a damp cloth from the woman and began to clean the blood from around the sheriff's wounds. After a moment he added dryly, "I expect I've seen a hurt man or two myself, here and there."

When he could examine the bullet holes closely, Ramsay decided their patient should at least have a chance for survival. The cold weather had kept the bleeding to less than it might have been otherwise, and exit wounds showed where both balls had passed entirely through his upper body. After pushing clean handkerchiefs through these openings, they poured turpentine on the raw flesh before binding it tightly with clean lint. The man on the bed struggled and cried out in pain as this process was carried out, but he never regained consciousness.

When they'd removed his trousers, Mrs. Steed applied her not inconsiderable weight to holding the sheriff down while Ramsay probed the leg wound with his fingers and the point of a knife. The injury was larger than he'd first supposed, and the flesh was torn badly. But no bones seemed to be broken, and after extracting three slugs of buckshot he was satisfied no more would be found. They treated this wound with turpentine as well, then applied bandages and finally drew the covers up over their unconscious charge to keep him warm.

When all this was finished, Chance Ramsay washed his hands in the tin basin beside him on the floor, then rose and crossed the room to recover his coat.

7 🖤

"My thanks, ma'am." He accepted a steaming cup of coffee from the homesteader's wife and took the offered chair by the fire. "I know it's not the kind of visit a woman alone could look forward to with much pleasure. But I am grateful for your assistance."

"Don't you fret about it." She filled a cup for herself and plopped down on a wooden box nearby. "If he lives, I'll be that pleased to have had a hand in it." Mrs. Steed took a swallow and shrugged her broad shoulders. "An' if he don't, well anyways we give it the best try that we was able."

For several minutes they drank their coffee in silence.

"Who'd you say he was?" she asked at last, glancing over her cup at her visitor.

"I don't know." The man in black met her eyes briefly before returning his gaze to the fire. "As I said, I came upon the bodies at dawn, not long after what appeared to be an ambush. There were six in all. This was the only survivor." He paused. "You saw the star that was pinned to his coat. That makes it fairly clear he is some kind of lawman."

The woman nodded and then said thoughtfully, "You reckon maybe he's got any papers about him which might tell us something?"

"Now I wonder why I didn't think of that." Ramsay smiled faintly. He got up and crossed to where the sheriff's pants lay across the foot of the bed. There was a folding knife and some change in the pockets, together with a leather wallet containing a little paper money but nothing else of interest. He turned and went to where the long woolen coat hung from its peg on the wall. After running his fingers through it Ramsay grunted softly and reached into an inside pocket. A moment later he returned to the fire with a thin sheaf of papers that he began to unfold as he resumed his seat in the chair.

"You'll have to read those to me, I reckon." Lucy Steed grinned shyly from her place near the hearth. "Neither I nor my mister ever did learn how to cipher out them words on a page."

Ramsay took his time studying the papers. At last he looked up at the woman across from him.

"There are several letters here addressed to Sheriff J. T. Braden of Ware County, Georgia. I expect that is who we have with us now. The address on the envelopes will provide a way of contacting his wife and family at least. It appears he was searching for some fugitives who had fled into Florida. Probably those others with him were members of a posse." He paused to swallow the last of his coffee before continuing.

"I've an idea perhaps they came upon the men

they were looking for this morning, unexpectedly."

"That's likely enough." The large woman shivered and tugged her woolen shawl more tightly around her shoulders. "There's all kinds of killers an' lowlifes makes their way into this Florida country now an' again. We see 'em come, Harold an' me, and we see 'em go. Try not to pay too much mind if'n we can help it. Just seems like anyplace where there's freedom enough for honest folks to have some kind of a fresh start there's others hankerin' after the same kind of freedom to keep up with their own murderin' ways." She looked at her guest. "We'll share a neighborly cup of coffee with travelers time to time, feed 'em if they appear hungry. But we don't ask no questions. And we don't tell 'em nothin' of ourselves. Just seems safer for everbody concerned thataway."

Ramsay nodded but made no reply. He set the papers on the floor beside him and bent to refill his cup.

Several minutes later, when his hostess had risen to go outside and draw another pail of water from the well, he took up two of the sheets and folded them together, thrusting them quickly into the pocket of his jacket. He had neglected to mention the contents of either of these items to the lady.

One was a warrant for the arrest of the killer of Beau Jordan, issued by a judge in Savannah some four days earlier. The other was a handbill advertising a reward for the same man, offered by Jordan's family in the amount of one thousand dollars. The money was to be paid upon delivery of the killer's body, dead or alive.

A half hour later Ramsay took his leave of Mrs.

Steed and her new charge to resume his journey south-ward. He would have liked to have stayed longer, at least until they could be more certain of the wounded man's condition. But time was clearly of the essence now. The papers in his pocket left no doubt that the Jordans were entirely serious about carrying out Quinn's threat of revenge.

Legal warrants issued from distant jurisdictions might or might not be enforced. But the offer of a thousand dollars was something else again. Its terms were sure to attract the interest of every hard case in the South who happened to get wind of it.

A sense of nagging guilt at abandoning such an uncalled-for burden with the lonely frontier wife had caused Ramsay to leave behind a portion of his care-fully hoarded stake to pay for the sheriff's care and upkeep. The lady had protested, but an extra mouth to feed and time away from daily chores were no small matters to a poor family like the Steeds. And he could be persuasive when he set his mind to it.

His present course was clear: He must shun people and settlements even more now, making his way ever deeper into the sparsely populated wilder-ness to the south. Perhaps if he traveled far enough he'd find some place beyond the reach of those damn-ing handbills, and the official curiosity of legally con-stituted authority as well.

That he was running away from his problem was something Chance Ramsay knew and freely acknowl-edged. It was not the first time, after all. Sometimes he felt as if he'd spent his entire life running from one thing or the other.

Not danger, necessarily. He'd faced that readily

enough on occasion, when it was man-to-man or one man against the elements. Yet something always seemed to keep driving him on just the same, from one town to the next, from one group of casual acquaintances to the other. With no real sense of belonging anywhere.

It was an hour past noon when he crossed the Alligator Road and struck out to the southwest among trackless sand hills and the huge boles of long-leaf pines. His thoughts went back to that family he had met on the road a few days earlier. What was their name? Carpenter. A good name for the sort of people who meant to build homes in this land and leave behind them something that was not here before.

Unlike Chance Ramsay, their journey was taking them toward a place rather than away from it. And they had all been full of hopes, dreams and expectations. Instead of . . . what?

The question struck him oddly and he shook his head as if trying to force it from his mind. Then, almost without thinking, the man in black leaned forward to gently stroke the neck of his Arabian mare.

A half-dozen rough cabins sprawled carelessly along the waterfront, partially hidden from view among stands of cypress, elm and live oak thickly overhung with Spanish moss. The settlement of Volusia lay some five miles upriver from Lake George, at a spot where Indians, Spanish and others had crossed the St. Johns since before recorded history, on their way from the Atlantic coast to the Florida interior.

Only a few residents could be seen pausing to

watch now as the steamboat rounded a bend and blew two short blasts on its whistle. When it slowed and steered toward a crude landing on the east bank there was no one waiting to greet its arrival.

The boat backed water to come alongside the narrow dock, and as it halted a large man in a broad-brimmed hat and scuffed calf-high boots stepped ashore. In his left hand he carried a small satchel, and over his right shoulder was slung a new Sharps carbine with the barrel pointed downward. The butt of a large Dragoon Colt revolver could be seen peeking from his open coat as he turned to signal the pilot with his free hand.

One of the boatmen fended off with a pole, and a black cloud huffed from the smokestacks. Then the boat pulled away to resume its progress upriver. The man watched while it disappeared around the next curve. As he turned back toward the poor cluster of buildings on shore, he scowled darkly, and with a shrug began directing his steps toward them. He'd gone no more than a dozen yards when a second man appeared from some trees nearby and raised a hand in greeting.

"Sorry to be late in meetin' you." The newcomer had waited until they were a few feet apart before speaking. He was lean and sallow-faced, wearing a slouch hat and a pair of single-shot percussion pistols thrust into the belt outside his long coat. "I was scoutin' the banks of that big lake all day yestiddy an' this mornin'. Didn't get back till just this minute."

"Not much of a town, is it, Luke?" The large man glanced at his companion before they resumed their progress toward the buildings. "You had any luck findin' me a horse?"

"Know where there's a couple good ones not too far off." The man named Luke shrugged. "Only the feller what owns 'em says they ain't for sale."

"Uh-huh." The large man kept walking up the low hill while Luke hurried to match his longer strides. "Real good horseflesh? Strength, bottom, an' a bit of speed too?"

"'Pears that way to me. I watched him an' his boy ride 'em a couple times. Those're prob'ly the best hosses we're goin' to find in this neck of the woods. I think they'd do the job."

"Well, let's go have a talk with the gentleman. Could be he's confused about whether they're for sale."

It took no more than half an hour to reach the homestead, riding double on Luke's horse. They drew rein and dismounted beside a brushwood corral some fifty yards in front of a log cabin backed up to a stand of pine and hardwood scrub.

As the two men stepped forward to look over the top of the corral, the door of the cabin opened. A thin, balding man came out and began walking across the sandy yard toward them. At his back, a young boy of ten or eleven appeared in the entrance and stood watching silently after him.

"Already told you them horses ain't for sale," the homesteader said when he was close enough for conversation. He carried an old flintlock musket in the crook of one arm, the muzzle pointed downward. "Don't care what you're offerin'. There ain't many more with Morgan blood like these out here in the scrub, and me an' my boy mean to keep 'em."

The large man turned toward him, his eyes dropping to the musket for an instant before settling on the other's face. "I'll give you a hundred dollars for both animals," he said calmly. "Cash on the barrel-head."

"Now, look here Mr. . . ."

"Jordan. Quinn Jordan."

"All right. I'm Milt Panner. Now look, Mr. Jordan, I don't mean to sound un-neighborly, but I already told this other gent them horses ain't for sale. Now I'm tellin' you again. Not for a hunderd, not for two hunderd. Not for any price. I just plain ain't a-sellin'."

Jordan met the homesteader's eyes for a long moment. Then he clasped his hands behind his back and continued in the same calm voice, "I'll give another fifty for the land and whatever's on it. A hundred fifty for the whole outfit." He paused. "That's a fair offer, Mr. Panner. You and your boy could start over again someplace else. Here's just liable to be trouble an' hard times for the both of you from now on."

The musket in the homesteader's arms started to lift. "Trouble's somethin' we already know about, Mister Quinn Jordan. And if you don't want your share of it you'll get on down the road now an' leave us be. Ain't nothin' here for sale, not to you nor nobody else." He reached up a hand to pull back the lock on the weapon. "You can both of you just climb back up on that horse there and . . ."

In a sudden quick motion Quinn Jordan bent and whipped the slung carbine up under his right arm, firing in the same instant his right hand gripped the action. Milt Panner took a step backward and dropped the musket, his eyes wide and staring. A moment later he slumped to the ground with his hands clutching feebly at his midsection.

"Pappa!" The boy came running from the cabin to kneel at his father's side. "No! Oh, pappa!"

Jordan let go the carbine so that it swung back to its place on his shoulder and stood looking down at the body at his feet. Luke had moved quickly to one side and now held a drawn pistol in his hand.

"You saw him try to throw down on us with that musket," the large man said, his voice cold and without emotion. "I had to shoot him, in self-defense." The boy lifted his tear-streaked face toward Quinn Jordan and shook his head in disbelief. He opened his mouth to speak, but no words would come.

"Luke, gather up the horses and see if you can't find a couple saddles there inside the house." Jordan reached into an inside pocket of his coat and took out a thick sheaf of bank notes. "A hundred an' fifty was the price we agreed on." He counted out the bills and offered them to the boy.

"You can go on and take whatever you want from the cabin you can carry. But you'd best head on out of here soon as you've buried your pa. We'd like to stay and help, but we got important business that won't wait."

"No!" The youngster rushed at him, ignoring the money and flailing his fists wildly against the big man's chest. Jordan took a step backward and gripped his assailant's forearms with both hands, squeezing so tightly that it brought a yelp of pain from the boy's lips.

"Now, son." He spoke quietly still, but with an air of menace which had not been there earlier. "Your pa was a foolish man who wouldn't listen to reason.

Don't you go making the same mistake. You take this money here," He turned the boy around so that he could grasp both wrists with one hand, then shoved the crumpled bills down inside the other's shirt, "and you be off this place 'fore night comes. You got friends or family hereabouts, you could stay with 'em a day or so. But then if I was you I'd find me some way to just leave out of this country entirely. Don't even waste no time lookin' back."

He let go his grip and gave the youngster a sudden push that sent him to his knees again beside his father's body. The boy hunched forward, rubbing his wrists and sobbing loudly.

"Luke, hurry up with them horses! We got us some places to see an' plans to talk over!"

An hour later the two men drew rein in a small clearing overlooking the broad placid waters of Lake George. They were four or five miles from the settlement of Volusia now, and perhaps two miles east of where the St. Johns entered the lake from the south. After they'd dismounted and tethered their horses, they walked forward and knelt together on a sandy point of land from which they could have a good view in all directions.

"This here's the spot I picked out," Luke said. "Mite closer to that town than I'd like, but there ain't no other parcels of dry ground nearby where we could build a fire big enough."

Quinn Jordan nodded. They'd had to cross a mile or more of low hammock to reach this place. He looked to east and west along the grassy tree-lined banks. "It'll do. From what I saw, they couldn't muster a dozen armed men all told back there anyway. And most of those probably won't feel much like coming through the swamp at night to investigate, no matter what they hear." He was thoughtful for a long moment.

"We got three days, at least. We'll camp here tonight and get a start on cuttin' up some wood. Then tomorrow you take a ride up-country to try and hook up with the others. You reckon you'll be able to find 'em all right?"

Luke nodded. "They'll be comin' acrost the Oklawaha somewhere near where it turns back south, an' I told 'em just keep followin' that east bank on down till they come up to the trail from Fort King, or I meet 'em first. Ought to be easy enough to find 'em thataway."

"Good. Bring 'em along here soon as you can, but be sure an' cross the St. Johns a ways up from that settlement, so as not to give the citizens too many more things to think about. I'll trade off between scoutin' the country and choppin' wood in the meanwhile."

Both men fell silent for several minutes. Jordan took a cigar from his pocket and lit it while Luke picked up a stone and skipped it far out across the water. At last the smaller man turned to his companion.

"You reckon them Budds'll be comin' along in time to do us any good with this business?" he asked. "I ain't heard ary word from them boys in nigh onto two weeks."

"They'll be along. They had to travel round about because of the wagons, but I expect they'll be showin' up on the road to Volusia 'most any day now."

"Sure could use them things they're a-carryin', if'n they'd get here soon enough." There was another long pause, then Luke asked in a lower voice, "What about that kid back there? You reckon he'll be able to make any trouble for us?"

Quinn Jordan shrugged. "I doubt it. I expect I scared him pretty good before we left. But even if he's got it in mind to start something, it'll be tough goin' for him. He's got our money, and it'd just be some kid's word against the two of us about what really happened back there."

Luke nodded. "That's how I figured it. But all the same it don't seem safe to just let him run free like that. Might of been better to shoot him too whilst we was about it."

"Uh-uh. The two bodies would look too much like murder an' robbery. Prob'ly get the whole neighborhood riled up once they'd been found." Jordan paused to draw deeply on his cigar. "This way the boy'll just bury his pa an' leave out, more'n likely. And if he doesn't, then it's still our word against him about self-defense."

His companion grinned. "That's what I like about you, Quinn. Always thinkin'. You're right as rain, and I'd never even a-thought of it." He stretched and pushed his hat back from his forehead. "Makes me feel better an' better all the time 'bout this here plan we got."

The big man said nothing for several minutes. Then he crushed his cigar out with the heel of a boot. "All right," he said. "Let's go see how much wood we can get cut before nightfall."

8 🌿

CHANCE RAMSAY HALTED THE MARE beside a swift-flowing creek that cut jaggedly across the leaf-covered floor of a forest of oaks, hickories and longleaf pines. They had been traveling among such dense woodlands almost since leaving Mrs. Steed's cabin the day before, with only occasional fields or lakes to give them a glimpse of the open sky.

It was late afternoon now, and though the days had been growing gradually warmer as he traveled south, there was a promise of the night's cold in the sudden breeze which came up to ripple the clear waters of the creek when Ramsay dismounted. Bending from the waist, he stretched his complaining muscles and then walked all the way around the mare twice before leading her to drink. It had been a long time since he had spent so many days in the saddle or so many nights on the hard ground as he had this past few weeks.

He'd been riding carefully, with frequent stops to survey the unknown country and keep his mount rested in case there was any need for sudden flight. But he expected less danger of that as they continued to move ever deeper into the wilderness of the central peninsula, where settlements were few and communication with the outside world infrequent. They had not crossed a traveled road since the day before, and this country west of the Oklawaha River had remained largely uninhabited since the Indians were driven from it a bare decade ago.

After he'd picketed the mare, he moved upstream to quench his own thirst. Then he rose and climbed the bank to a fallen log a few yards away. Sitting and carefully taking the last of his cigars from his jacket pocket, Ramsay bit off the end and lit it between cupped hands. For a time he smoked in thoughtful silence.

He still had no ultimate destination in mind. His knowledge of the country was slight and based mostly on his recollection of a crude map drawn on the wall of a trading post where he'd risked a visit several days earlier. Yet it was not entirely ignorance of the terrain that was responsible for his indecision.

To the south were the fewest people, and so the best chance of avoiding those who might be bent on enriching themselves at Ramsay's expense. The question was not so much which direction to take, but where to stop. And what to do with himself when he did.

It was obvious his gambling career was at an end, at least for the time being. The earlier life on riverboats and in city saloons was far too visible now, even assuming there would be such places in the Florida wilderness. Any poor homesteaders he'd be likely to meet in this place would have little ready cash and probably less inclination to risk their slim resources on cards or dice.

In truth, Ramsay was not entirely disappointed at the prospect of leaving his former occupation behind. He'd come to it as to most things in his life, by the path of least resistance. And since his pride had compelled him to run an honest game, the lean times had been almost as frequent as the good. Yet when he won, the losers were no happier with the outcome than if they had actually been cheated. Beau Jordan was hardly the first to try canceling a gambling debt with guns or steel.

But what else could a man like him do?

He might homestead. The federal government was offering 160 acres of former Indian lands to any able-bodied man with a gun who'd defend it and improve upon it. Perhaps that was the sort of anchor he needed. After all, it was his father's indebtedness and the loss of their plantation in South Carolina that had made Chance Ramsay a wanderer in the first place.

Or was it? He wondered now if he might have chosen such a life for himself at all events. So far he'd felt little temptation to settle down in any of the locations he'd visited during his travels.

And though the idea of owning land had its appeal, an endless struggle to grub his living from this sandy soil did not. It wasn't so much the prospect of hard work, for he'd done that willingly enough whenever his dwindling resources required it. But he could see little future for a simple dirt farmer, here or elsewhere. He'd watched too many become bound to the land by debt and poor crops, in a manner not very different from Medieval serfs.

There was a small sum of money left from his original stake. Perhaps if he could think of some way to invest that in connection with a homesteading interest . . . . But nothing promising came immediately to mind.

Chance Ramsay shook his head abruptly and turned to rub the ash off his cigar on the bark beside him. Then with moistened fingers he quenched the remaining sparks and replaced the two-inch stub in his pocket before rising and stepping forward to untie the mare.

With or without any definite plan for the future, his immediate problem remained clear enough: He was a hunted man. And if he failed to keep moving now he might never get the opportunity to make additional plans.

The map he'd seen earlier had indicated that the only roads in this central part of the peninsula ran from north to south near the two coasts, with nothing connecting them but an occasional old military trail. Two rivers, the Oklawaha and the St. Johns, offered the only ready access to the interior. As the land between them appeared to be trackless wilderness with few if any settlements, it seemed made to order for a man who wished to avoid new acquaintances.

Ramsay gathered the reins and mounted, crossing the creek and then turning the mare's head to the east along a faintly visible animal trail among pine, hardwood and occasional thick stands of palmetto. He hoped this would eventually lead him to some shallow place where the Oklawaha could be forded.

But after reaching the river and searching for an

hour along its low-lying banks, he was forced to admit defeat. Though not especially wide, the clear waters ran swift and deep at every point he came to.

Yielding at last to the inevitable, he selected a place where the cypress roots on both sides were less frequent and presented fewer dangers of a misstep which might cripple the mare. Then he unfastened his gunbelts and hung them around his neck before urging his mount into the cold, strong current. She took the water well, and it was only a matter of minutes before they climbed dripping and shivering onto the opposite shore.

After dismounting, Ramsay led the mare into the trees on the east side of the river and halted in a low depression gouged out by spring floods. Quickly he cleared a place among the fallen leaves, gathered some pieces of dry wood, and lit a small fire.

It was a risk, he knew, for the winter day was almost spent and a fire could arouse unwanted curiosity if any strangers happened to be in the neighborhood. But he and the mare were both soaked from the crossing, and the air was growing steadily colder. They needed the warmth and a chance to dry off a bit before moving deeper into the forest to make their camp.

The inside of his bedroll had stayed dry for the most part, wound tightly in a tarpaulin behind the saddle with his other belongings. Ramsay untied it now and shook out one of the blankets. After spreading this across the mare's back he removed his outer garments and hung them on branches near the fire. When he'd laid his gunbelts within easy reach and wrapped himself in the remaining blanket, he took a seat on the ground a few feet from the flames. Reaching out for a burning twig to light the stub of cigar he'd recovered from his jacket, the man glanced over at his equine companion.

"This is just about what you can expect, you know, traveling with the likes of me." He drew deeply on the cigar and pulled his blanket more tightly around him. "Wet, cold, short rations, and not much better to look forward to in your old age." The mare tossed her head and extended her graceful neck to crop some dry grass near the crest of the low ridge beside her.

Ramsay shrugged beneath his blanket. "Well," he said quietly, "if it doesn't bother you I suppose it shouldn't matter so very much to me. 'Any port in a storm,' as the sailors say."

He finished his stub of cigar and then took up his weapons, cleaning and reloading each with care. After a time he rose to dress himself in the partially dried suit. When he'd removed the blanket from the mare's back and reassembled his bedroll, it was completely dark. The moon had not yet made an appearance, and the tall trees overhead would have shut out most of its light in any case. After scattering the coals with the toe of a boot he spoke softly as he bent to draw the cinch tight again.

"Only a little farther now, lady. Just enough to put a bit of distance between us and the fire's smell, in case there should be others in the neighborhood." He gathered the reins and mounted. "Then we'll make a dry camp until morning."

Once they'd climbed the rise, Ramsay let the mare continue at a walk among the pines and hardwoods, moving slowly away from the river toward the higher ground to eastward. They had covered no more than a mile at this pace when he became aware of a faint glow among the trees some four or five hundred yards distant. Drawing rein gently, he sat in his saddle and studied the light for a long while. At last he dismounted and began to lead the mare cautiously forward on foot.

He was tired and had meant to make his final camp nearby. But Chance Ramsay had no wish to remain this close to others if it could be avoided, especially strangers whom he knew nothing of. There was always the possibility, remote as it might seem in this place, that the strangers were hunting him.

When he drew closer he could see that the light came from an open fire in a clearing among huge overhanging live oaks. From time to time men's voices could be heard, but they spoke quietly and their words could not be made out distinctly. Halting beside a clump of scrub oak some fifty yards away, Ramsay tethered the mare and continued his stealthy progress alone.

He thought about hailing the camp, but decided against it for the time being. It would be far better if he could learn something more of the nature and the number of these strangers first.

Suddenly he drew back with a sharp, silent curse on his lips. He'd only barely managed to avoid tumbling into a dry creek bed which crossed his path almost in sight of the fire. After a moment's hesitation he descended the low embankment, treading lightly so as not to disturb the thick covering of leaves at its bottom, then made his way up the opposite side in a wary crouch.

Upon reaching the top he froze instantly in his tracks. A half dozen large forms loomed ahead of him, silhouetted now against the bright glow from the fire. Two of the horses had raised their heads and turned to look in his direction.

Ramsay inhaled deeply and then let his breath out again, slowly and carefully. He was about to retreat back the way he had come when one of the voices from the clearing became louder:

". . . best be saddlin' up and gettin' on the way, boys. Sam, you an' Jimmy go fetch the horses an' bring 'em in here closer by the fire."

There were sounds of men stirring about and a moment later two figures were moving through the trees toward him. When he turned to make his departure a branch cracked under his boot and there was a sudden shout:

"Hey! Who's that out there?"

A bare second before he descended the embankment the boom of a pistol broke the night's stillness and Ramsay felt a sharp blinding pain at the base of his skull. He tried to keep moving, but his legs would not respond. Then he was falling down onto the soft cushion of leaves at the bottom of the creekbed.

His arms and legs were numb and useless. From above, the voices grew closer, then gradually moved away again.

"I got him Ab, I know it. Saw him fall. Body's got to be around here somewheres."

"Mebbe. An' mebbe you was just seein' some of them spooks an' haints ol' Dud was talkin' about earlier. It don't matter none. Either you got him an' he ain't no problem no more, or you didn't an' he's out there still a-runnin'. We ain't got time to go lookin' for him in any case. We got to make us some tracks here 'fore it gets on to bein' daylight."

"Yeah, but . . ."

"Come on an' get them horses in here so's we can saddle up an' be ridin'!" a third voice called out sharply. "Or else we'll leave y'all back in there to keep company with them haints!"

The voices began to fade and Ramsay felt a warm silken blackness closing around him. He barely managed to shut his eyes before the night and his ebbing consciousness merged into one.

❖   ❖   ❖

A pale light flickered fitfully, catching brown and yellow highlights from the mass of dry palmetto a few inches before his face. He could feel the warmth of a fire against his neck, and the comforting weight of a blanket laid across his body and shoulders. It seemed he was lying on some sort of pallet spread upon the bare ground.

Ramsay's mind labored sluggishly, trying to grasp the meaning of these new sensations. Where was he? He had been in the forest, approaching a campfire in a clearing. There had been men's voices. And a shot . . .

When he tried to turn his head to get a better look at his surroundings, brilliant streaks of white and crimson flashed before his eyes. The searing pain that accompanied them forced him to give up the attempt, and he moaned softly as he closed his eyes again. His voice sounded far away, as if it had come from someone else's lips.

After a moment he felt a cool, gentle hand resting lightly against his forehead.

He lay still, and the hand remained where it was

for a time, then he heard someone speak quietly close to his ear:

"You take it easy, mister. You had a nasty crack on the noggin and it scrambled your brains some. Best you don't try to talk or move too soon yet." The voice was that of a woman. Or a girl.

"You're safe enough here, and I'll be lookin' in on you through the night. Go ahead an' sleep awhile." The hand moved to tuck the blanket more tightly around him.

Ramsay tried to answer, but no words would come. Once more consciousness was slipping from him and he could not muster the will to stop it. He felt himself sinking into a warm, deep cavern of oblivion.

When he woke the next time daylight was filtering in from someplace behind him, and the smell of wood smoke was strong in his nostrils. His mind was clearer now, and he could tell that his outer garments had been removed and his wound was covered with a sort of poultice held in place by strips of cloth around his head and neck. He was lying on his stomach on woven mats and blankets covering a dirt floor, inside what appeared to be some kind of cabin made out of thick layers of palmetto.

After remaining motionless for several minutes, he at last managed to stir himself, and with an effort that brought tears to his eyes, rolled over on his side to take a better look at his surroundings.

The light was coming from a blanket-covered opening in one wall which served as a door, and from a hole in the thatched roof overhead that took the place of a chimney, letting out at least some of the smoke from a fire in a circle of stones at the center of the hut. Beyond this a hand-hewn table and chair rested against the far wall, with a hanging shelf above them containing cooking utensils and other small items. The entire living area was no more than fifteen feet long by ten feet wide.

He was alone at present. But after lying there for a time trying to decide if he could gather enough strength to move about and locate some means of slaking his raging thirst, a shadow darkened the opening and the blanket was pulled aside. A moment later a slim figure stepped from the bright sunlight into the dark interior.

She was tall and had to lower her head to pass through the doorway, moving with an easy grace as she crossed to the table to put down a large wicker basket filled with leaves and herbs. When she turned back her eyes grew accustomed to the dim light, and she became aware that Ramsay was awake and watching her. For a long moment she stood motionless, looking down at him.

Her clothing seemed to be made entirely of animal skins: skirt, tunic and cape of light deer hide, and soft boots of rabbit with the fur turned inward. A mass of jet black hair was piled loosely on top of her head, framing an oval face with high cheekbones and piercing dark eyes that revealed neither fear nor shyness as she regarded her visitor with curious interest.

She was very beautiful, Ramsay thought. And very young. He raised himself on an elbow with difficulty, smiling up at her.

"Good morning, ma'am. I don't suppose I might trouble you for a drink of water? My injury seems to have left me with a considerable thirst."

The effort of speech made him unexpectedly light-headed, but he was able to maintain his smile as she went to a bucket and returned, kneeling beside him with a gourd dipper which she held carefully to his lips. He drank gratefully, nodding his thanks when she took the dipper away.

"That ought to do you for now," she said. "You can have more after a bit. But first I'm going to make a kind of a broth that I'll want you to drink ever drop of. Go on and lay down again now. You get some rest whilst I make things ready."

Ramsay eased himself back to a prone position, with his face toward the fire. His head was throbbing, and he hovered between sleep and wakefulness for an unknown time while the girl finished her preparations at the table, then returned and knelt to set up an iron tripod and add fresh wood to the flames. When she'd hung a small iron kettle from the tripod she crossed to his pallet and began removing the bandage and poultice from his head.

He moaned softly as she parted his hair and examined the wound, probing with gentle fingers. After a minute or two she uttered a satisfied grunt and began to replace the poultice from a bowl she'd brought with her across the room. It felt warm and moist on the back of his head, stinging slightly when first applied but then gradually starting to ease the pain and soothe his ragged nerves.

"You'll live, I reckon." She reached around his neck to begin re-tying the bandage. "Little crease on the bone, but it don't appear to be nothing broke or cracked. Might see double and have some funny dreams for awhile. But you seem healthy enough, so I imagine you'll get over it 'fore too long." When the bandage was in place she helped him up onto his elbows and then turned to remove the pot from the fire.

"Luckier than any man has a right to expect, I'd say. 'Nother half inch and I'd of been out there diggin' a hole to plant you in, 'stead of tryin' to get some nourishment into you." She dipped a gourd in the pot and held it near his mouth. "You ready?"

The broth was partly soup and partly medicine, Ramsay decided. It had a strong, pungent odor that was not unpleasant to the taste. With occasional pauses to rest and breathe deeply, he was able to finish the small quantity the girl had prepared before sleep overtook him.

As he stretched out again and she reached to pull the blanket over his shoulders, it occurred to him that he had not even learned her name. He tried to open his eyes and ask, but the effort was more than he could manage.

Introductions would have to wait for another time.

9 🌿

It was thirty miles to Jacksonville from where the Carpenters and Merriweathers had made their first camp in Florida. They reached that river town — "city" would have been too generous a word at this stage in its history — on the evening of the third day.

The sun was low by the time they managed the crossing of the Trout River and located an open place where they could park their wagons. The animals were exhausted, and the humans in the party little better off. After a hastily prepared supper, everyone was content to climb wearily into their blankets and give themselves over to sleep, with only an occasional thought for the new adventure which lay ahead on the broad St. Johns.

When breakfast was over the next morning, 'Lias and Mr. Merriweather rode the mules to town in order to find out what arrangements could be made for their passage to Lake Monroe in the distant south. The number of steamers making the trip were few at this time, and their schedules were far from regular. The travelers might have to wait several days or perhaps even a week before one large enough to accommodate their wagons and livestock was ready to set out on the two-hundred-mile journey upriver.

Yet as it turned out they were in luck. A large converted stern-wheeler was in the process of tying up when they reached the wharves. It had a small cabin area but ample deck space, and there were even a few crude stables built forward below the pilothouse. The captain had expected to lay over for the night and depart the following day in order to have sufficient passengers and cargo to make his trip worthwhile. But since a number of the cabins had already been reserved ahead of time, he seemed more than willing to negotiate for deck passage with these latest arrivals and make ready to leave that same afternoon. To a man whose living depended on water transport, time was money, and any delay was money out of his pocket.

The newcomers would have to sleep with their wagons in the open, and like other deck passengers would be expected to help in the loading of firewood when the boat made its periodic stops for fuel. But the cost would be modest in view of this, and after consulting briefly with his companion, Mr. Merriweather agreed to it willingly.

"Spendin' four, five days on the deck of a riverboat still beats hikin' the couple hundred miles down to that lake country," 'Lias observed as they returned to bring their families and belongings into town. "Save us two weeks or more of travel and a heap of trouble any way you cut it. Give us that much longer to find some good lands and get ourselves situated on 'em too." He glanced at the man beside him. "Reckon you didn't find the price too steep?"

The older gentleman laughed. "No, I don't expect the sum of fifteen dollars for our entire party will break me. The captain seemed anxious to reach an agreement and be under way. I think the chance to return a day earlier and take on new cargo made the difference." After a moment he added quietly, "Jessie and I will still have adequate resources after the transaction, I assure you."

They rode for several minutes before 'Lias spoke again. His voice was thoughtful. "Y'know, Mr. Merriweather, it ain't any of my business and you're welcome to tell me so. But if'n I was a man with some 'resources' like you say, comin' into this here new country without no special knowledge nor knack for farmin', I might give me some consideration to settin' up as a merchant somewheres. I mean they's folks movin' south 'most ever day now. And it strikes me that if a man was to put him up a little place an' lay in a stock o' goods, and if he'd sometimes take things in trade from those who hadn't no ready cash — well, he might just make hisself a right fair go of it."

"That's an idea," the older man agreed. "A very good one, in fact." He turned to look at his companion. "You've a head on your shoulders for business, Mr. Carpenter. I've little doubt that you'll be 'making a go of it' yourself in this new land."

"Mebbe — Whoa, mule!" They had reached the wagons, and both men climbed to the ground. "But I reckon there'll still be a deal of hard work and strivin' first, for all of us out there in the wilderness."

The chance to depart on a steamer that very night

was welcome news but it meant leaving their just-kindled dinner fire behind and making haste, for it was some six miles to the waterfront with another small river to cross in between. They would have to settle for cold rations at the moment and try to make other arrangements after arriving on board, where there'd be a good possibility of trading a portion of their preserved meats for hot meals from the boat's galley.

While the women packed, Josh set about hitching up their team of oxen. The prospect of a long journey on a riverboat was something new and exciting to him. Though he'd seen them often enough from a distance as they plied the Cape Fear River near his home, and on other waterways during their trek into Florida, he had never been aboard one. And like all boys his age, he found the noisy, smoke-belching engines with their huge pistons, iron driving rods and broad paddlewheels almost irresistible.

The winter twilight had faded to darkness by the time they reached the landing, and for the past hour Josh had had only brief glimpses of lantern-lit windows and the shadowy outlines of several large buildings — some more than two stories high — before the party finally drew rein alongside the boat with the bright red letters ANDREW JACKSON beneath its wheelhouse.

The captain ordered up a full head of steam in anticipation of their departure, and Negro dockhands moved quickly to help get the livestock and wagons aboard and securely tied down prior to giving the signal to cast off. By seven o'clock, they were chugging slowly upstream into the dark unknown of the Florida interior.

Even after the long day and a supper of chicken, biscuits and sweet potatoes provided by the boat's crew, Josh found himself unable to sleep. The sounds and smells of this latest leg of their journey were too exciting. The rhythmic lapping of water against the boat's hull, the huff and clank of machinery, and the unseen vastness of their surroundings, broken only occasionally by dim lights from plantations along the shore, spoke to him keenly of fresh discoveries and high adventure.

For many minutes he stood alone at the bow, leaning with both hands on the rail and breathing deeply of the moist, cold air with its faint hint of salt and more pungent odors of the river. His eyes searched the black expanse ahead eagerly for some clue to the country they were moving into, but found there only darkness and mystery. Ghostly clouds had swallowed the moon and cloaked the distant shorelines in formless shadow. It seemed almost as if this boat, its crew and passengers, had become the last remaining outpost of light and humanity in an unbroken sea of gloom.

After a time Josh felt rather than saw the man standing next to him. When he turned his head, Mr. Merriweather looked briefly in his direction and nodded before shifting his gaze back to the dark void that lay ahead. When he spoke, his voice sounded odd against the night's stillness:

"I traveled some in my younger days, you know. To New York, Boston, New England, even across the ocean once to Britain and the Continent. But I don't believe I've ever felt so isolated, so completely apart from my fellow man, as I do now. By tomorrow most of the large plantations will be behind us, and with them the last traces of anything faintly resembling the life Jessie and I once knew. When night falls again there will be nothing for a hundred miles in every direction but trackless wilderness, with only the occasional rough homesteads of those few like ourselves."

He fell silent, and Josh offered no immediate reply. He understood well enough what the older gentleman was saying; he could admit to being more than a little afraid of this vast unknown himself. But there was something else in his present mood, a kind of eagerness and anticipation that went hand-in-glove with his fear — a suddenly discovered yearning to face these dangers now, head-on and with a challenge on his lips. His every sense was sharpened, and Josh Carpenter was aware of a fierce desire to conquer this wild country before him, or give himself up fully in the trying.

Someone with added years and experience might have called it the pride of youth or, perhaps more generously, the pioneer spirit. A cynic might have labeled it simple folly. Josh had no name to give it. He only knew that with all the prospects of hardship and danger which still lay ahead of them, he felt more alive at this moment than at any other time in his brief life.

Finally Mr. Merriweather spoke again, oddly echoing the boy's thoughts: "It's a bold new country for a young man, isn't it? There was a time I'd have felt that way myself. When I was twenty-three or so I considered leaving my home to journey across the western mountains. No good reason for it that I can recall, except to see what was there and perhaps find a place to settle down and start a different life. But I'd responsibilities at home, the family business and a small amount of property to look after. And I was the oldest." He paused, then shook his head.

"Now in the fullness of my fifty-seven years, I have become a pioneer at last. Only it's late in life for me and Jessie. Maybe too late. I'm an old man, and . . ."

"No, sir." Josh turned suddenly and met his companion's eyes in the dim light from the boat's running lanterns. "No, sir, it ain't too late. There's no time's too late to start in to makin' yourself a better life when you need one. Not for any man what's got the gumption to set hisself about doin' it." He hesitated at the older man's curious expression, but then decided to go ahead and finish saying his piece.

"And you ain't too old, not by half. Nor Miz Merriweather neither. You're spry an' you're capable, and you both know 'bout all kinds of things me an' my family ain't prob'ly ever goin' to learn." Josh paused again as the truth of what he was about to say sank in and lent conviction to his words: "Why, you know what? I'll bet whenever enough folks has come into this country so they start dividin' it up into new towns an' counties, you'd be just the natural choice to go into politics. 'Alderman Merriweather,' or 'Commissioner Merriweather,' or maybe even 'Senator Merriweather.' You'd sure have my vote, sir, whenever I'm old enough!"

The man at his side smiled and shook his head. "My thanks for your confidence, son. But that all may be a bit much to hope for where we're going. And perhaps a little more than I'd want for myself. Let's see if we can't just make it 'Farmer Merriweather' for the time being, and maybe 'Storekeeper Merriweather' after a while. Either of those would suit me quite well."

He placed a hand on the boy's shoulder. "I'm grateful for your words of encouragement, though. You're entirely right about there being no time too late to make needed changes. I suppose I only wanted someone with your fresh viewpoint to tell me so. A man's never too old to start over again, as you say, if he's willing to do the hard work required." He paused, then shrugged and added quietly:

"And the dead past can just stay behind and bury its dead."

Josh wasn't sure what Mr. Merriweather meant by that last remark. But it was with a good feeling that he watched the older gentleman turn and square his shoulders before walking slowly aft to where their wagons were secured.

A short time later the boy felt his eyelids grow heavy, and finally he made his way back to where their bedrolls had been laid out among some soft sacks of grain on the deck. He barely had time to take off his shoes and roll himself up in his blankets, before he was fast asleep.

Dawn had not yet come to the St. Johns when Josh was roused from his sleep to help take on wood at a crude landing on the west bank. A huge bonfire had been lit to guide the boat through the dense mists which concealed the far shore and lay like an icy blanket over the dark waters of the river.

After he'd crawled from his covers and joined his brother and Mr. Merriweather at the rail, the boy could see two rangy men in tattered clothes on shore, waiting beside a large pile of cordwood a few yards from the fire. Behind them a young woman stood in the shadows holding a blanket-wrapped baby in her arms. Such families of woodcutters could be found along all the rivers of America at this time, supplementing their meager livings with the small amount of cash money they received in return for hours of back-breaking work.

When the boat had slowed and come to a stop adjacent to the landing, Josh and the others formed a line to begin transferring the split logs from hand to hand onto the deck of the steamer. Under the captain's watchful eye and with his constant and vocal urging, the loading went quickly. In half an hour the lines had been cast off again and the *Andrew Jackson* was once more pulling out into the stream to resume its progress upriver.

'Lias and Mr. Merriweather returned to their blankets to gather what sleep they could before daylight found its way onto the fog-shrouded river. But Josh was wide awake now, and he had no desire to miss even another hour of this fabulous journey. After a quick turn around the deck he followed his nose to the pungent smell of coffee brewing in the small galley near the stern of the boat.

A burly engineer was filling his cup from the pot on the stove as the boy entered. He glanced at his visitor, then reached up to take a second cup from the cabinet overhead and began filling it as well.

"Thanks," Josh said, accepting the cup and holding it so as to let the steam warm his face before taking a tentative sip of the strong brew. "Right nippy out this mornin', ain't it?"

"I reckon." The big man plopped down on a bench beside the open window of the galley and inhaled deeply of the cold morning air. His face was streaked with soot and sweat, and he was dressed only in trousers, shoes and a faded flannel undershirt. "But that suits me fine. Them boilers an' fire box back there gives off all the heat I'll ever need, winter or summer. If'n they'd give me a choice I'd take twelve straight months of January ever single time."

"Where you reckon we are about now? I mean how far down the river since we left Jacksonville last night?"

"It's pert' near fifty mile to where we wooded up there at Whetstone Point. Passed Picolata around midnight, but then afterwards the pilot had to slow her down some 'cause of this here fog. Ought to be gettin' into Pilatka in another hour an' a half, give or take. We'll make a stop there right soon after first light, then head on up into the narrer part of the river."

Josh nodded, though the place names meant little to him. What he could tell from the engineer's words was that they'd now come a little over a fourth of the way to their destination. At this rate they would be arriving at Lake Monroe some time late tomorrow night, in the heart of the Florida interior.

He finished his coffee and went out on deck again, pulling his coat around him more tightly against the pre-dawn cold. There was still nothing to see but an occasional navigation light on shore, gleaming yellowly in the distance through thick layers of fog. Josh was full of restless energy, however, and decided he might as well work off a little of it by seeing to the task of feeding and caring for their livestock.

After finding a lantern and lighting it at one end of the small row of stables, he began to fork hay to the animals from the supply nearby. Mr. Merriweather had arranged with the captain for fodder at an additional cost of fifty cents a head, a total of two and a half dollars for the entire journey.

The boy whistled cheerfully as he worked, grateful for the opportunity to exercise his young muscles. Apart from occasional stops for fuel, this was almost the only labor he'd have to perform until they went ashore again; and compared to the past few months it made their trip upriver seem almost like a vacation. Once he'd fed the livestock he set about cleaning the stables, then went to wash his hands and returned to the galley for a fresh cup of coffee.

When he stepped out on deck the rest of his party were awake and stirring about, pulling on boots, rolling up blankets, and generally getting things shipshape for the day ahead. After a smile and a few words of greeting, he took his coffee and went forward to the rail where he'd stood the night before. Breakfast would be served to the cabin passengers first, so it would be some time until he and his fellow travelers could have their turn.

The eastern sky was finally growing light now, blue and cloudless as a sign of fair weather to come. Josh watched in fascination while the fog lifted to offer him his first view of the Florida interior.

The river was over a mile wide at this point, with a strong current that churned and frothed the dark waters around the boat as it made its steady progress upstream. Its banks were lined with cypress, hickory, live oak and other lush growth which gave the impression of two long, impenetrable walls of green. Huge vines climbed the trees and dropped from their limbs in long tendrils amid heavy beards of gray-green Spanish moss.

Some of the branches had lost their leaves with the season, and brown patches were visible. But still the dominant color was green: rich, luxuriant, and of every shade imaginable. Bright red and yellow accents testified to the fact that in this land even winter could not halt its endless cycles of growth, propagation and rebirth.

There was a light breeze off the river which nipped at his cheeks and ears, yet Josh believed he could feel the promise of more temperate days ahead. He realized suddenly that it had been almost a month since he had seen even a hint of snow on the ground or in the sky.

10 🌿

THEY'D SCARCELY TIME to wolf down their breakfast of corned beef and fried potatoes before the boat was tying up at a landing on the west bank where the town of Pilatka sat on low bluffs overlooking a broad bay to eastward. Egrets and herons skimmed close to the water against the dark forest background, while sailboats and other small craft plied the river casting nets, transporting passengers and goods, or simply drifting lazily along with the current.

The *Andrew Jackson* had cargo to unload, and several passengers would be debarking here as well. But as the stop would be no longer than necessary, those continuing on were advised to resist the temptation to go ashore exploring lest they find themselves abandoned when the boat resumed its course upriver. Josh watched from his place at the rail as dockhands carried barrels and boxes down the short gangway and into a rough-hewn warehouse extending out on pilings over the water's edge. Before long he saw two men manhandling a large steamer trunk onto the wharf, closely supervised by a sharp-faced woman of middle years with her bespectacled husband in tow. When everything was in place, the man went off to engage a wagon while his wife stood guard over their belongings.

A few minutes later two other passengers left the boat, one a drummer lugging his heavy sample case behind him, and the other a man in a threadbare suit with only one small carpetbag to carry his worldly goods. Josh hadn't met or talked with any of these, and he watched curiously as they glanced at their new surroundings, then strode purposefully up the bank on their way to town. It seemed clear they were all newcomers to Florida, and he couldn't help wondering what it was that had brought each of them into this unsettled land.

He was struck by the sudden realization of how many different kinds of people it must take to open up any new frontier. Not just farmers and homesteaders like themselves, but merchants and bankers, lawyers, saloon-keepers, carpenters, masons, blacksmiths . . .

Thieves and confidence men too, no doubt. And worse. It was not only the honest and peaceful members of society who would be seeking fresh opportunity here. The wilderness was open to all, and all kinds might try their luck.

After a time his attention was drawn to three new arrivals on the dock. The first, a tall man in a silk hat and dark frockcoat, was talking earnestly with the captain. From the valises at his feet it seemed clear he was some new passenger making arrangements for the journey upriver.

The other two were more of a mystery. They hung back slouching beside the warehouse with occasional stealthy glances from the captain to the boat and back again. Both were unshaven, and their clothing was rough and well worn. Josh could see that the shorter of the two had a long ugly scar running the length of his face from temple to jawline. Neither appeared to have any luggage with him, but their long shabby coats bulged suspiciously in the middle where a pistol or other object might be thrust down into the waistband.

The man in the silk hat finished his negotiations and handed several dollars in coin to the captain. Then he picked up his bags and strode across the gangway, nodding briefly to the boy and to 'Lias, who had just arrived to stand beside his brother at the rail. When the newcomer turned to climb the stairs to the upper deck, Josh saw that beneath his open coat he wore a large revolver in a shiny leather holster. And one of the items in his hands appeared to be a long case containing a rifle or a shotgun.

He glanced over his shoulder at 'Lias. "Right fair heeled for a gent, ain't he?"

"I reckon." The older brother looked at him. "But this here's fierce country, and a man's liable to need some kind of a weapon just for his own peace of mind."

"A six-shooter *and* a long gun? For a gent what don't appear like he's ever spent a night in the woods sinct the day he was weaned?"

His brother shrugged. "Might be he's one of them New York sportsmen I heard the crew talkin' about last night. Seems some of them gents travel all the way down here to Florida just so's they can blast away from the deck of a boat at anything that moves. Don't even bother catchin' up most of it, an' then give away whatever they do catch." 'Lias shook his head. "Ain't got nothin' better to do I suppose. They call it 'sport.'"

"Sounds like plain foolishness to me," Josh said. "What they want to go shootin' anything for if they ain't got no plans to use it?"

"No accountin' for what some folks'll do when they got too much money an' too much time on their hands. You 'call there's a few back home likes to spend half the day chasin' a little bitty fox out'n the scrub with horses an' dogs. I never seen a awful lot of sense in that brand o' tom-foolery neither."

Josh nodded and fell silent, directing his attention once more to the two rough-looking men on the dock. They'd come forward and were speaking to the captain now, and after another minute one of them took out a sack of coins from his coat pocket and began carefully untying it. When the money had changed hands, his companion disappeared behind the warehouse and came back leading two horses, a sturdy buckskin and a handsome white and tan stallion with a dark mane. The other man joined him as they started across the gangway.

"Couple more deck passengers," 'Lias whispered close to his brother's ear. "And from the looks of 'em they'll bear a deal more watchin' than that gent in the high hat you was concerned about earlier."

Yet after stabling their horses, the two did not remain on deck, but mounted the same stairway the gentleman in the frock coat had taken before them. Despite their appearance and lack of possessions, it seemed they'd had the resources to pay for private cabins after all.

Mr. Merriweather's watch showed a few minutes past nine o'clock when they steamed across the bay to turn back south where the St. Johns narrowed. With luck they'd be past the mouth of the Oklawaha and out onto the broad expanse of Lake George before darkness came again.

❖ ❖ ❖

The day on the St. Johns passed slowly. Sooner than he might have expected, Josh grew weary of standing at the rail watching the unbroken forest glide by as the steamboat steered right and left and back again around countless bends in the winding river. He spent the morning wandering from one part of the deck to the other, exploring the limits of their small world and looking in on the engine room, the galley and stables, but finding little to occupy his interest for long.

After the noon meal he returned to his place at the bow. He felt restless and strangely on edge, for reasons he could not fully understand.

Perhaps it was just that he'd known so little idleness in the past three months it felt odd now to have nothing which really needed doing: no miles to walk, no chores to perform, no camp to be made. . . .

Perhaps. Yet there seemed to be something else, some subtle difference in the air like an unseen storm brewing in the distance. He glanced up at the sky almost without thinking, but saw there only fleecy clouds against a background of clear and brilliant blue.

Finally he shrugged and thrust his hands in his pockets, turning idly to look back along the length of the starboard deck. There was little to see there either at the moment. A couple of Negro hands were drowsing in the shade of the stable entrance, and Mr. Merriweather was trolling a line from the side rail with little apparent success, while beyond him the big paddle wheel splashed and lifted in its constant lazy rhythm driving the boat steadily upstream. No one else was in view. His family and Mrs. Merriweather were somewhere out of sight behind their wagons, probably, or on the far side of the cabins.

The boy's eyes were gradually drawn to a small veranda overhead which thrust forward from the upper deck directly below the wheelhouse. The man in the dark frock coat was there, tall and motionless with his hands on the balustrade gazing out toward the line of trees where the river curved before them. Josh had a feeling he'd been standing like that for a long time.

There was something about the man's icy stare and grim, tight-lipped expression which aroused both curiosity and a strange feeling of apprehension. Josh watched him for several long minutes from under his hat brim, trying not to betray more than a casual interest. In some way he could not explain, he knew instinctively that this was a cruel and dangerous man, a man to be wary of anytime — and perhaps especially here on the frontier where so little law existed to restrain men's baser motives.

Not long afterward the other two passengers from Pilatka appeared on the veranda, stepping up to the balustrade a few yards beyond the man in the frock coat. There was no sign of recognition between them, but after a moment one of the newcomers spoke and the tall man glanced briefly in his direction before nodding and saying something in reply.

Suddenly Josh realized that the men had become

aware of his presence. All three looked down sharply at him over the rail, and then the tall man turned away quickly to disappear through the door to the cabin area. It seemed he made some low-voiced remark to his companions as he was leaving, but the boy could hear nothing over the steady huff and clank of the boat's machinery.

The two rough-looking men were still watching him, and Josh grew increasingly uncomfortable under their hard-eyed gaze. At last he glanced up and smiled in brief acknowledgment, then shrugged and started walking aft to a place where he could be out of view of the veranda and its occupants.

He stopped briefly next to Mr. Merriweather, long enough to confirm that the older gentleman was having no luck fishing from the moving steamboat, and then continued his round of the deck to halt a few yards beyond their wagons where Mary and little Sara Jane were gathering articles of clothing to pull in their wake as a crude means of doing laundry. Mrs. Merriweather was standing nearby, uncoiling a rope to which the garments could be attached.

Josh knelt and took up a heavy homespun dress which the six-year-old girl had been struggling to drag across the rough planks to her mother.

"Better let me give you a hand with that, tadpole. You're game enough, but it's a right big load for such a little girl." He grinned at her. "You're liable to get splinters all the way through it before you get it over to where you're goin'."

"I won't neither!" She continued tugging at the fabric for a few seconds, then let go and put her hands on her hips as the boy rose to carry the dress to Mrs.

Merriweather. "I can do just fine without your help, Josh Carpenter. You ask my mama!"

Mary smiled up from where she was separating shirts and blankets beside the rail. "I reckon you can, honey. But still you might ought to learn that when a man's willin' to help a lady, you'd best not refuse him. Besides bein' impolite, it ain't too awful smart neither. We can all of us use a helpin' hand now an' again."

After he'd spent another few minutes carrying more items to the rail for the women, Josh continued around the stern of the boat to find 'Lias sitting on a wooden box where he was making delicate incisions on a chunk of hickory with the tip of his knife. It was a talent his brother had, carving likenesses of birds and forest animals from cast-off pieces of wood, but something the older Carpenter rarely found time to work at.

When the boy came near and hunkered down beside him, 'Lias looked up and grinned.

"Kind of a lazy day today, ain't it?" He set his work aside and arched his back, then reached down into a coat pocket for his battered pipe. "Just look at this weather though, would you? Fair an' sunny an' gettin' warmer ever day. Why, I bet we could get in two crops a year if'n we could manage all the plantin' and tillin' needed to be done in between times. 'Pears to me that . . ." He stopped suddenly and glanced at his brother out of the corner of his eye. "You got something on your mind?"

"No. . . ." The boy waited while 'Lias finished crumbling tobacco into his pipe from a twist of leaf he'd taken from the same pocket. Then he shrugged. "It ain't nothin' really. Only . . ."

"Only what?" 'Lias looked at Josh while he fished a match from his shirt and bent to strike it on the heel of a boot. "Nothin' don't appear to be what's been makin' them two creases up there between your eyes. Liable to crack your face wide open if'n they was to get any deeper." He paused to puff his pipe to life. "Somethin's troublin' you, son. You might's well out with it 'stead of givin' yourself the vapors because of frettin' over it."

"Well, it's just that . . . You 'call them men we was a-watchin' come on board here this mornin'?"

"Uh-huh. Them two rough-lookin' fellers was down here a mite earlier, skulkin' about an' puttin' their noses into this an' that. Give me a right peculiar feelin', though I can't exactly say why. I reckon maybe they was only curious, same as you an' me or anybody else what never rode a riverboat before." 'Lias paused, then grinned slyly. "But I still didn't feel much like turnin' my back on 'em. Not even onct."

"What about that other gent, the one in the high hat? You see him come down on deck anytime earlier?"

"Nope. Wouldn't of expected to. Gent like that's prob'ly rode the rivers plenty of times, so that it's got to be kind of a ordinary thing with him. He didn't strike me much like the curious sort anyhow."

Josh nodded. "What I'd thought too at first. Only now I ain't so sure. You wouldn't expect him to be havin' much truck with them other two types neither, would you? I reckon maybe that's the thing started me in to thinkin' just now." He described what he had seen on the veranda a short time before.

'Lias listened attentively, but only shrugged when

the boy finished.

"Ain't none of that prob'ly means too much, if'n you was to take a step back an' look at it. Strangers speak to one another right regular when they're travelin', just a part of bein' polite. Or they might of met whilst they was havin' dinner an' got to be on speakin' terms then."

"I reckon," Josh said without conviction. "But there was somethin' else, somethin' about the way they all looked up there, which give me a real funny feelin'. 'Specially that high-hatted one." He hesitated. "Don't know as I can rightly explain it 'less you was there to see it." The boy fell silent, then suddenly turned and met his brother's eyes.

"You know how it is when a ol' owl swivels its head around to stare at the sound of some kind of critter rustlin' out in the brush? That's the way I felt when they all looked down on me after they'd realized I was watchin' 'em. Like I was some little field mouse with three big ol' barn owls a-perched up in a tree just lickin' their chops!"

'Lias was silent for a long moment. Then he grinned and shook his head.

"Sounds to me like you maybe just got a mite more imagination than's rightly your share, is all. I expect them gents was took some curious theirselves, about why a tow-head ragamuffin would be starin' at 'em so hard an' suspicious-like." He paused to knock the ash from his pipe and gaze over the rail at the green tangle of wilderness moving slowly past on shore. When he spoke again, his smile had disappeared.

"I don't reckon it costs nothin' extra though, to

keep a eye out and have your wits about you whenever you meet up with folks this far from the settlements. Takes all kinds to make a world, an' that's a
fact."

Josh decided he'd keep his eyes open, but would
keep any other thoughts about the three men to himself for the time being. Maybe if he could watch them
privately and learn something about their activities on
board, his brother and the rest would be more inclined to take his misgivings seriously.

He spent the next two hours wandering about
the deck with frequent stealthy looks up toward the
veranda and the row of ports on the second level. But
neither the man in the frock coat nor his two earlier
companions made any fresh appearances. At last, his
resolve slowly weakening, the boy found a seat forward of the engine room and returned his attention to
the constantly changing panorama of the tree-lined
shore.

They passed by a forested island and then found
themselves moving out onto the broad dark waters of
Lake George, chugging steadily onward toward the
gray wooded banks some ten miles to the south. The
sun was low on the horizon now, and the air off the
water was growing colder by the minute. Josh stuck
his hands in his pockets to warm them, and almost
without thinking his fingers closed around the golden
locket. He took it out and opened the cover to gaze
once more into the smiling face of the lady within.

After a moment the back of his neck prickled,
and he became aware of an eerie sensation as if someone were watching him from a place not far off. Snap-
ping the locket closed with an almost guilty start, he

held it the palm of his hand and shifted his position to glance quickly in both directions along the deck.

The crate on which he sat was next to the bulkhead a few feet forward of the engine room door. Beyond this opening he had the sudden vision of two long-coated men as they turned and strode rapidly toward the stern and the stairs leading up to the cabin deck. Just before they disappeared from view the man with the long scar on his face looked back and met Josh's eyes for a brief instant.

And once again the boy had that heart-stopping feeling of some helpless field mouse, trapped in the open under the predator's baleful stare.

11 🌿

Her name was Abigail Marianne Macklin. Abby for short. It was not the kind of exotic name Chance Ramsay had perhaps imagined when he first laid eyes upon her dark-haired beauty and graceful buckskin-clad figure. Nor did it seem to match her strange and solitary living arrangement here in the wilderness. But he decided it had a pretty sound and seemed to suit her well enough.

Her father had been a trapper who'd moved to Florida from Alabama some twenty years earlier, when the Seminoles still inhabited this part of the peninsula. Her mother was Choctaw, and they'd come into the wilderness to make a life apart from the prejudices of both their peoples, white and red. Zebediah Macklin was a peaceful but fiercely independent man who neither sought nor welcomed the company of others. For a time they'd made out well enough, trapping and farming the rich hammock lands, trading furs on the rivers for what little else they needed.

But the long, bitter Seminole war had changed

all that. Abby was just five years old when it began, and though her father had tried at first to remain neutral and have no dealings with either side, there was small chance of avoiding the six years of constant fighting which ravaged the territory from Pensacola to Lake Okeechobee. After a few months, their cabin was burned — whether by Indians or white men they never found out — and their crops were laid waste. Within another year Abby's mother had died from a fever made worse by exposure and lack of proper food.

Her father had retreated deeper into the wilderness, moving his small daughter and their meager belongings often and refusing to build any structure more permanent than a cabin of palmetto thatch such as the one where she now made her home. They'd never learned exactly when the war was over, but continued to live in this nomadic fashion until Abby became a young woman.

Almost a year ago Zebediah Macklin had been attacked by a panther after going out at night to fetch more wood for the fire. Bitten and horribly clawed, he'd lingered for over a month while his daughter tended his wounds and took over his earlier tasks of hunting and trapping for food. When he finally died, Abby had buried him in the forest and continued on much as before. It never occurred to her to leave and start over somewhere else. This was the only life she'd ever known.

Her story was an unusual one, and Ramsay learned it only gradually during the two days he remained at the cabin recovering from his wound. The young woman seldom spoke without being spoken to first, although she seemed willing enough to answer questions when he put them to her. Yet she always answered with a frankness and economy of words that left him wanting to know more.

Clearly she was one of those rare persons who feel no need for idle conversation but can be content with silence even after months of living apart from others of her kind. His questions did not seem to offend her, but Ramsay had the impression Abby Macklin herself saw little value in words except to convey some necessary or useful information.

As the hours passed his mind grew clearer and he was able to spend longer periods awake and sitting up, even managing in time to make his way across the dirt floor to the water pail and back before exhaustion overtook him. He was weak from the concussion and loss of blood, but the actual damage to his flesh seemed relatively minor. The poultices on his head that the young woman changed regularly seemed to prevent infection and speed healing, as well as soothing somewhat the dull throbbing at the back of his skull.

His thoughts were jumbled at first and his memory was spotty, with particular gaps around the time of his injury. But as he rested and slept that first day they gradually began to sort themselves out, so that by the time his hostess returned to the cabin in late afternoon, he'd recalled enough to make a worried inquiry about his Arabian mare.

"She's fine. I got her picketed out in the trees a little ways where there's a bit of grass by the run-off to the spring." Abby favored him with a quick half-smile before returning to her preparations for the evening meal.

"Wasn't for her you might be still layin' out there in that crick bed. I was sneakin' up on them men's camp to try an' see what they was about, and found her tied to a bush. After they'd rode off I took her along to have a closer look at the clearing, and that's when she found you." Abby crossed the room and knelt to set the tripod over the fire. "Right big help gettin' you back here to the cabin too. Not sure how I'd of managed that all by my lonesome, you bein' a good-sized man an' all."

"Well, I'm grateful to both of you for taking such good care of me," Ramsay said seriously. "And to you as well for looking after the mare."

"No trouble. She's a right pretty animal. Smart too." The young woman began adding sticks to the fire. "She got a name?"

Ramsay hesitated. "You know, I never did get around to giving her one. I've just been sort of calling her 'lady' as we rode along."

"I'd say Lady suits her fine. Anybody can tell that's what she is, and I reckon she knows it too."

The following day Ramsay's mind was clearer and he was strong enough to rise from his pallet and walk a few steps without help. That afternoon he sat in the sun outside the cabin while Abby cleaned and scraped some animal furs for trade or possibly to make fresh garments for herself. There was little talk, and he simply watched while she went about her tasks with practiced ease and efficiency. It was the way she seemed to approach everything in this world of hers: calmly, knowingly, and with a minimum of wasted effort.

Her list of skills was impressive too, based on the little Ramsay had seen so far. That morning she had killed two rabbits with a bow and arrow, homemade by either herself or her father, dressed and skinned the animals, prepared a tasty stew from wild herbs and greens she'd gathered the night before, and then stretched the skins for scraping — all before the sun was much above the tree-tops. He knew from their conversations that she made and used traps, caught fish, and maintained a small kitchen garden to supplement her diet in spring and fall.

He'd an idea she might have built this shelter also, or at least had the knowledge to make another like it should the need arise. And Ramsay himself was proof of her skill at medical care. There seemed no limit to what this quiet, dark-eyed young woman was capable of once she set her mind upon it.

She gave the impression of being entirely self-sufficient here in the wilderness, not only with regard to practical matters like providing herself with the necessities and a few small comforts, but emotionally as well. It made her unique among the women Chance Ramsay had known until now, and different from most men of his acquaintance also.

He watched in silence for a long time with his back against the trunk of a tall cedar, drowsing off and on in the warmth of the afternoon sun while Abby finished her task and returned the racks of skins to the shelter. When it was time to start supper, she came and helped him back inside.

He took a chair at the table and looked thoughtfully up at her as she began removing items from the shelf overhead.

"You were following those men in the forest?" he asked finally. "The ones who shot me?"

"I try to keep a eye on everbody comes into this neck of the woods. From a distance mostly, an' without lettin' on I'm here. Not so many of 'em that's any big chore. But it pays to be careful."

"Had they been there long?"

"Only the one day at that place, day before yesterday. Come down from the north, made a early camp, then left off again right after the shootin'."

"Which way were they heading when they rode out?"

"East an' south. There's a lake over yonder with a salt spring on t'other side. Could be it's the place they was headin' for." She paused to meet his eyes. "Why'd you want to know? Was they anybody you was acquainted with?"

"Not that I'm aware of. I never got a good look at them."

"So?" She studied him curiously.

"It's not every day a man gets shot and left for dead, by strangers or anybody else. Maybe I'd like to meet up with them again."

Abby shook her head. "I wouldn't, was it me. They was rough men, rough as pine bark, appeared like. And ever one of 'em was armed to the teeth. Pistols, knives, an' most carryin' long guns besides."

"How many were there?"

"Six. Six when they left, that is. One wasn't with 'em when they first made camp. Seems like he met up with 'em sometime before dark." She shrugged. "I wasn't watchin' the whole time, though, just off an' on as I had the chance."

Ramsay nodded and fell silent. It was a damn fool idea anyway, to seek revenge for a shooting that appeared as casual and thoughtless as this had been. And dangerous too. He'd do better to just count himself lucky and keep moving south, trying to forget it ever happened.

But he wasn't quite ready to make up his mind about that yet. Tomorrow, or the next day, would be soon enough.

When they'd finished supper Ramsay returned to his pallet to begin cleaning his long-neglected pistols. Some minutes later a deep muffled roar in the distance brought his head up sharply — and painfully — to glance toward the blanket-covered entrance.

Thunder? Possibly, although the sound had seemed different somehow. And there'd been no clouds or other indications before dark that a storm was brewing. A second low boom that came crashing and rumbling through the trees moments later brought a surprised comment from Abby to confirm Ramsay's private doubts:

"What in the world is that? Ain't like nothing I ever heard before. Too short an' spaced out for thunder, but it surely ain't no rifle nor pistol shots neither." She glanced at him, then cocked her head to one side listening intently into the night.

A third explosion reverberated through the forest and Ramsay felt a tinge of recognition. He'd heard something like it a few years earlier when the yellow fever had come to Charleston and the town's militia had been called out to purify the air with fire from their batteries. But he could scarcely believe it was the same sound he was hearing now in the Florida wilderness.

Cannons! But how could that be? The war with

the Seminoles was long over and what little military presence remained was in the distant south. He rose and stepped to the entrance, thrusting his head outside the blanket just as a fourth deep boom pierced the night's stillness. Faintly beneath its dying echoes, he thought he could detect a crackle of small arms far off to the southeast.

As he withdrew inside again he glanced at the young woman who had crossed the cabin to stand next to him. Their eyes met in the flickering glow from the fire and he told her what he had heard. She made no reply. For several long minutes they stood together in silence, each thinking private thoughts.

The distant bonfire was a lonely beacon drawing the boat steadily on across the dark featureless void of Lake George. Night had fallen quickly and the moon was not yet up; the flickering yellow light of the woodcutters' blaze was the pilot's only guide to the river's southern entrance some five miles off.

After a hasty supper, Josh had resumed his place at the rail, straining his eyes into the night for some clue to the land around them but without success. Water, shore and sky seemed everywhere merged into a cold, murky veil of blackness. They were a hundred miles deep into the Florida wilderness now, and the sense of hidden mystery was almost overwhelming.

Despite the coming of dusk it was early yet, and when he turned his head the boy could see several passengers taking the air on the lamp-lit veranda above him. Two ladies were seated in wicker chairs near the rail, and three or four gentlemen stood talking with them in low tones. He watched the group for some time, partly out of curiosity but also in the hope of perhaps another view of the man in the frock coat or those he had spoken with earlier. But none of those three seemed inclined toward socializing. They made no appearance on the veranda or anyplace else Josh could see from his present vantage point.

After a while he noticed Mary and little Sara Jane strolling hand-in-hand along the deck, crossing from where it skirted the cabin area on the port side. When they stood next to him the girl's mother put her free hand on the rail and gazed out silently into the darkness ahead. As Josh turned back to look he could see that the blaze on shore had grown noticeably closer in the few minutes since his attention was drawn to the passengers on the veranda. A thin stretch of sandy beach was faintly visible now, with marsh grass and dark trees in the background.

"That's a right sizable fire they got over there," Mary said mildly, the softness of her voice blending easily with the night's stillness. "Some of them flames seem to reach up almost to the tree-tops."

"I reckon it's got to be good-sized," Josh answered, "or folks wouldn't be able to see it all the way acrost this big ol' lake. 'Specially if there was fog an' all." He leaned with his elbows on the rail and went on casually, "One of them boatmen told me that's built out on a point of land right west of where the river comes into the lake. We'll wood up there, an' then make a stop a couple miles farther on at this settlement they call Volusia. Got to pick up a new pilot there, after he's hung lanterns up along the river to steer by."

Mary turned her head toward him and smiled.

"Sounds to me like you're gettin' to be a reg'lar expert at this riverboatin' business, Josh. Maybe you'll turn out to be a pilot or a master yourself one of these days."

The boy shrugged. "Might be. Too soon to tell yet. I ain't rightly made up my mind what it is I mean to do in this new country once we get ourselves situated an' all. Reckon it'll be somethin' besides just farmin', though. I been studyin' on that some since we started up the river here." He looked at her.

"Way I figure it, a man's got hisself all kinds of chances to do important things when he makes his way into a brand-new country like this. Important to him, I mean. What he was before don't amount to a hill of beans. Nor what his daddy was, nor his granddaddy neither. All that matters is what he sets his own mind to doin', and how hard he's willin' to work at it."

Mary studied him for a long minute in the faint light of the boat's lanterns. Then she placed a hand on his arm and said seriously, "I think you're right, Josh. It's a powerful lot for a boy your age to be considerin', but I reckon what it means is that you've just stopped bein' a boy an' started to become a man." She gave his arm a quick squeeze.

"An' you'll do it too. You're a hard worker and steady, an' smart as a whip besides. I got a idea you'll find the way to become anything in this world you set your mind upon."

Josh was embarrassed by her sudden praise. "Only trouble of it is," he went on shyly, "I still ain't got no real good ideas about what that ought to be."

"You'll work it out. You got lots of time yet. An'

. . ." She was interrupted by Mrs. Merriweather's call from the direction of their wagons near the stern of the boat:

"Oh, Mary! Would you come here and take a look at these things for a moment, please? I think they will do, but I'd like your opinion."

Mary glanced down at the child at her side, then pulled her closer and placed her small hand in Josh's. "If you'll look after Sara Jane for a minute, I'll be back. I got to see to some things Miz Merriweather's took out of her wagon." She caught the boy's surprised look and winked just before turning away. "It's for a B. D."

A 'B. D.'? Then Josh recalled Sara Jane's birthday came at the end of January, less than a week away. That would explain 'Lias's carving project this afternoon, too. He'd forgotten all about it himself, and had nothing put by to give her. It was something that would need some serious thought in the next few days. Perhaps when they reached that new settlement of Enterprise . . .

He took a firmer grip on the girl's hand so she'd have no chance to slip under the rail toward the water, then shifted around to look once more at the firelit clearing on the south shore of the lake. They were less than a mile off now and closing the remaining distance quickly. Josh could make out details of a small reed-lined stretch of ground at the water's edge, with flickering red-gold reflections off the dark tangle of water oak, bay, palmetto and royal palm beyond. There was no sign of the woodcutters who'd built the blaze, but probably they were waiting somewhere beyond the fire's light.

In another few minutes they began slowing their

progress and had come near enough for Josh to feel a flush of warmth from the hot blaze against his cheeks. He glanced over his shoulder, wondering if Mary would remember to come get Sara Jane before it was time for him to go ashore and help with the taking on of wood.

Wood? He brought his eyes back quickly to the fire in the clearing. Something peculiar had been nagging about the edges of his mind, and now he realized what it was. There was no large stack of firewood beside the water as had been the case with their other fueling stops so far. In fact he could see no cut wood at all, except what was being consumed by the flames.

Suddenly a surprised shout rang out from the wheelhouse, followed almost immediately by a clash of gears as the pilot ordered the boat into reverse. He'd just thrown the wheel hard over in an effort to turn and back away from the landing when a blossom of flame erupted from the dark trees beyond the bonfire. There was a loud splash as the vessel swung sharply parallel to the shore and a fountain of water rose from the lake several hundred yards away.

The sharp turn had thrown Josh off balance and he clutched desperately at the rail with his free hand to steady himself. Moments later the riverboat lurched to a grinding halt as it ran up onto a hidden shoal some dozen yards from the water's edge.

The boy cried out in alarm as he felt little Sara Jane's hand slipping from his grasp. He tried to turn and catch her but fell to his knees and could only watch in horror as her small body tumbled over the bow and plunged into the dark waters below.

12 🌅

In another instant Josh was past the rail and into the water himself, trying to locate the child from the faint sounds of her thrashing amid a furious din which seemed to be exploding around them now from every direction. The night was filled with pistol and musket fire, running feet, angry shouts of men and occasional high-pitched screams from women passengers.

After what seemed like an eternity, he came upon the girl's flailing body and desperately tried to calm her, holding her head above water as they both struggled against the heavy weight of her sodden home-spun dress. At last he managed to wrap one arm around her tiny waist and strike out for shore. Minutes later his feet found the sandy bottom and he was able to stumble up onto a patch of dry ground some fifty yards from the fire and the continuing fury of the battle.

They were in darkness here behind a stand of scrub oak and saw palmetto, but Josh could hear musket and pistol balls rattling among the brush not far off. He laid Sara Jane on the ground and moved to cover her body with his own just as the cannon roared again from the dark trees beyond them. She started to cry out and he clapped a rough hand over her mouth to silence her.

"Keep quiet, tadpole!" His voice was a harsh whisper. "I ain't so sure what all this is about, but I expect we'll do best not to let nobody know where we're at for the time bein'." He glanced down and saw her nod, then slowly removed his hand.

"What is it, Josh?" she asked, her voice small and frightened. She clutched at his coat as they both lay shivering in the night air. "What happened to the boat?"

"Ran aground when the pilot tried to back us off from that bank over yonder." He kept his voice low as he scanned the darkness for any sign of movement nearby. Small arms fire could still be heard from the lighted area beyond them. "I got a feelin' this ain't the place we was supposed to put into a-tall, but somewheres else around the lake. When the pilot realized it he tried to get away, but he didn't make it."

The cannon thundered a third time and the boy shifted his position to look at Sara Jane. She remained silent, pressing her lips together and closing her eyes in an attempt to shut out the fearful sound.

Once the echoes had died away Josh concluded softly, "Them ambushers must of done somethin' to the reg'lar woodcutters and built this fire so's to lead us here where they could jump us. But as to the rest of it, who they are or why they done it, I ain't got ary idea." He raised himself up on one knee and looked all around them again before lowering his head to speak close to the girl's ear: "Now you just stay put a couple minutes longer and I'll take a look-see an' try to find out some of what's goin' on."

He moved away from her on hands and knees, keeping a few low shrubs between himself and the lighted clearing until he was twenty feet from the girl and had managed to crawl under a yaupon bush not far from the water's edge. After lying there for several minutes to let his breathing become more regular, he raised his head and slowly began easing the spiny branches aside so that he could look out upon the narrow coastline and the lake beyond.

The *Andrew Jackson* lay dead in the water not fifty yards off, its big paddles still churning and complaining noisily as the crew desperately tried to free it from the sandy shoal where it appeared to be lodged fast. The decks were brightly lit in the flickering yellow glow from the bonfire, out of sight now to Josh's left behind intervening stands of cedar and cabbage palmetto.

The shooting seemed less frequent than earlier, with most of it coming from the shore and only occasional flashes of answering fire visible from defenders aboard the boat. Upon looking more closely, the boy could make out two motionless figures sprawled on the vessel's lower deck, and a third on the promenade above where one of the cannon balls had ripped a gaping hole through the passenger cabins. He could see nothing of 'Lias, Mary or the Merriweathers from his present position.

As he watched, there came a sudden lull in the firing, followed seconds later by a fierce shout from the bank as a half dozen men appeared from the trees and plunged into the water. They held their weapons high while they swam and waded across the narrow interval to begin climbing and pulling each other on board.

One of the first to reach the deck held a Bowie knife in one hand and a cocked pistol in the other. He rose to his feet and glanced around him, then started aft just as 'Lias appeared from behind a barricade of wooden boxes with his rifle aimed at the invader's chest. The man dropped to one knee and tried to bring his pistol to bear, but instead was thrown sprawling backward by the force of the spinning ball.

Josh shifted position excitedly and opened his mouth as if to shout encouragement. Then he caught himself and froze in place, letting his breath carefully out again in silence. Moments later he choked down a cry of horror as he watched his brother drop the rifle and clutch awkwardly at his chest before slumping to the deck beyond the barricade.

There was a plume of smoke on the deck above, and the boy glanced up to see the man in the silk hat holding a strange-looking rifle with what appeared to be two barrels, one over the other. After pulling on a ring below the breech, making no other move to re-load, he raised the weapon to his shoulder and fired a second time toward the place where 'Lias had fallen.

Josh could not see the result of this latest shot, and a moment afterward his attention was drawn by a sudden rush of the attackers from bow to stern along both sides of the boat. They seemed to carry before them what little resistance was left. In a matter of minutes, all firing aboard the vessel had ceased.

The man in the silk hat called out to those still ashore to come aboard. Then he paused to issue a few terse orders to the men on deck. As he turned and began to mount the steps to the wheelhouse a voice came from the darkness some dozen yards from where Josh lay hiding. It was so close and unexpected the boy almost cried out in spite of himself.

"What about this here cannon? An' them other guns, an' the powder an' such? We ain't goin' to get all that acrost there without no help, not an' keep it dry to boot!" The voice sounded oddly familiar, but Josh couldn't imagine where he'd heard it before.

"Gather it all together at the water's edge then, there by the fire. We'll pick you up after we get the boat free. But we've no time to spare, so shake a leg and be ready when we come!"

The top-hatted man disappeared inside the pilot-house while those on deck made their way to the rails with long poles to begin putting their backs to the task of moving the riverboat off the sandbar. Josh watched a moment longer, then eased back on his belly from under the yaupon bush and silently returned to where he had left Sara Jane. She was shivering when he knelt beside her, and as he put an arm around her shoulders to draw her close the boy realized he was trembling too. It was not merely from the cold.

"What's happenin', Josh?" Her tiny voice was muffled against the damp fabric of his coat. "Who are those men? What was they doin' whilst you was off watching?"

"Bad things, tadpole." His low whisper sounded hollow in his ears as the vision of 'Lias' collapse came back to him with frightening clarity. "Real bad." After a minute he gave the girl's shoulder a squeeze and got to his feet.

To his right was the dark expanse of the lake, its low waves illuminated fitfully in the waning light of the bonfire. To his left beyond a narrow patch of grassy clearing he could make out the dim silhouettes of tall reeds against a sky made paler now by the recently risen moon. They seemed to be on a point of land surrounded on three sides by either water or low marshes. The only way out was toward the fire and those men who remained on shore.

"Josh?"

"What?" The boy's whisper was sharp and impatient as he knelt again to place his head close to hers.

Catching the warning in his voice, Sara Jane spoke in a barely audible murmur. "Are Mama and Poppa . . . Are we goin' to see them again?"

"Not soon, Tadpole. The boat's took an' ain't nothing going to help us there. Nor aught we can do for them neither, at least for right now." He glanced around, then added under his breath, "We best be gettin' away from this place right quick ourselves, 'fore somebody thinks to come a-lookin'. We're goin' to have to move awful quiet and careful to get around them men near the fire an' into the woods on t'other side. You take my hand an' follow my lead. Try to move quiet, holdin' your skirts up an' steppin' where I step. And don't you cry out nor say nothing, no matter what happens." He paused and turned his face toward her in the darkness. "Not a sound. You hear?"

The girl nodded. "I c'n do it, Josh. I'll be quiet as ary mouse you'll see. You go on ahead and I'll follow."

With Sara Jane's hand clasped tightly in his, he led the way quickly across a moonlit stretch of ground toward the forbidding blackness of the forest beyond. As they came in among the trees and the limbs closed above them he had to slow their pace, picking his way gingerly among fallen branches and clinging vines, high weeds and spongy earth that held the thick hidden roots of palmettos. This was land that would be under water during the wet season, deeply carpeted now with leaves and crisscrossed by dry creek beds which presented constant danger of a misstep that could twist an ankle and send them sprawling headlong to the ground.

Josh knew they'd no real hope of moving silently through such terrain. But he counted on the crackling flames and the noise of the men's own movements to mask what small sounds he and the girl might make in passing, together with the steady chuff and plash of the steamboat's paddles in the distance.

When they'd advanced perhaps thirty yards among the dense trees and hanging vines, he stopped and turned to look back in the direction they had come. It was not in his plans to leave the light of the bonfire entirely, for the danger of losing their way in these dark woods was too great. They could easily spend the night walking in circles, only to find themselves almost back where they'd started from by daybreak.

After a brief halt to let his young charge catch her breath, he began moving on a course at right angles to his original one, in such a way as to keep the firelit clearing in view while remaining well back among the shadows themselves. He hoped in time they might come to some trail or opening among the trees which would lead them away from the lake and the site of the battle for the *Andrew Jackson*.

His first thought was to get Sara Jane to a place of safety and away from these ruthless attackers. He'd no idea where such a place might be, for his knowledge of the country was scarce at best. But it seemed clear that if they controlled the riverboat, nowhere near the water would be safe. Sooner or later they would have to start traveling inland, and from that point simply hope for the best.

He had no plans for the future after that. Except . . .

Josh Carpenter thought of his brother and realized there was one other thing he meant to do, after Sara Jane was safe and he could take stock of their situation. He meant to meet up with that man in the silk hat one more time. Someplace. Somehow.

He'd been following the path of least resistance through the trees, and it had taken him closer than he'd intended to the clearing and the men around it. When he felt the firelight in his eyes he stopped so quickly the girl behind him collided and tripped over his leg. He tightened his grip and jerked roughly on her arm as she started to fall. She opened her mouth to cry out but then clamped her lips tightly shut, letting only a tiny muffled grunt escape through her nose.

A moment later the boy had found cover behind a clump of palmetto and pulled his companion down beside him into its shadow.

"Sorry, tadpole," he whispered softly. "My fault. Wasn't watchin' where I was goin'." He glanced around them and started to say something else. But there was a shout from the direction of the lake, and when Josh raised his head cautiously he saw the *Andrew Jackson* backing slowly into view beyond the smoke and dwindling flames of the bonfire. The men aboard had finally managed to push her free of the sandbar. While the boy watched, the big paddle wheels shifted direction and she began swinging her bow to bring it in next to the thin strip of beach nearby.

Four men appeared from the darkness to start carrying boxes, barrels and a small cannon aboard from the hastily-assembled stack of goods in the clearing. As others hurried from the boat to help, it was Josh's turn to open his mouth suddenly and then clamp it shut again.

The men who'd appeared from the trees on shore had been Levi, Clyde, Jake and Reuben Budd!

He watched in silent astonishment as they completed their loading and then led a half-dozen horses from the woods up the ramp to the boat; there was no sign of the Budds' original wagons and mule teams. Josh could make little sense of this latest development, except it was clear the men they'd accompanied into Florida were in league with these others. Apparently it had been part of some long-standing plan from the beginning.

Soon the boy's attention was drawn to two new figures who came forward quickly, leading their horses across the deck and down the narrow ramp to the ground. The long-coated men paused and turned back as one of those standing at the rail called out to them:

"Hey! Where you two think you're goin'? This job ain't finished, and we ain't waitin' around for nobody to take no sight-seein' tours on shore!"

"We got us a li'l job of our own needs doin' about now," the man with the long scar answered calmly, "and it won't wait neither. You just go on about your business and we'll catch up to you later on."

"Yeah, well what'll I tell *him*? You know he said for everbody to stay together on board here till we can wood up an' get along to our next stop."

"You tell him it's a li'l unfinished business for the both of us," the second man said. "We done searched that boat stem to stern and ain't found hide nor hair of that boy was there earlier, nor his little girl niece neither. Might be they got ashore an' could make it to one of them settlements sooner or later. And they'd have some mighty interestin' stories to tell folks if'n they did." He reached inside his open coat and took out a large Colt revolver, shoving it into his pocket and starting to re-button the outer garment before continuing: "We'll just have us a look around an' see can we maybe find 'em first, before they get a chance to do any talkin'."

"You better ask him 'bout that 'fore you go off half-cocked. He ain't liable to be too pleased about a couple men takin' off on their own like this."

"Mebbe." The scar-faced man turned his back on the speaker and slid his own gun from his waistband. "But we're a-goin' just the same."

"That boy's got somethin' belongs to us," his companion added after a brief pause, as if he owed the man on the boat some further explanation. "Somethin' we lost back along the road a ways. It's right important to us, and we mean to have it back."

Josh heard these last words while he was edging away from the palmettos on hands and knees, still clutching Sara Jane's small fingers in his own as they retreated toward the sheltering darkness of the woods behind them. She was being remarkably cooperative in view of all that had happened so far, and he meant to be sure and tell her so when — if — they managed to escape from their present situation.

The men in the clearing exchanged a few more words with those aboard the boat before taking up their reins and mounting. In the meantime Josh and his young companion reached the deeper shadows of the trees outside the circle of firelight. Turning quickly with a final glance over his shoulder, the boy made a sudden dash for the jungle-like thicket beyond, with little Sara Jane close on his heels.

The sound of their footsteps drew the attention of the horses and riders. A moment later there was a rough shout behind them:

"Hey! What'd I tell you? There they are! Come on!"

Josh had been aware of the risk their noisy flight might bring, but he also knew that with mounted pursuers the place of greatest danger was in the open. Men on horseback would have a difficult time following into the dense tangle they'd entered now, even in daylight. With trees to hide the moon and the fire well out of sight behind, it would take uncommon luck for anyone to overtake them as he slowed their pace and began moving silently once again.

The chance of losing their own way in the darkness still existed, but the boy had in mind not to try covering too much ground before daylight. Although he wanted badly to be away from this place, he could control the impulse. It was more important to give these men no further clues to their whereabouts. If necessary they would stop moving altogether and go into hiding when the horsemen came near.

His mind was filled with plans and fears as they picked their way gingerly among the fallen limbs and hidden ravines of the dry swamp. There was little opportunity to think about the last thing he'd heard that taller man say — about some object he had which belonged to them. When it did occur to him briefly, Josh realized he had no idea what it was they'd been talking about.

Unless . . .

But how would two cruel, hard men like those come to own a golden locket with a beautiful lady inside?

13 ⚜

I<small>T WAS A LONG, BITTER NIGHT</small>. Josh's hands and face were numb from the cold and bloodied by the countless limbs and brambles they'd stumbled upon unseeing in the dark. His trousers were torn at the knee, and he could not recall how he'd lost his hat. He could guess little Sara Jane wasn't much better off, though she rarely cried out or complained as they felt their way blindly among the clutching vines and brush-filled hollows of this seemingly endless tangle of wilderness beyond Lake George. Perhaps her heavy woolen dress gave her a bit more protection from the briars at least.

The one good thing among all their difficulties in the dark was that it had been a long time now since they'd had any sign of the men pursuing them. Several hours earlier they'd seen a brief light in the distance, perhaps the flare of a match as someone lit a pipe or a cigar. It had lasted only seconds and had not been repeated, but Josh changed course to lead them in the opposite direction all the same. Since that time they had seen and heard nothing. No lights, and no sounds but the occasional faint rustle of some forest creature stalking food or evading a predator.

As the sky began to turn pale the boy brought them to a halt in a small thicket of cedar, hawthorn and scrub oak where they could remain out of sight until daybreak. They both needed rest, and with the coming of dawn he'd have a chance to look over their surroundings before deciding what course to follow next. He scooped fallen leaves around them and burrowed in beside the girl to share body warmth against the pre-dawn cold. Then he lay quietly trying to form some picture in his mind of their present location.

He could only guess at the distance they'd covered since leaving the lakeshore. Five or six miles perhaps, possibly less. Surely no more than ten. It had been slow going through these rugged low hammock lands, with frequent stops to rest and listen cautiously into the night. At one point they'd halted for a longer time while Sara Jane took a much-needed nap.

That had given Josh his first chance to think about their situation, between the brief snatches of sleep he'd found himself unable to resist. It occurred to him then that despite the danger all waterways seemed to present with the *Andrew Jackson* in the hands of those vicious attackers, the lakes and rivers still offered his best hope of coming across people or settlements in this forbidding wilderness. Almost all travel hereabouts was done by water, and that was where he must look for towns and trading posts, too.

At the moment he could not even be certain where the attack on the boat had taken place. It seemed likely it was somewhere on the south shore of the lake, for otherwise the pilot might have suspected the deception of the bogus woodcutters' fire sooner. If that was correct, the direction of their own flight must have been roughly south also, away from the water. Josh had tried hard to keep them moving on a straight line through the night, but he'd no way of being sure how well he'd succeeded.

They'd come across no major waterways in their journey so far. Yet if they were south of the lake the St. Johns River must lie not too far away, flowing from south to north. The trouble was, the boy had no idea whether they were to the west or the east of it now. Any effort to reach it might just as easily take them in the opposite direction. And that river was the only landmark he'd even the slightest knowledge of in this untracked wilderness.

He listened to the girl's steady breathing at his elbow for a long time, forcing himself to think things through calmly and deliberately as 'Lias would have done. At last he arrived at a plan. They would travel east no matter what. If they were west of the river they would soon come to it, and a short distance away would be the settlement of Volusia he'd heard about. If they were already east of it then an eastward course must eventually bring them to the Atlantic Ocean, where coastal fishermen or passing steamers offered at least some better hope of rescue than they could expect at present.

The longer journey might be a hard one for a boy and a small girl on foot without food, matches or weapons. But it was all Josh could think to do, and any plan was better than none. Perhaps they'd come upon some well-marked road or trail in the meantime.

An early morning mist and overcast skies forced them to remain in their hiding place longer than he wished once the boy had fixed upon this course of action. But in time the fog lifted and the clouds parted long enough for him to see shadows on the ground and gauge the direction of the rising sun. He rose and carefully made his way from the thicket to a nearby clearing, watching and listening intently for the slightest sign of danger.

After satisfying himself there was nothing nearby to concern him, he took his bearings from the shadows and then shifted his focus a little to the left to compensate for the sun's winter position. A tall stand of junipers rose in that direction, and he picked one with a distinctive arrangement of limbs to use as a landmark. He would move toward that and select some other tree beyond it as he came near, continuing the process as long as needed. It was a surer method than trying to rely on periodic glimpses of the sun through limbs and clouds overhead.

When he'd checked and double-checked the location and appearance of his landmark, he dug a heel into the ground to mark his position in the clearing before returning to the thicket to finally rouse his sleeping companion. Little Sara Jane yawned and rubbed her eyes with her fists while Josh helped her gently to her feet. "Time to get a move on, tadpole. Rise and shine."

"I'm hungry, Josh. An' thirsty too." She looked up at him blankly, as if having difficulty realizing where they were. "C'n I have a drink of water?"

"Later, tadpole. We'll try and find us a crick or a spring 'fore too long, where we can both drink our fill." He made no mention of food, for Josh knew that might take a bit more doing. His own stomach had been growling since first light.

Suddenly the girl's eyes grew wide and she spun on her heel to look at the silent trees and the forbidding expanse of trackless woods beyond. A moment later she uttered a small choking sob and threw her arms tightly around the boy's waist, burying her face against the rough fabric of his homespun coat.

"I . . ." Her first attempt at speech was cut short by another gulping sob and she had to take several deep breaths before trying again. "I . . . I thought it was a dream. The boat, them men yellin' and shootin', us runnin' away in the dark . . ." She shuddered and then began hiccupping. "A bad . . . dream . . . was all . . . all I . . ."

Josh's arm was around her shoulders and he stroked her head awkwardly with his free hand. "T'weren't no dream, tadpole. It were a bad time an' we only barely got out of it by the skin of our teeth." He tried to make his voice sound soothing and confident. "But we done it, and we left them bad men out there somewheres in the dark whilst we was about it. Now we're on our own, and we just got to make do the best we can from here."

After a time she stopped sobbing and hiccupping and clung to him tightly for several long minutes. At last she looked up at his face and gave him a shy smile. Josh grinned back at her, then took her hand to lead her out of the thicket into the clearing.

He said a silent prayer that she hadn't seen the worry behind his grin, nor the fear which made him miss a step and almost forget to look for his landmark tree before leading her off among the tall grass to east-ward.

❖   ❖   ❖

The sky was a pale metallic gray when Chance Ramsay stepped outside the palmetto cabin to greet the coming morning. Tall trees rose from the black-ness around him like the tapering spires of some enor-mous darkened cathedral, silent and majestic in those cold first minutes before light touched the forest floor.

In his left hand he carried his gunbelts wound tightly together to forestall any random clink of metal against metal. His boots and saddle-roll were clutched in his right as he crossed the few yards of bare sand in his stocking feet to set them before a felled log that was used as a bench. With deliberate care he un-wrapped each weapon and buckled it quietly in place beneath his coat. Then he sat down to draw on his boots.

"You goin' somewhere?" Abby's voice was vel-vet-soft in the pre-dawn stillness, barely spanning the distance between the log bench and the cabin behind it.

Ramsay froze for an instant, then smiled wryly to himself in the dark. "Caught," he said as he finished tugging on the second boot and stood up to stamp them both into place. He turned to face the unseen speaker. "When I woke I felt so much recovered that I thought I'd take a little early morning ride in the for-est. I expect the mare and I both could use the exer-cise."

Her slim figure was barely visible in silhouette against the lighter rectangle of the cabin's entrance.

After a moment she asked mildly, "Wasn't plannin' on ridin' southeast by any chance?"

Ramsay hesitated. Then he shrugged. "I might be."

"Lookin' for them gents you come crosswise of earlier?"

He hesitated again before closing the few steps between them.

"No," he said in a more conversational tone. "Not exactly. I thought I'd have a look around in the direction of those noises we heard last night, see what I can find. Curiosity is one of my fatal flaws. Besides, there's a possibility someone might be hurt and in need of help."

She'd folded her arms and seemed to be studying him thoughtfully. It was a long time before she spoke again, so long that Ramsay thought perhaps she'd nothing more to say. He was on the verge of turning to go saddle his mare when the young woman gave a half shrug and started back inside the cabin.

"Wait here. I'll gather up a couple things."

When she returned a few minutes later, the day had grown noticeably brighter. Ramsay could see that she carried her bow and arrows in her left hand and had a light deerskin pack across her shoulders. Hanging from a leather belt at her waist were a large hunting knife, powder horn and pouch for ammunition. Across her back she'd slung a short-barreled flintlock trade rifle of the kind often carried by Indians and hunters on the frontier.

She glanced at him briefly as she emerged, and then without a word started walking toward the grove where the mare was tethered. Her stride was the lithe, broad-ranging tread of the long hunter. It took Chance

Ramsay a half-dozen hurried steps to bring himself alongside her.

"Now, wait just a minute Miss Macklin . . . Abby." She continued on for another few yards, then stopped and turned toward him curiously.

"When I told you I meant to go have a look around I didn't mean for you . . . that is, I'd no intention you should . . ." He paused and she continued to regard him in placid silence. "There is no need for you to come along," he concluded finally. "This is not anything that concerns you, and . . ."

"Nor you."

"Yes I know. But . . ." He sighed and gently reached up to shift his hat from where it was binding against the bandage at the back of his skull. As he did so he met her eyes. "Miss Macklin, each man's private folly is his own personal business. If I choose to risk my neck, it's mine to risk. But to bring someone else into it needlessly . . ."

"You ain't bringin' me. I come on my own."

"But . . ."

"Mr. Ramsay, these here're my woods. Leastways that's the way I look at it. Anything happens in 'em is of concern to me. And I got just as much reason — more — for wantin' to know what-all happened last night as you do. My neck's my own to do with as I please too. And I'm comin'.

"Besides . . ." She smiled at him with her eyes only. "I get around this country pretty good, huntin' game an' all. So far you ain't showed me you can even sneak up on a bunch of half-drunk men in the dark without gettin' your fool head blowed off. More'n likely it'll be me who's got to be lookin' out for you if we come acrost any trouble."

Ramsay sighed and shook his head in resignation. "You've made your point," he said with a wry smile. "Let's saddle the mare."

As he was tightening the cinch he glanced over his shoulder at the silent young woman behind him. "I don't know if I like the idea of this little lady carrying double for any distance. Perhaps we could take turns. . . ."

She shrugged her pack into a more comfortable position and took a few steps away into the forest. "You been hurt, and you still ain't feelin' so chipper as you'd like to let on. Go ahead an' mount up. I'll walk."

❖   ❖   ❖

Josh and Sara Jane had not been traveling for more than an hour when the boy caught his first faint whiff of wood smoke. He halted immediately, wrinkling his nose and sniffing lightly at the crisp morning air. His eyes shifted warily to look in every direction.

They'd entered a grove of hardwoods and live oak not long before, where the ground was higher and there was little undergrowth to slow their progress. It made for easier walking, but the dense trees here kept them from seeing more than thirty yards in any direction.

After a minute Josh glanced down and met the young girl's curious look. He bent and put his mouth close to her ear.

"Smoke," he said softly. "That means folks is about." When he'd raised his head again to study their surroundings, he knelt at Sara Jane's elbow and went on in a low whisper: "If they's settlers it'd be a blessin'.

A warm fire an' a bite to eat, maybe some help with them men been huntin' us too." He hesitated. "But if it turns out to be them fellers theirselves . . ."

He felt the girl shudder as he rested a hand on her shoulder. "What we goin' to do, Josh?"

The boy was silent for a long moment. At last he shrugged. "Try an' find out, I reckon." He rose to his feet and led her to the shelter of a huge live oak some dozen feet away. "You stay put here and I'll scout around a bit. Be back to get you soon as I find out that it's safe." When he turned away she took hold of his arm tightly with both hands.

"No!" Her whisper was shrill and harsh, so that Josh glanced around in sudden panic. Sara Jane saw his look and hesitated, then swallowed and went on more quietly, "No, Josh." She shook her head firmly. "No. I ain't stayin' here by myself. What if them men is out there? What if they's to take aholt of you?" Tears had appeared at the corners of her eyes. "What'd I do if'n you don't come back?"

He moved closer and squatted on his heels beside her, reaching out gently to place an arm around her waist.

"Reckon I didn't think about that, tadpole." He paused, meeting her eyes. "Reckon I just plain didn't think things through all the way for a minute there. But you're right. It's you an' me together out here, and we'd best keep it thataway." After another minute he took her hand and helped her to her feet. "Pardners?" She nodded silently. "Okay. Let's you an' me take that look around together then. But we got to move quiet. So quiet even a ol' she-panther wouldn't know we was in the neighborhood. You understand?"

Sara Jane nodded again. Suddenly she threw her arms around him and clung tightly. "Thanks, Josh. Thanks for not leavin' me. I was so scared when I thought about you maybe never comin' back. Scared almost to death!"

The boy patted her shoulder and gave her a brief hug before moving to separate them. "Reckon you ain't got no corner on that bein' scared market, tadpole, tell you the truth. But we got it to do."

They began making their way slowly and cautiously among the boles of lichen-covered trees, treading softly and pausing to listen after every few steps. When they'd covered perhaps a hundred yards, a faint clink of metal against stone froze them both in their tracks. It seemed to come from a small clearing a short distance off on their left. Josh glanced down at his companion, indicating the direction with a nod of his head.

For a long time he studied the woods between them and the clearing, selecting a route he felt offered the best concealment while taking them toward a large fallen log almost at the edge of the open space. Then with a finger to his lips as an unnecessary reminder for silence, he led them forward on tiptoe from tree to tree until they were a dozen yards from the log and partly hidden behind it. Here he dropped to the ground and began easing forward on hands and knees, with Sara Jane close behind. They reached the log after what seemed an eternity of crawling, yet Josh kept still for several long minutes more while he listened intently to the sounds coming from the clearing.

There was not much to hear: a faint crackle of flames, a mild scuffling from time to time as someone shifted position near the fire, the occasional repetition of that metallic sound which Josh decided was some kind of cooking utensil after he'd caught a clear scent of bacon on the morning air. No voices could be heard, nor any suggestion of other humans or animals nearby. It sounded as it they'd come upon some hunter or trapper cooking his solitary breakfast in the open.

Yet he was unwilling to gamble their safety on these slight impressions, and after another long wait Josh eased his way to one side in order to raise his head cautiously between two broken limbs at one end of the fallen tree.

He saw the clearing's occupant, alone and cooking breakfast as he had guessed. But still the view of this unattended pioneer of the Florida wilderness caught him off guard, so that he had to swallow quickly to keep from voicing his surprise.

Squatting on his heels beside a circle of stones and a battered cast iron skillet over the fire, wearing dirty homespun trousers and a tattered jacket, was a boy some two or three years younger than Josh himself!

14 🌿

Josh studied the scene carefully, his eyes flicking from the boy to the crude palmetto-thatched lean-to at the edge of the woods and back again to the old flintlock musket which stood against a young pine tree a few feet from the fire. Finally he glanced at Sara Jane and reached out to take her hand. They rose together and stepped from behind the fallen log.

"Howdy," Josh said mildly.

The other boy jerked his head up and turned to take hold of the musket with both hands.

"You won't need that shootin' iron. We're both friendly." There was a faint grin on his lips as Josh led the girl into the clearing. "More'n likely too wore out to do nothing about it even if'n we wasn't."

"You alone?" The other boy spoke warily. He held the musket with his right thumb on the hammer, but Josh saw that he had not yet cocked it.

"Yep." The musket lowered slightly. "An' like I say, we're both of us plumb near wore to a frazzle after a night out in them woods. Sure would admire to warm ourselves at that fire for a bit. An' maybe take a drink of water if you've got some handy." He glanced at the few lonely strips of bacon in the frying pan and made himself resist the temptation to ask about food.

"Come on ahead then. They's some spring water in that bucket back yonder by the lean-to." The younger boy had caught Josh's look, and when he'd set the musket aside he reached into a burlap sack lying on the ground behind him. "Got a couple extra sweet potatoes here if you want 'em." He took them out and placed them near the coals to warm. Then he shrugged. "Bacon's about played out, but I reckon we can share what's left of that too."

"Thanks," Josh said. "We're mighty grateful." He went to fetch the water bucket while Sara Jane squatted beside the fire and held out her hands toward the low-burning flames. The younger boy watched them both in silence.

"You say you spent all night out there alone?" he asked finally. "Just the two of you?"

"Uh-huh." Josh handed the gourd dipper to Sara Jane. When she'd finished he refilled it from the bucket and drank in his turn. The spring water was cool and sweet.

"Got folks around here somewheres?" The younger boy's eyes narrowed slightly. "Anybody lookin' for you?"

"Well . . ." Josh refilled the dipper from the bucket and drank again. "Yes an' no." He hesitated. "That is, I reckon maybe it's kind of a long story."

The other boy shrugged. "Wasn't plannin' on goin' noplace right away."

Josh looked over the fire at him. After a moment

he said, "All right. Why not?"

He settled himself more comfortably and started at the beginning, describing the journey on the riverboat, the bonfire, the night attack, and how he and Sara Jane had escaped to shore after plunging into the lake. The younger boy listened attentively, interrupting with questions from time to time and nodding thoughtfully at the answers. He'd heard the sounds of battle, but seemed most interested now in the appearance of those men who'd had a hand in the attack. Apart from the Budds and the man in the silk hat Josh could offer little of interest in that regard.

Sara Jane sat hugging her knees beside the circle of stones, listening in silence. When they came to the part about the wounding of 'Lias she closed her eyes and began to cry softly. Josh moved closer and put an arm around her shoulders before finishing his tale, ending at last with a description of the two men on horseback who'd pursued them into the night.

The younger boy's eyes grew watchful when he heard about the riders. He retrieved his musket and glanced around the clearing before finally asking, "How was them two mounted? I mean, what did their horses look like?"

"Shorter one with the scar had him a buckskin gelding. T'other was on a big white-an'-tan stallion." Josh paused, struck curiously by the other's agitation. "Why'd you ask?"

"'Tain't them." The boy spoke quietly, almost to himself. Then he looked at Josh. "But I got a idea they's part of that same bunch." He hunkered down near the fire again, and after a minute went on in a low, deliberate voice:

"Couple men come up on our cabin some four, five days ago. Kilt my pappa and stole our two horses, then threw down money and ordered me off the place. Said they was buyin' the land an' the horses, and for me not to make no fuss about it or I'd wind up the same as my pa." He stared into the flames for a long time. When he spoke again his voice was cold:

"I didn't make no fuss about it. Didn't say nothin' to nobody a-tall. Just buried Pappa and moved what I could from the cabin out here in the woods, an' set up housekeepin'." He paused to spit and glanced around the clearing briefly. "Figured maybe I'd run acrost them two again sooner or later. And I didn't want no others along for company when I did." The younger boy raised his eyes to look at his visitors.

"Me an' Pappa's from the mountains, y'see. Up Nantahala, Shootin' Creek way. Got no kinfolks back there now, nor anywheres else that I know about. And no partic'lar friends since we come here into Florida. But we got our ways. And one of 'em is that a man skins his own coons. I got business with them men who shot my pappa. And us Panners is knowed to have a real long memory."

There was a silence after he'd finished speaking. At last Josh nodded soberly.

"Reckon I know what you're sayin'. Seein' my brother cut down by that dude in the high hat give me pretty much the same kind of feelin'. I'd a mind to meet up again with that partic'lar gent my ownself sometime." He paused and met the other boy's eyes. "I'm Josh Carpenter. Short for Joshua. This here's my little girl niece, Sara Jane."

"Pleased to make your acquaintance. Matt Panner's

my name, short for Matthew." The boy set his musket aside and removed the pan from the fire, taking out a piece of bacon as he did and putting it in his mouth. After a moment he started pulling sweet potatoes away from the coals.

"You go on ahead an' eat up now, Josh an' Sara Jane." He rose and went to the lean-to, kneeling there to begin rolling his meager belongings in the blankets that lay on the palmetto floor. "We best be makin' some tracks away from this place pretty quick now, 'fore them gents was huntin' y'all has any chanct to make their appearance."

Josh took a potato and cooled it briefly by tossing it from hand to hand before giving it to Sara Jane. "We done left them two back in the swamp hours ago," he said calmly. "Sometime before midnight I'd reckon. Ain't seen hide nor hair of 'em sinct." He picked up the second potato for himself.

"Uh-huh." Matt Panner finished tying the blankets and made a rope sling to hang them over his shoulder. "Only you-all didn't cover half so much ground as you thought you did durin' the night. It ain't no more'n two, three mile to Lake George from here as the crow flies. And they's game and Injun trails all through these woods. Shucks, the main road from Pilatka to Volusia don't pass no more'n a thousand yards to the east of this place!"

Josh glanced quickly around and then fell thoughtfully silent. When the younger boy returned to the fire, he was carrying an old flintlock pistol. He handed it to Josh before kneeling and starting to scour the frying pan with handfuls of clean sand.

"That there was Pappa's, same as the musket. Ain't

too much for shootin' nothing 'less you're nigh up close enough to spit on it. But she's all charged and loaded, and I reckon maybe it'd be better'n nothin' if you was to run acrost them men who's after your scalp." He finished by rinsing the pan with water from the bucket and pouring it over the coals to douse them. Then he shook out the drops from both items before putting them into the burlap sack.

"Since you two are travelin' light, I'd be obliged if you'd tote this here whilst I carry the bedroll an' musket." The boy who'd called himself Matt rose and took up the long gun, then glanced at Josh and Sara Jane. "You 'bout ready to travel?"

Josh got to his feet and shoved the pistol into his belt. "I reckon." He bent to pick up the sack. "But where was it you had in mind for us to be goin'?"

"They's a place back up in the brush not too far from here where I hid out first after leavin' the cabin. It's a mite low an' damp, but a deal better hid than this one. Won't nobody find us there unless they come lookin' with dogs, or is part coon dog their ownselves."

Josh took Sara Jane's hand and they followed Matt quickly through the hardwood hammock and toward a deeper stand of palmetto scrub some hundred yards beyond. When they'd come to a dry creek bed a little farther on, well hidden among low-hanging branches and dense undergrowth, the younger boy paused briefly to let them rest and catch their breaths.

"Not too much further now to that place I was talkin' of," he said in a low voice, kneeling on the damp leaves to look back in the direction they had come. "'Nother quarter mile maybe, right along this little ol' draw here."

Josh set the sack down and squatted on his heels, glancing from Sara Jane to Matt and frowning in thought. At last he spoke quietly, matching his voice to that of his companion: "What then?"

"Huh?"

"What'll we do onct we get to that hidin' place of yours? I mean we can't set out here holed up in these woods forever. You got any plans for what we'd ought to do afterwards?" He paused and the other boy shrugged.

"We can stay holed up till them men what's after y'all gives up the chase at least. Seems to me that's the most important thing to be thinkin' about just now."

"Maybe. An' maybe them two are a sight more determined than you'd expect. Anyways there's family of ours aboard that riverboat was took last night, and I got to try an' get help to 'em if there's any way I can manage it."

Matt looked at him oddly. "Now, how you think you're goin' to do that? We three ain't exactly no high sheriff's posse. In fact we're about as sorry a outfit as I ever seen to be takin' on no armed outlaws, even two of 'em to say nothin' 'bout a dozen or more."

"Seems to me I recall little while ago you 'lowed you'd a mind to take on two of 'em all by your lonesome."

"When . . . whenever I get the chanct I will. Sometime. Somehow." He was looking at the ground, avoiding Josh's eyes. "Mebbe by ambush, I don't know. That is, if'n I ever do get the chanct . . . .." The younger boy fell silent for a moment. When he went on his voice was hoarse and he seemed to speak with difficulty.

"They kilt my pappa. I got it to do. Or at least try.

Ain't never had nobody else, Momma dyin' when I was born an' all. And Pappa hadn't nothin' to show for a life's hard work but that little bitty homestead an' them two Tennessee horses, what was stole out from under us." Matt paused again, then said quietly: "Reckon maybe they'll kill me too, if'n I ever do see 'em again. I ain't no match for men like that an' prob'ly never will be, but . . .. Dang it all anyway!"

He swallowed hard, then turned to Josh with reddened eyes. "What else can I do?"

The older boy hesitated before finally sitting back on the leaf-covered ground and folding his arms across his knees. He deliberately tried to make his voice sound calm and matter-of-fact.

"I been studyin' on that some. 'Pears to me what all three of us could use right now is a mite of help. It's high time we quit tryin' to do everthing on our lonesome and started huntin' up reinforcements. Now I heard tell there's this settlement on the river called Volusia . . ."

At a sound from Matt, Josh glanced up to see the younger boy's lips pressed tightly together and a hard expression in his eyes. "What you got stuck in your craw now?"

"Them settlement folks ain't no friends of ours. Treated us like trash mostly, the whole time we been livin' here." Matt took a breath and went on slowly:

"Pappa weren't so much for socializin' anyway, I reckon. He were accustomed to keepin' his own counsel. But if folks asked his opinion on somethin', he didn't have no hesitation a-tall about tellin' 'em. I guess maybe there was some talk up there to the store a time or two, of states' rights an' dissolvin' the Union an' such. And Pappa told 'em what he thought. He were agin it. Said it was a dang fool notion that could only lead to war an' killin' sooner or later, brother against brother." The boy paused. "Reckon that wasn't just exactly what they all wanted to hear. Afterwards we was right unpopular folks hereabouts. Pretty much they left us to our own devices, and we stayed shut of them too."

Matt Panner lifted his eyes and shrugged. "That's why I didn't bother goin' down there after Pappa was kilt, lookin' for help or nothin'. Wasn't sure they'd be willin' anyhow, the way they all acted when he was alive. And I knowed he wouldn't never of asked 'em for it hisself, no matter what happened. So I decided that I wouldn't neither. Just made up my mind to hole up in them woods an' take care of things my ownself."

Josh nodded when the other boy finished, and sat in silence for several long minutes. At last he said:

"I reckon I can understand how you feel, Matt. Us Carpenters been knowed to have a good-sized streak of pride our ownselves. But it still don't change the fact that us three kids ain't goin' to do nobody no good out here in the woods all by our lonesome. We just flat ain't got the hosses."

He hugged his knees and cocked his head, listening for a moment into the silent forest. Then he went on thoughtfully, "It strikes me that this here ain't no business what concerns just the Carpenters or the Panners anyhow. Not no longer. Men who'd kill one homesteader or run him off his land would as like do it to another. And attackin' a riverboat comes right close to declarin' war on this entire country. I think maybe it's time we spread the word an' let the rest of 'em have a hand in what's goin' on." He glanced at Sara Jane, then met Matt's eyes.

"My brother 'Lias said onct that whenever there's the need folks on the frontier's got to pull together, without concernin' theirselves too much 'bout any personal differences they might feel at the time. I guess now is maybe just the sort of case he was talkin' about." Josh paused, studying the other boy's face. "I ain't too proud to go lookin' for help, anyplace we can find it. And I don't reckon you ought to be neither."

The younger boy sat without speaking for several minutes. Finally he nodded. "All right, Josh Carpenter. I expect you done made your point. There ain't a awful lot else we can do anyhow. So we might's well go ahead up there to that settlement and see can we find somebody who'll listen to our story."

Josh grinned, then stood and reached out to take up the burlap sack. "You lead on, and we'll follow. How far you reckon it is to that Volusia place?"

"'Nother couple miles mebbe. Say a hour and a half through these woods an' trails hereabouts."

"Okay. But let's keep takin' it real easy and watchful whilst we're a-travelin'. I'd sure hate for them trackers to come up on us 'fore we get to someplace we might find help."

15 🖤

I⊤ WAS A LITTLE AFTER SUNRISE when Abby and Ramsay crossed the trail left by the riders three nights earlier. On a hunch — Abby's — they had taken an eastward route from her cabin rather than heading directly southeast, and the signs left by the six horsemen were still plainly visible. Fortunately, there had been no rains to wash tracks out in the meantime.

Both had a suspicion there was some connection between that party of well-armed men and the distant sounds of battle they'd heard the previous night. Their presence in this sparsely populated wilderness seemed too great a coincidence otherwise. Yet even if this did not prove true, it would still be well to know where the men had ridden. The dull ache at the back of Ramsay's skull was a constant reminder of the danger they presented by themselves.

As it happened, the riders' trail did lead to the southeast, skirting a good-sized lake a few miles farther on and eventually coming to a salt spring at the lake's eastern outlet. Shortly before noon Abby and

Ramsay followed the tracks across a marshy creek, then turned aside toward a log cabin several hundred yards away and partly hidden among the trees of the south bank.

"I know the folks that lives here," the young woman explained in a half whisper as they stopped by the opening in a brushwood fence. "Keeps to theirselves mostly, an' don't favor strangers. But if anything's happened hereabouts, they'd know it." She put warning fingers on her companion's arm as he moved to dismount. "You stay put. Just rest easy up there with your hands in the open, an' let me do the talkin'."

A lean, sunburned woman in dark shawl and faded bonnet had appeared on the narrow porch, cradling a blanket-wrapped baby in her left arm. Her right was at her side, where the muzzle of an ancient flintlock pistol could be seen partly hidden by the ragged apron that covered her homespun skirt.

Chance Ramsay sat very still while Abby spoke a word of greeting and allowed herself to be recognized, then entered the yard and approached the cabin. He'd noticed immediately that the pistol in the woman's hand was cocked and ready to fire. It took a minute longer to catch the faint movement and glint of metal from the woods at his right which told him she was not alone.

The conversation seemed to last a long time. Abby asked questions and the woman answered, always in a few words and seldom taking her eyes from the mounted visitor in the black suit. Their voices were low so that Ramsay could make out nothing of what was said. At last Abby nodded and turned away, lifting a hand in parting as the woman disappeared back through the open doorway with her infant and her loaded pistol.

He looked down at her curiously when she came near, but Abby only motioned with her head and continued silently past him away from the cabin. After turning the mare, he followed at an easy walk back along the creek toward the southbound trail. It was not until they'd traveled perhaps another half mile that the young woman in buckskins slowed her pace and dropped back beside him.

"That Maude Tabor and her man's all right, I reckon," she said. "But notional. Didn't see no sense in hangin' around there after I'd found out what we come to ask 'em." She paused to adjust her pack and Ramsay brought the mare to a stop beside her.

"What did she tell you?"

"Big doin's over t'other side of the lake last night. Shootin', yellin', firin' off that cannon you was talkin' about." She straightened and met his eyes. "Sounded like a real for-sure battle, Maude said. Her man was out giggin' fish by torchlight an' he pretty much seen the whole thing."

"On the opposite side of the lake?"

"South bank. Some eight, ten mile from where his boat was at. But the sound carries good over water like that."

"Could he tell anything about what what was happening?"

"Not so much he could see from that far off. Nothin' 'cept the flashes from the guns an' this big ole bonfire next to the water. But he'd a idea or two all the same." Abby glanced around, then moved to a large stump where a tree had been felled to make the trail more passable.

"You might's well light an' set. This could take a bit of explainin'. And we're about due for a break anyhow." She leaned her bow up against the stump and sat, then waited in silence while Ramsay dismounted and tethered the mare nearby. When he'd approached and taken a place beside her she continued as if there'd been no interruption:

"Harley, that's Maude's man, he knows ever inch of this lake. Fished an' hunted all round it sinct before the Injun wars. When he seen that bonfire on the south bank towards dusk, an' the steamboat passin' him not long after headin' thataway — well, he didn't think too much about it. Them boats allus likes to wood up at the point there west of the river before headin' up to Lake Monroe. But then after little while Harley looked again an' something struck him kind of odd. He got to studyin' on it, and decided that fire weren't nowhere near the river's mouth. 'Peared like it was maybe two, three mile t'other side to the east of it."

Ramsay gave her a curious look, but said nothing. After a moment the young woman continued:

"'Bout the time he'd decided that, he sort of lost interest in fishin' and kept on a-lookin' off towards that bonfire, tryin' to figure out what it was doin' at the place where it was. He seen the lights of the boat comin' closer, and then all of a sudden it seemed like the entire woods over yonder just kind of exploded with rifle an' musket fire and the boom of that big ole cannon spittin' flame an' sparks off acrost the water." She glanced at Ramsay out of the corners of her eyes and shrugged.

"Said it kept on like that for maybe a quarter hour, with them on the boat shootin' back ever now an' again, before they was a great big yell from shore together with even bigger noise from the guns. And then after that everthing got real quiet. Harley didn't wait around to see what happened next. He'd already doused his torch soon as the shebang started, and by the time it was over he was pullin' hard for the mouth of that crick what runs past his cabin. Beached his boat and hid it up under some brush, then went inside and bolted all the shutters an' doors. They ain't hardly set a foot outside sinct yesterday evenin', and didn't see nor hear nobody else till we come callin'."

Ramsay sat in silence for a long time after Abby finished, close beside her but not looking at her. At last he said thoughtfully:

"It would appear that bonfire was deliberately set at the wrong landing place in order to lure the boat into an ambush." He glanced over his shoulder and saw her nod.

"Seemed that way to Harley too. Reckon it was some kind of outlaw gang after whatever they could steal from them folks on board."

"Maybe." Ramsay frowned. "But remarkably well armed for such an enterprise, even to include a cannon." After another silence he turned to meet the young woman's eyes. "What about those men whose trail we've been following? Did Mr. or Mrs. Tabor have any knowledge of them?"

"Heard somebody passin' a couple nights back, but didn't pay it no special mind. It was late an' they was both turned in already, so when whoever it was kept on ridin' they figured everthing was for the best.

Trouble comes soon enough in this country without havin' to climb out of a nice warm bed to go lookin' for it."

Ramsay nodded. "So it is possible at least that those men had a hand in the fighting." He fell silent again, and it was several more minutes before he asked, "Is there anyplace close where we could look out over the lake toward the scene of the attack?"

Abby considered. "'Nother four, five mile down this trail's prob'ly the nearest spot. Comes out right almost beside the water there, with lime rock bluffs where you could climb up an' have a good look-see. Still a right long ways to the place Harley was talkin' about, though. Hard to tell much at that distance." She cocked her head to one side and asked, "You got somethin' partic'lar in mind?"

"Only that I'd be curious to know if the boat is still there." The man in black shrugged. "Assuming robbery was the motive, it ought to be. Sunk or burned down to the waterline maybe, but still partly visible in the shallows. If there is no sign of it at all . . ."

She nodded, completing the sentence: ". . . then somebody's done made off with it durin' the night. And if that's the case it was more'n likely what them bushwhackers planned from the git-go."

"Yes. Though why it should be, I can't imagine." He fell silent for a moment, then turned to look at her questioningly. "If we're to reach your cabin by night-fall we should start back now. It is past noon and I would guess we've already traveled a dozen miles since morning. At least we have gained some general idea of what happened during the night. . ." When he paused Abby shook her head and smiled one of her rare smiles.

"Oh no, Mr. Chance Ramsay. No you don't. Now you got me near 'bout eat up with the curiosity over this riverboat business, you're sayin' just leave it all behind an' forget it? Not likely." She rose from the stump and bent to take up her bow and arrows.

"If *you're* fearful of a night out in the wilderness you can just head on back your ownself. Me, I'm a mind to keep goin' till I can find out what happened to that boat!"

Ramsay smiled faintly to himself, admiring the lithe movements of her body and the determined set of her shoulders as she walked away a few steps, then turned back to meet his eyes. He nodded and got up quietly to go untie the mare and join her.

He'd felt obliged to make the suggestion, but was more than pleased with her decision to proceed around the lake. In truth, his own curiosity would not have allowed him to ignore the questions of the previous night for much longer.

The store at Volusia looked out over the river from a high shell mound, some fifty yards to landward from an ancient live oak tree which Matt Panner said had been a landmark for Indians and trappers since earliest times. There were several other widely scattered buildings visible among the woods to either side, and in a low clearing beyond the board-and-batten store stood a rough warehouse and boat landing at the water's edge.

Josh and his companions crouched to survey the scene behind a stand of palmettos a short distance away with the shell mound between themselves and the river. The sun was well overhead now, and it appeared most of the villagers had retired to their homes for the noon meal. There was no one in sight.

"Reckon that store'd be the place to start," the older boy said quietly. "They'd know most everbody in these parts, and likely could help spread the word if need be." He glanced at Matt, who shrugged and nodded.

"Ol' Brooks ain't such a bad sort, I guess. An' prob'ly curious to know 'bout all the shootin' an' hooraw up to the lake last night anyhow." He stretched and seated himself on the ground with his back against a pine tree, laying the musket across his knees. "You go on ahead an' talk to him. I'll wait here."

Josh looked at him. "I'd a mind for all of us to go in together. You got things to tell 'em too, 'bout your pa an' the horses an' all."

"Maybe." Matt was avoiding his eyes. "But I'm just old man Panner's kid. They ain't likely to care too much 'bout anything I got to say."

"I ain't sure of that. And anyways you'd ought to tell 'em. It's important for other folks to know what's been goin' on hereabouts."

"You think so, you tell 'em. I ain't of a mind to make no social calls at the moment."

Josh shifted his position to study the other boy's face.

"Nope," he said finally, shaking his head. "We're in this together, Matt. And I reckon we'll just stick together now until the game is over." He rose, glancing briefly over his shoulder before looking back at the boy on the ground. "Come on and get to your feet."

Matt Panner set his jaw and stared up at him stubbornly. "Who's goin' to make me?"

"You're lookin' at him." Josh put his hands on his hips and took a step closer.

There was something in the Carpenter boy's eyes which Matt had not seen before, and it did not encourage argument. He glanced away and shrugged, then slowly rose from the ground. "Oh, all right. If'n it'll make you happy."

Josh grinned and took Sara Jane's hand, turning and stepping into the open toward the river and the store. "Seein' them folks ain't ever goin' to get no easier if you keep on puttin' it off. We might's well all just go ahead an' have done with it."

They crossed the clearing and climbed the shell mound to the broad front porch, with Matt lagging slightly behind. The younger boy remained outside while Josh and Sara Jane entered the long narrow sales room. It was empty, but a minute later a tall bearded man emerged grumbling from a back door which apparently led to living quarters beyond. He was wearing no coat, and a soiled napkin had been thrust into the neck of his collarless shirt.

"You'd think just onct a man ought to be able to have his dinner in peace, 'thout everbody in the county come bargin' in here to . . ." He stopped suddenly and regarded his young visitors with surprise. "Hello. Somethin' I can do for y'all?"

"I'm Josh Carpenter, this here's my niece Sara Jane. You'd be Mr. Brooks?" The bearded man nodded. "Well, we come in off the *Andrew Jackson* last night after she was attacked an' boarded by a bunch of murderin' outlaws." The man's eyebrows lifted and he slowly removed the napkin to wipe his lips. "Thought maybe you'd want to hear about it."

Mr. Brooks studied them narrowly. "I reckon we would, son." He paused. "That is if you ain't just a-funnin' me."

"We ain't funnin'. They shot my brother an' kilt maybe three, four others. Two of 'em chased me an' Sara Jane through the woods last night on horseback. It ain't somethin' we feel partic'lar light-hearted about."

The storekeeper regarded them in silence for a moment longer. Then he called over his shoulder toward the back of the building: "Mother, set a couple more places at the table. We got us some company."

Josh turned and saw that Matt had still not entered the room. He stepped outside and took the younger boy's arm in a firm grip, leading him through the door to stand between himself and Sara Jane.

"Three sir, if'n you don't mind. I reckon maybe you'd know Matt Panner. He's got some things to tell you too. 'Bout how his pa was murdered a few days back, and their horses stole an' the homestead took over by what we expect was some of that same bunch."

The man with the beard gave Matt a long, hard look. Yet Josh had the impression it was more a look of surprise than any kind of resentment. He nodded and called out: "Three places, Mother." Then he turned and started through the doorway, indicating with a wave of his hand that they were to follow. "Mind you leave them shootin' irons out here in the hall 'fore you come to table. We don't serve dinner to no armed men."

They followed him into a large high-ceilinged room that served as both kitchen and dining area. Two younger children were seated at the oak table, where a plump woman with a cheerful face was bustling about laying out extra dishes and silverware. She looked up in surprise as the visitors entered. But all she said was, "Y'all can wash up at that basin there on the counter. Then come ahead and set 'fore it starts to get cold."

It took some time until Josh and Matt had both finished their stories, between generous helpings of fried fish, cornbread and home-canned vegetables. When the younger boy finally fell silent after describing his father's death and his days alone in the woods, neither the storekeeper nor his wife spoke for a long while.

At last the bearded man pushed his chair back and rose from the table. "Reckon I'd best have a word with the other men in the settlement. Ain't too sure what all this means yet, but it won't hurt none to be ready and on the look-out for trouble. We've seen our share of it this past fifteen year, with the Injun wars and raidin' afterwards an' all. A touch more wouldn't hardly come as no surprise." He reached up to take a long Kentucky rifle from its brackets over the fireplace, then glanced at the Carpenters and Matt.

"You kids can stay here for the time bein'. This ol' store was built like a fort from the git-go. It's 'bout as safe as any place you're liable to find this side of Pilatka. Them boards outside is only for show. Underneath she's solid heart pine, through and through."

When he disappeared out the doorway, Mrs. Brooks rose and examined her new charges with a critical eye. "'Pears to me the three of y'all ought to be just plumb near wore to a frazzle. Shouldn't wonder, spendin' nights alone in the woods an' such. Come on." She led them through a second door toward another part of the house. "We got a couple extra beds we rent to drummers time to time. You can settle in there and have yourselves a nice long nap."

Josh and his companions made no argument, for they were exhausted by the night's difficulties and their long trek through the wilderness. Little Sara Jane was asleep almost the moment her head touched the pillow and Matt Panner was not far behind. For a short while Josh lay awake thinking about his brother and wondering what had become of the others aboard the riverboat. But soon he too was unable to keep his eyes open, drifting comfortably into a warm, deep slumber.

16 🌴

For a time Chance Ramsay and Abby Macklin walked the trail side by side, the man leading the mare and enjoying an opportunity to stretch his legs on the soft forest floor. He had been feeling stronger and more alert as the day progressed, nourished by the sun and the mild air filled with fresh scents of growing things. He felt sure it would not be long now until he would become his former self again.

Their route led them to the southeast, and in less than two hours they had come to the low bluffs overlooking Lake George. The sandy ground here was thick with yaupon and scrub oak, spread beneath towering stands of cypress, white cedar and royal palm. Another half hour of searching was needed to locate an open place where they could gaze out over the blue waters of the lake.

Abby pointed toward the south where Harley Tabor had described seeing the flashes of gunfire, and for a time they stood in silence, studying the far shoreline. At last Ramsay shifted his position slightly to take in a broader view of the lake. He let his eyes roam from south to north and slowly back again. There was no sign of a riverboat in any direction.

"It would seem," he said quietly, "that our hunch was correct. Whoever attacked the vessel intended to take possession of it, and succeeded. Now the larger question is, 'Why?'"

"Might still have burned it." Abby was facing away from him, shading her eyes to peer out over the expanse of gently rippling waters. "Wouldn't likely notice it from here, 'specially if they sunk what was left." After a minute she turned to him and shrugged. "Don't see no sense to it anyway, takin' a big boat like that when everbody knows whose it was right along. Alls they'd be buyin' is trouble onct the word got around."

"Yes." He nodded. "So either they are very foolish — or perhaps they don't think it will matter in the long run." Ramsay hunkered down on his heels and the young woman knelt beside him.

"With a cannon and a large company of armed men on board, they could stand off an attack from virtually any source except a naval flotilla. And it might be a long time before the authorities would believe there is any need for such steps. In the meanwhile they'd control not only Lake George, but communication with the settlements upriver as well."

Abby shook her head. "Still don't make no sense to me. What's to be gained from it? It ain't like there's gold or nothin' else much worth takin' from them places down south."

"There's land." He met her eyes. "Millions of unclaimed acres, with more cattle than settlers all the way from here to the Florida Cape. It's something ambitious men have thought of before, on this as well as other frontiers."

He fell silent and she watched him without speaking for several long minutes. At last she stirred and got to her feet, brushing the sand from her skirts and observing matter-of-factly:

"Could be you're right. But ain't neither of us goin' to learn no more about it just sittin' here makin' guesses. We got two, three hours of good daylight left, and I figure we might's well move on down the road a piece. If we're a mind, we can be to that spot where the ambush took place before noon tomorrow. Maybe we'll find out somethin' then."

Ramsay nodded and rose from the ground, ignoring the small voice at the back of his mind which kept asking fitfully why this should be any of his concern. Viewed in the clear light of reason, the attack on the riverboat and its aftermath might be the best thing for him: a useful distraction to occupy the authorities until he could lose himself deeper in the Florida peninsula.

Yet there was something about the arrogance and brutality of the men who'd commit such a deed, quite apart from their attack on him earlier, that aroused feelings of anger, even outrage, in the gambler's breast. It was a feeling he could not explain — reckless perhaps, even dangerous. But it seemed enough at present to warrant postponing his flight south, for one more day at least. . . .

Their trail led them parallel to the lakeshore now, sometimes in view of the water and sometimes not. Ramsay finally managed to persuade the young woman to take her turn riding while he walked alongside, arguing that each of them would remain fresher as a result, and so better prepared to deal with any unknown dangers which might arise.

That such dangers existed, lurking deadly and unseen around the circumference of Lake George, was a thing both appeared to accept now without further discussion. A captured riverboat could be hidden anyplace among dozens of sheltered coves or creeks along the waterway, and armed riders might be abroad too, perhaps ahead or behind them on this very trail.

With that in mind, and with a strong desire to avoid known springs and stopping places, Abby soon struck out cross-country toward the southwest, over trackless sand hills grown up thickly with pine, palmetto and hardwood scrub. It was slow going, and they paused frequently to listen and let their eyes roam carefully left to right, forward and back, among the trees and shadowed closeness of the surrounding woods.

The sun was low and dark clouds were gathering in the east when they finally entered a deep ravine to halt at a clear-flowing creek under barren branches of water oak, sweetgum and red maple. Thick vines of buckthorn and wild grape climbed the trees and returned to earth in knotted, serpentine shrouds. Ramsay was struck by the eerie stillness of the place, interrupted only by the restless murmur of swift-moving water near his feet.

They found a narrow sand beach where the mare could drink. Afterwards the man and woman knelt upstream to cup handfuls of cold, sweet water to their own lips. It was several minutes before Ramsay glanced at his companion and ventured softly, "We ought to be making camp soon, don't you think? There might be rain before morning."

She nodded. "Uh-huh. 'Pears likely." She got to her feet and looked around them. "Best move off from this crick a little ways first, though. Never can tell who else might be . . ." Suddenly she froze, then quickly lifted a hand to her lips for silence.

Ramsay continued squatting on his heels by the water, straining his ears for the faintest hint of a sound. His right hand found its way instinctively to the butt of a pistol and he eased it stealthily from its holster. Still he heard nothing. A moment later he saw Abby notch an arrow and begin making her way slowly downstream, silent as a ghost. Just before she disappeared from view, she turned and made it clear by hand signals that he was not to follow.

It seemed he waited like that for hours, the Navy Colt in his fist, every sense alert for some warning of danger. In time his legs began to cramp and he shifted them slightly, overcoming the temptation to stand and look about him. Once he believed he heard a distant murmur of voices, but so faint and indistinct that afterward he wondered if it might have been his imagination.

At long last Abby reappeared and motioned for Ramsay to come with her. Still clutching the pistol in his right hand, he gathered the mare's reins in his left and advanced cautiously beside the twisting, tree-lined creek, straining to keep the young woman's swiftly moving form in view while negotiating the treacherous tangles of roots and vines growing close by the water's edge.

When they'd covered what he guessed to be some

three or four hundred yards, he saw that Abby had halted near a place where the stream curved around an ancient live oak, so massive that its trunk and branches concealed everything which lay beyond it. She spoke quietly and received a low-voiced reply, then disappeared around the tree with Ramsay following a few yards behind.

Here long-ago floods had gouged a broad notch from the sandy bank, leaving a dry, level shelf some thirty feet wide by half that deep. It was hidden from view in every direction by trees and high outcroppings of earth where the stream turned sharply to the right and then back left again.

Huddled together on the ground in this sanctuary were eight or nine bedraggled figures, their faces smeared with dirt and their clothing torn and sodden from earlier encounters with the forest and the creek. At least four of the figures were women.

"Mr. Ramsay?"

He stared hard at the slight, gray-haired lady who rose from the group and stepped toward him. Then with sudden embarrassed recognition, he holstered the pistol and reached to take Mrs. Merriweather's outstretched hand.

"Mr. Ramsay, if you aren't a welcome sight in this ungovernable wilderness, I surely don't know what is!"

It was a moment before he could find his voice. He looked past her at the others, then released his grip and reached up to push his hat back from his forehead.

"I'm pleased to see you too, ma'am. Although the circumstances . . ."

". . . are hardly the best. That goes without saying." She turned and took his arm, leading him closer to the weary band of refugees. "You recall my husband." Ramsay nodded to the gentleman who had risen to greet him. "And Mrs. Carpenter, I'm sure."

When he touched his hat to the young woman seated on the ground she glanced up and nodded briefly. Her face seemed drawn, her eyes haunted and rimmed with red.

Ramsay looked beyond her and realized with a shock that there were wounded among the party. The still form of 'Lias Carpenter lay on a coat spread over the damp earth. His eyes were closed and he appeared to be breathing shallowly. Abby came forward and knelt beside him, removing her pack as she did.

"You can see," Mrs. Merriweather said quietly, "that Mrs. Carpenter's husband is in very serious condition. He was shot through the upper body."

Ramsay turned his head to look at her. "Last night?"

"Yes. Our riverboat was set upon and captured by a vicious company of brigands. We were their prisoners until only a few hours ago, when we finally made good our escape." She raised a curious eyebrow. "You knew about it?"

"We heard the sounds of shooting from far away. Today we had a report from someone who saw the fighting at a distance. It was these things which brought us here to investigate." The man in black shrugged, smiling faintly. "Idle curiosity, perhaps."

"Or fate." Mrs. Merriweather looked up and met his eyes. "Never underestimate the power of fate, Mr. Ramsay."

A tall, heavy-set man in a battered top hat and

broadcloth suit, ripped at one shoulder, had come forward while they were talking. He held out a thick-fingered hand in greeting.

"Ramsay, is it? I'm Gil Davies. Master of the riverboat *Andrew Jackson*. Or I was until last night."

Ramsay took the hand. The big man's grip was firm and strong. "A pleasure, Captain. You seem to have fallen upon hard times."

"Hard enough. They killed a damn fine pilot and four of my crew, hurt two more so bad we couldn't bring 'em with us when we escaped." He indicated 'Lias with a nod of his head. "Prob'ly ought to of left him too, only these ladies wouldn't hear of it. He's a right tough man to have made it this far."

"Where was the place you made your escape from?"

"Some several mile northeast of here's a great spring with a broad run out into the lake. Them men got a reg'lar camp set up at this end of it, tents, wagons, supplies an' everthing. Brung us there on the *Andy* last night after they'd whupped us an' took aholt of her."

Abby looked up briefly from where she was examining 'Lias' wounds. "I know the place. Kept away from it a-purpose today, just on a hunch."

"Right good hunch," Davies agreed. "They's a couple dozen of 'em been camped up there more'n a week from the looks of things. Five or six was holdin' the fort when we got in, besides them what attacked us earlier."

"It seems they've quite a sizable force," Ramsay said. "I'm surprised you were able to get away."

"Couldn't, whilst everybody was there with the

boat an' all. They kept us aboard an' penned up real close durin' the night. Put us off with our wagons an' livestock this mornin' so's to make more room for theirselves and their horses. Then some three, four hours ago everbody loaded up an' steamed on down the creek. Left two behind to watch over us, and I guess it might of been enough the shape we was in." He nodded toward 'Lias on the ground. "Only they didn't count on that gent's big bull mastiff."

When he paused, Mrs. Merriweather took up the story. "Satan had been very quiet since Mr. Carpenter was injured, so I guess the men guarding us didn't think he would cause any trouble. They had him on a long rope under the trees, tossing food at him from time to time and arguing about who was going to get him after his owner died. He just lay there looking at them, never touching a morsel. At last one of the men got up and went to prod him with a stick. To see if he could get him to move, he said."

Davies grunted. "He moved all right. Like to tore that man's throat right out of him. The other one managed to get his pistol out and shoot into the critter, but he had to take his eyes off the rest of us whilst he was doin' it. That's when we seen our chance, and we took it."

He shook his head sadly. "Hate like the dickens to see a good dog get kilt thataway. But he seen his duty an' he done it. And I snapped the neck of the man what shot him right afterwards." The riverboat captain fell silent for a moment, then went on.

"All of us what could travel, we took off an' headed southwest till we come to this here creek, then followed it upstream to where you see us now. Wasn't thinkin' of nothin' a-tall at the moment but puttin' distance behind us, 'fore them men with the boat could make it back."

"Where do you suppose they went?"

"Couldn't even begin to guess. They wooded up real good this mornin', after unloadin' us and the cargo, enough to take 'em most anywheres between Lake Monroe and Pilatka without stoppin'. Once they'd got all their horses an' men aboard, the last we seen of 'em was steamin' down the creek this afternoon towards Lake George."

Ramsay was thoughtful for several minutes. Finally he asked, "How many men would you estimate they have in all?"

Davies pushed his hat aside and scratched his head. "Well, they was maybe fifteen or so opened up at us from the shore last night, together with their leader who was already on board. They lost a couple in that go-round, so I'd guess thirteen or fourteen time we tied up at the spring. Six more there comes to twenty, less the two they left behind to guard us who won't be no trouble no more. That makes a total of eighteen." The big man looked at Ramsay. "Give or take. You understand I wasn't takin' no real careful nose count."

"What we heard last evening seemed to sound like cannon fire. Were they . . . ?"

"Uh-huh." The captain nodded sourly. "Had 'em a little eight- or ten-pounder it looked like. Sure played hell with my pilothouse an' superstructure. I wouldn't mind meetin' up again with the boys shootin' that thing neither, somewhere along the line." He hesitated, then snapped his fingers. "I just plumb near forgot. You can add two more to that eighteen I give you. They was leavin' the boat whilst that cannon was comin' on. Both rode off into the night a-chasin' after them youngsters."

"Youngsters?" With a sudden chill Ramsay realized he hadn't seen Josh or the little girl among the boat's survivors. "You mean . . . ?" He glanced down at Mary Carpenter again. She'd lowered her head to her chest, and her shoulders shook now with silent sobs.

Mrs. Merriweather reached out and placed a hand on his arm. "One of the crew saw them fall overboard during the attack. With any luck they made it safely to shore, for the boat was quite near land at the time." She met his eyes, then looked away.

"To abandon them alone in the wilderness seems terrible enough, but for some reason those men were not satisfied. They appeared desperately afraid the children might escape. So much so that they left the boat against their leader's orders to pursue them."

"That makes no sense." Ramsay frowned. "What danger could a young boy and girl be to them?"

"They could spread the word about the fightin' maybe." Davies seemed doubtful. "If they could make it to a settlement, that is."

"No." Chance Ramsay shook his head. "If their leader was concerned about such a thing, he would have ordered the pursuit himself."

The other man shrugged. "Beats me then. They was a couple strange ones from the beginnin'. Paid for two cabins in hard cash at Pilatka, though I'd a-swore when I laid eyes on 'em they couldn't find the price of a cup of coffee between 'em. Kept pretty much to theirselves afterwards, near as I could tell. But they sure made it clear enough where their loyalties was once the shootin' got started!"

Ramsay looked at him and nodded. "I don't suppose their reasons matter much anyhow. It's the danger they've placed those youngsters in that's the real concern."

"It ain't a awful lot of pleasure for me to think on neither," the captain agreed soberly. "But might be you're forgettin' somethin' too." He gestured with his arm.

"Take a look around. What you s'pose we could do to help them young-uns, when we can't do no better for ourselves than this here? 'Pears to me we got to see to our own situation first before plannin' no rescue missions for others!"

17 🖐

WHILE THE MEN AND MRS. MERRIWEATHER were speaking, Abby had been giving her full attention to 'Lias Carpenter. After removing the soiled bandages and examining the entry and exit wounds carefully, she'd had Mary clean them with water from the creek while she made poultices using materials from her pack. Once fresh dressings had been tied in place they lowered their patient gently back to the ground and Abby lifted her eyes to meet those of the woman across from her.

"He's a strong one, ma'am. There ain't no corruption set in yet, so I reckon he's got a chance. You done good to bind him up an' stop the bleedin' when you did." Mary smiled faintly as the girl turned her attention to the group's other casualty, a boy of about seventeen with a broad freckled face and his left arm in a sling.

His injuries were minor by comparison: a rough gash where a bullet had creased the flesh, plus numerous cuts and bruises from an unsuccessful attempt to grapple with one of the boat's attackers. He told her his name was Dan Hester, then gritted his teeth as she began cleaning his hurts, finally managing a shy grin while she rebandaged his arm.

As Abby sat back on her heels and wiped her hands she glanced at the sky, then announced to the others: "We best be thinkin' 'bout some kind of a shelter right soon. Goin' to rain sure come nightfall, more likely early than late."

She rose and made a brief circuit of the clearing, studying the layout thoughtfully and then gazing up toward the scrub- and palmetto-covered hills around them. After several minutes she returned to where Ramsay and Davies were standing beside Mrs. Merriweather.

"I reckon here's 'bout as good a place to stay as any. Creek'll swallow up most sounds we make, and she's hid pretty good from folks comin' up or downstream. Them ridges on either side is growed up thick so we'd be able to hear most anybody short of a Injun comin' thataway." She indicated 'Lias with a nod of her head. "Best not move him no more'n we have to anyhow, after what he's been through already."

She turned and pointed to two young trees growing some ten feet apart nearby. "Cut a couple saplin's to lash crossways an' we'll rig us a lean-to right there. When it's thatched over with palmettos it'll make a fair to middlin' shelter. Might even chance a li'l bit of a fire underneath one end of it, while it's still light an' the branches'll hide the smoke."

As she looked back at her companions Ramsay lowered his head to conceal the faint smile that was playing about his lips, brought on partly by admiration for the no-nonsense manner in which Abby had assumed command of the refugees' camp, and partly by amusement at the others' reaction to it. He was used to her plain-spoken ways now, and had few doubts about her qualifications in wilderness survival. It was taking the rest of them a bit longer to become accustomed to the idea.

When no one stirred right away the young woman caught Ramsay's look and frowned briefly, then shifted her attention to those nearby.

"Well," she said with a toss of her raven-tressed head, "what're we waitin' on? Sooner everbody pitches in and gets things done, the sooner all of us'll start in to feelin' some better."

With Ramsay and Mrs. Merriweather leading off, the company set about the tasks of making camp without further discussion.

Once the lean-to was underway Abby gave directions for thatching it so that water would run off into shallow ditches to be dug around the perimeter. Then she took up her bow and arrows and disappeared along the creek to westward. By the time the shelter was finished and a small pine-knot fire was burning brightly close by, she had reappeared carrying several rabbits and small birds, together with roots and leaves collected along the way. The other women moved to help while she knelt and began skinning her meager catch.

"Hoped for a deer," she told them, "but I reckon they was spooked by all the noise an' to-do in the neighborhood lately. We'll have to make it with a mite of stew an' broth for the time bein'. Maybe have better luck tomorrow."

Before long the slim provisions were ready, and

the pot Abby had brought in her pack was filled and placed to simmer over the coals. It was too small to feed everyone, so they would have to cook and eat in shifts. By agreement 'Lias and the women would be served first, and the others afterward.

While they waited, the young buckskin-clad woman spoke to the men and assembled them at the opposite end of the lean-to. "Council of war," she explained briefly as they gathered to sit or squat on the ground nearby. There were five besides herself: Davies, Ramsay, Mr. Merriweather, Dan Hester, and a pale, sour-faced man in what appeared to have been at one time a very expensive woolen suit.

"We got to decide what to do about this situation," she continued, "an' the sooner we make some plans the better. First thing I'd like to know is how much trouble we got to look for tonight." She turned to Davies. "You got any ideas 'bout where them men with the boat went, or when they're liable to come back? It's only a couple, three miles to that spring from here I'd guess. If they made it in 'fore dark an' found y'all missin', they could follow your trail pretty quick on horseback."

The captain shrugged. "Can't say for sure. They was a right closed-mouthed bunch when it come to their plans an' all. Still, from the way they was wooded up and took everbody an' their horses along with 'em, I'd a idea it was someplace partic'lar they meant to go tonight. And somethin' they'd in mind doin' once they got there."

"Another attack?" Ramsay looked at him curiously.

"Wouldn't be surprised. Seems like I heard somethin' about pickin' up another half-dozen men or so too. On the way to where they was headed maybe."

The man in black frowned. "I don't care much for the sound of that, neither the attack nor the reinforcements." He met Abby's eyes, then glanced at the others. "But I suppose for us it's a help of sorts. If they've other work to do they may have less time for chasing escaped prisoners."

"Likely," the young woman across from him agreed. "Leastways they'd be busy somewheres else for a time. Prob'ly wait till after dark for whatever they got in mind, like before." She paused. "But I don't expect it'd do no harm for us to take turn-about standin' watch through the night anyway, just in case."

"You reckon we'd ought to pack up an' move on instead?" It was Dan Hester who asked. "Put some more distance behind us whilst we can?"

"Might," Abby replied, "if we was able. But I don't figure we'd get far enough in the shape y'all are in to make much difference. Best thing's to rest up now an' leave out at first light tomorrow, or a hair before."

"Which raises the next question," Ramsay said. "Where do we go once we leave here?"

The well-dressed man spoke for the first time. "I'd think that would be obvious. We must find the nearest seat of government, and report this outrage at once! To the law enforcement and military authorities both."

Chance Ramsay studied him thoughtfully for a moment, then turned to Davies. "You know this country better than the rest of us, Captain. Where would you say the nearest such 'authorities' might be found?"

The big man hesitated. "Pilatka maybe, a hundred mile downstream. But this here ain't their sheriff's jurisdiction. Mellonville'd be the seat of Orange County, a mite farther in the other direction. There's Marion County to the west, too. But last I heard they ain't even got a lawman now. One they had quit 'em to go into ranchin'."

"And the military?"

"Jacksonville, St. Augustine. Maybe Fort Brooke, but it's four, five days ride southwest, without no roads to get there." He glanced at the well-dressed man and shrugged apologetically. "I reckon Florida ain't too much like what you been used to up there in New England, Mr. Tallman. The 'authorities' are right few and far between. Most folks hereabouts take care of their own troubles, if they get took care of a-tall."

"Well," the other man said, "what about towns and settlements then? At least we might find some help in such a place, for ourselves and our wounded."

"That's true," the captain agreed. "And I reckon Volusia'd have to be it in this part of the country. Three, four mile upriver from Lake George." He turned to Abby. "How far'd you guess from here by land?"

"Five hours maybe, walkin' steady. Prob'ly more with the women an' the hurt man."

"That must be our answer then." Tallman looked at the others. "The only one available to us, evidently. If we leave at first light we should be safely there before dark."

Ramsay kept silent among the general sounds of agreement. Then he nodded. "I expect you're right. It would certainly be the best place for Mr. Carpenter and the women, if we can get there without further trouble." He paused. "Still . . ."

"Yes?" The New England man sounded impatient.

"Nothing. A passing idea. Probably a poor one at that."

Abby looked at him curiously, but he avoided meeting her eyes while Gil Davies turned the conversation to more general matters.

". . . Them river pirates is somethin' got to be dealt with, no matter what happens to us. A big gang like that, takin' riverboats and murderin' innocent travelers an' all, is goin' to get the attention of this entire country. Folks'll be wantin' to take steps right soon."

"Steps?" Mr. Tallman asked quietly.

"First thing to do is spread the word," the captain responded grimly. "Send out riders an' boatmen all up an' down the river here. Then get together ever good fightin' men we can find, an' . . ."

"I still think it might best be dealt with by the proper authorities." The other man spoke more mildly than before. "If they can be reached in time, a company or two of soldiers from one of those posts you mentioned . . ."

"Maybe. But mostly they're way south of us now, down around Tampa Bay an' Lake Tohopekaliga. And besides, them federal officers is notional. Might come when we asked 'em to, an' then again they might not. Seen it happen more'n once, durin' the Injun wars." The big man shook his head.

"Nossir. This here's a local problem, and it's local folks got to take care of it. Them I know wouldn't ask others to do their fightin' for 'em anyhow."

Chance Ramsay stirred and pushed his hat back from his forehead. "I just wish we'd some better idea of their plans and motives. I can't seem to shake the idea that there's more involved here than simple river piracy." He looked at the others. "Did they give you any clues while you were with them as to what they might have in mind?"

"They wasn't much for conversation," the captain answered, "like I said. But you could guess a couple things, maybe. Like about their leaders. Most of the others wasn't nothin' but hired guns an' river trash. But them three or four in charge, they kind of had the look of Quality about 'em. Specially that Mr. Mason Coltrane what come on board at Pilatka. He was dressed real fine in a frock coat an' top hat. Awful well-spoke. Never give us no reason to believe he was anything but some well-to-do passenger till the shootin' got started. Then it turned out he was bossin' the whole she-bang!"

"You mentioned 'hired guns,'" Ramsay said. "Do you mean they're in Mr. Coltrane's employ?"

"'Peared like it. Or at least somebody's payin' 'em. I overheard one say they'd like to take on more if they could find 'em hereabouts."

"There's money behind the operation, then. From someplace. It is beginning to sound more and more like . . ."

"Excuse me." Mr. Merriweather spoke suddenly from a corner of the lean-to. He'd been so quiet since the group sat down together that Ramsay had almost forgotten he was present.

"I believe I can save you all a good deal of time and speculation," the older man said, raising his eyes from the ground where he had been drawing meaningless figures with a twig of hickory.

"As it happens, I am familiar with the man you call Coltrane, though it's been several years now. I expect Jessie and I have changed a bit in the meanwhile, since he evidently did not recognize us." Ignoring their surprised looks, the older gentleman continued in a calm voice, "I think I can guess his intentions too, from what I knew of him earlier. You are quite right that he has money behind him. He has been collecting contributions for a long time. From wealthy slaveowners, as well as others. . . " He paused, smiling oddly.

"I believe he plans to use those resources now to establish a separate government in the Florida peninsula, one that may in time be brought under his exclusive control — a private empire, if you will."

For a moment no one spoke. Then the riverboat captain struck a fist in his palm and exploded in frustration: "But damn it, man! If you knew the kind of trouble he meant, why didn't you say something earlier? A word of warning, even a hint of suspicion, might have saved us all a world of grief!"

"I know. I should have come to you when I first saw him aboard the *Andrew Jackson*. But you must understand that . . . I was afraid."

"Afraid?"

Mr. Merriweather paused to take a breath and let it out again in a long, slow sigh. "Yes. For to do so would have required me to explain the circumstances around our earlier acquaintance with this man you know as Mason Coltrane. And that is something I hoped to avoid. Until now." He glanced quickly at the others, then straightened his shoulders before continuing.

"He called himself Jonathan Winthrop at that earlier time, though I doubt if it was his real name either.

Jessie and I attended a lecture he presented while visiting friends up North. It was a meeting of the Anti-Slavery Society of New England." The older man hesitated again, briefly. "You see, for more than twenty years my wife and I have been, and remain, confirmed abolitionists."

Mr. Merriweather eyed his companions warily under his hat brim, as if fearing some personal attack. But his announcement was met only by silence.

"I'm sure you understand my apprehension in revealing this," he went on quietly. "Over the past several years it has become increasingly dangerous for Southerners to hold such views, though our own Washington and Jefferson did in earlier times, and even the aristocratic old John Randolph.

"Our convictions remain important to us: we see slavery as a hateful blight upon an otherwise noble heritage. But openly opposing it has cost us much in the past, and we'd hoped to reach this new frontier without bringing that extra cloud of prejudice along with us." The older man paused, removing his hat to wipe the band with a soiled linen handkerchief.

"Forgive me. You've no cause to be interested in our private difficulties, but only in how they relate to the twisted ambitions of this man Jonathan Winthrop — or Mason Coltrane.

"He sounded at the beginning like any other passionate believer in the cause of freedom. But unlike many such, he had a plan. And as he described it in glowing oratory, we began to hope that it might offer some slim chance for a peaceful solution to the slavery question. Until then, between the hot-blooded rhetoric of abolitionists in the North and secessionists in the South, we had almost begun to despair of any such resolution short of armed conflict."

The women had finished eating now, and, as a fresh pot of stew was being readied to place among the coals for the men, Mrs. Merriweather approached and took a seat beside her husband. The expression on her face was unreadable as she adjusted her skirts and nodded a silent greeting to the others. But Chance Ramsay had a feeling she'd been listening; and he suspected her arrival at this time was not entirely accidental.

"Simply put," the older man went on, "Mr. Winthrop proposed to establish a new territory in the unpopulated Florida peninsula, where former slaves could be sent and allowed to establish their own government. Owners would be asked to free their Negroes voluntarily for that purpose, or face the threat of widespread escape to this new and easily reached haven." He shrugged slightly.

"It might have worked, or so we thought at the time. Especially since we were led to believe there was already support from influential leaders in Washington. With sufficient funds to purchase land in Florida and establish a political base for the task ahead . . ."

His words trailed off and he shook his head sadly. Mrs. Merriweather placed a hand on his arm, then after a moment took up the narrative in a quiet and bitter voice: "We invited him to visit us in Charleston, and at the end of a week had agreed to donate the bulk of our savings to his cause. It seemed a small price to pay for the ransom of so many human souls." When she paused Ramsay could sense a smoldering anger behind the lady's pale blue eyes.

"But the man was a complete and utter fraud! He'd no more interest in freeing the slaves than I have in becoming Empress of China!" The older woman clasped her hands in her lap, composing herself with difficulty. "Within hours of receiving our money he departed Charleston in the middle of the night, without even a word of thanks or farewell!"

Her husband sighed heavily. "We accepted our loss and went on. There was nothing else to do. For a time we managed to survive on the income from a few small investments. But our antislavery views were well-known in Charleston, and when our meager holdings were wiped out in a financial panic there was no hope of credit or other assistance. I was fortunate to gain an offer of employment with a small shipping firm in Savannah, and we moved to that city in the spring of '47.

"We expected never again to see or hear of the man we'd known as Winthrop. But that was not to be. Some three months ago we received a letter from a favorite nephew, one who knew our situation and had remained close to us through all our troubles. He was traveling in north Georgia when he came across the villain, now in league with those very slaveowners he'd earlier denounced as criminals! His plan with them was to partition the Florida peninsula and create a new slave state, in response to the recent admission of California and Wisconsin to the Union!"

Mrs. Merriweather shook her head grimly. "He was no more sincere about that than his earlier scheme. It was all a pretext to collect additional money in order to raise an army of vicious trash like those who attacked us last night." She looked at the others.

"He's quite mad, you know. Totally obsessed with his extravagant dreams of empire. You could see it in him this morning, even at a distance — the way he preened and strutted, barking out orders and treating his men like servants. . . . And yet for all of that, he remains a horribly cruel and dangerous enemy." The lady fell silent for a moment and closed her eyes. When she spoke again her voice had become strangely dull and lifeless.

"Our nephew Kirby was a proud young man, and he knew the story of how Winthrop defrauded us of our savings. He denounced the man publicly as a liar and a thief, offered his card, and was accepted. But before dawn the next morning, on his way to the dueling ground, Kirby was shot dead in cold blood along with the friend who was his second. No one ever saw their assailants.

"We found it out in a sheriff's postscript to that same letter Kirby had written the day before. When it was already too late . . ."

18 🌿

Mrs. Merriweather paused, lowering her chin to her chest. There was a moment of silence before she looked up with reddened eyes and continued: "Even after Kirby's death this Winthrop, or Coltrane, was not satisfied. He sent a message to a contact in Savannah who spread the word that we were abolitionists, a fact we had kept secret since arriving there, in order to avoid risking my husband's meager employment. The announcement had the desired effect, and we were forced to leave town. After selling what we could, all that remained was the single covered wagon you saw us arrive in Florida with." She paused, then added softly, "And now it appears we have lost even that!"

For a time no one spoke. At last Chance Ramsay rose and stepped forward, placing a hand gently on the lady's shoulder.

"You're among friends, ma'am. It's little enough to say maybe, but it is the truth. For my part your views on slavery are your own affair, and I would not hold them against you even if I were so rigid a man as the late Mr. Calhoun himself." He glanced around the campsite. "I cannot speak for the others — except to suggest that if anyone here feels so strongly as to make an issue of the matter, they bring their objections to me first!"

The only response that could be heard was a general murmuring of assent and acceptance. Mrs. Merriweather looked up at the man standing over her.

"I thank you, Mr. Ramsay." She paused, pale drops glistening at the corners of her eyes. "I'm a foolish old woman. And a selfish, complaining one to boot. At least we've been spared our lives, when others were not so fortunate. And we have our health. In fact, I feel more vital now physically than I have in years. The outdoor life must agree with me."

She smiled, tentatively at first, then more brightly. "Life is full of trials and new beginnings. We've started over before, and if we manage to escape those pirates we will do it again, if need be, as often as it takes."

"Yes, ma'am. I've the feeling you'll make it, too. You'll do just fine, the both of you."

She reached out to take her husband's hand as he sat beside her. "Thank you again, sir. We shall make out, God willing. Or know the reason why!"

The others were beginning to drift slowly toward the cook-fire now. Several had stopped to wish the Merriweathers well as they did. When Ramsay started to turn away he saw Abby still seated on the ground, watching him curiously.

"And what will you do, sir?" Mrs. Merriweather's question caught him by surprise, and he looked back at her sharply.

"Ma'am?"

"What plans do you have in mind for dealing with our Mr. Coltrane, and those murderous cutthroats in his employ?"

"I don't know. To be honest, I'd thought little about it beyond our escape tomorrow." He hesitated, then shrugged. "I'd not have believed it my place to decide in any event."

"Someone must decide. And you at least are a man of action."

"I?" It was not a phrase he would have applied to himself. Though when Mrs. Merriweather said it . . .

The older woman smiled as she allowed her husband to help her from the ground. "I believe you are too modest, sir. And I believe you know it. You are the most dangerous fighting man in this part of Florida at the moment, and unless I've misjudged you greatly, you are already thinking of how we might bring those villains to account." Her expression sobered as she placed a hand on his forearm.

"Do what you must, Mr. Ramsay. Have faith in yourself, as I have faith in you. Yet remember you are not alone. There are enough enemies here for each to have his share. And you will need the help of all to bring this business to a successful conclusion!" She took her husband's arm and turned away without another word, leaving Ramsay to watch after her curiously.

It was a moment before he realized Abby Macklin had risen and approached to stand beside him. When he glanced at her, her hand was raised as if she meant to rest it on his arm. But as their eyes met she lowered it quickly, hooking both thumbs in the belt at her waist and cocking her head to one side before leaning close to whisper in his ear: "You'd somethin' in mind earlier. Somethin' you decided were best kept to yourself." She hesitated, smiling faintly. "Had to do with them outlaws' landin' place up there to the spring, I'll bet."

"Perhaps." He turned to look at her, wondering if it had become so easy for everyone to read him lately. It could be just as well he'd been forced to give up the cards when he did. "Yes," he answered, studying her finely chiseled features in the late afternoon light. He shook his head. "A foolish notion, probably . . ."

"Uh-huh." Abby Macklin took a small step backward and shrugged her shoulders. "Could be I'd a idea or two like it myself though. Wonderin' what we'd find in the way of goods or information that might prove useful."

"And there are a couple of wounded men out there, also."

"If we was to take your Lady along, we might rig up a travois an' bring 'em back here with us."

"We?"

Her smile became broader and she gave him a taunting look. "I'm the one with the Injun blood here, 'member? You're liable to need me a heap more'n I'll need you on this kind of a expedition." She favored him with a hearty nudge to the ribs as she stepped past him toward the fire.

"Come on. Let's grab us a bite to eat an' tell the cap'n what we got in mind."

The burly river man nodded thoughtfully as Abby and Ramsay explained their plan. He agreed there might be valuable supplies left behind by the outlaws, possibly including weapons. Concern for the women and the wounded 'Lias had led them to depart without making a careful search earlier, and they'd brought only a single cap-lock pistol with them. A second captured weapon had been left with the injured crewmen as some slight protection for themselves.

"I reckon it's worth a try," Davies said, "'long as them others ain't made it back in the meantime." He rubbed a dark-stubbled jaw with the palm of his hand. "But I'm a mind to come too. Those're my men out there, and I'm responsible for 'em. Besides which, you-all could prob'ly use a hand with the totin' if we find anything much worth carryin' with us."

Ramsay opened his mouth to protest, then closed it again and glanced at Abby. Mrs. Merriweather's words about the help of others came back to him, and he nodded his agreement. There would still be three men left to mount guard, and some of the women could take a turn as well.

Minutes later Abby handed her rifle and ammunition belt to Mr. Merriweather, content to rely on the silent but deadly bow and knife for the work ahead. After a brief hesitation Ramsay unbuckled one of his gunbelts and passed it to Davies.

While they were completing their preparations, Mr. Merriweather took Ramsay to one side and spoke in a cautious whisper: "I forgot to mention to you that I recognized several others among the outlaws who attacked the *Andrew Jackson*. I believe they recognized me as well, though they gave no obvious sign of it." He paused meaningfully before continuing. "The men who were operating the cannon from shore during the battle were Levi Budd and his three sons!"

Ramsay stared at him. "You mean . . ."

"Evidently they were in league with these cut-throats since the beginning. It appears their task was to transport the cannon and other supplies into Florida aboard their wagons. That would explain the heavy loads as well as their secretiveness and impatience to reach their destination."

It was interesting information, offering further evidence of the thoroughness of Coltrane's plan. Yet beyond satisfying a certain suspicion about the motives of the Budd family when Ramsay first encountered them, it seemed to add nothing of value to what he already knew of the river pirates. Except that they had made the journey into Florida with eight good mules . . .

A low grumbling of thunder echoed among the trees as they left the lean-to and advanced along the creek bank into the gathering twilight. Abby was in front, followed by Davies and then Ramsay leading the Arabian mare.

"No cannons this time," the gambler observed wryly. "But I've an idea we'll all be wet before this adventure is over with."

"Rain'll help cover the sounds of our travelin'." Abby had paused to peer cautiously around the first bend in the creek. "An' wash out our tracks too, with any luck. Be thankful for small favors."

A moment later she'd disappeared ahead of them with a curt whispered, "Come on!"

The heavy drops beat a steady tattoo on the cypress shingles overhead as gusts of wind hissed through cracks to rattle the bolted shutters next to the bed where Josh had been sleeping. He was wide awake now, propped on one elbow and staring into the shadows, trying to recall where he was and how he had gotten here.

There were faint traces of daylight outside, but the storm and the closed shutters made it almost like night within the small bedchamber. His eyes came to rest on the cot a few feet away where the small form of Sara Jane, still peacefully sleeping, brought back the memory of their arrival at the store in Volusia.

After a moment he sat up and swung his legs to the floor, bending to pull on his shoes. Then he crossed the room on tiptoe and opened the door. From the brighter light in the hallway he could see the now-empty bed where Matt Panner had been asleep. It was late afternoon, and Josh realized suddenly that despite the generous meal some four hours earlier, he was ravenously hungry.

There were voices at the front of the store. Mrs. Brooks seemed to be in conversation with several men, probably customers. They sounded vaguely familiar, though Josh could not place them right away. Neither appeared to be the lady's husband.

The kitchen was empty, and at present no one else was in the living quarters at the rear of the building. He crossed the hall toward the large front room and saw that Matt's musket was missing from the corner where he'd stood it earlier. Josh wondered where the younger boy had gone, noting that the old flintlock pistol he'd borrowed was still resting on a shelf nearby.

As he stepped through the doorway he turned to

his right where the long counter stood, intending to ask Mrs. Brooks about the possibility of a snack until supper might be ready. He was beginning to form the words when his eyes fell upon the two customers.

He froze in his tracks, recognizing them instantly.

The long-coated men were leaning against the far end of the counter in earnest conversation with the storekeeper's wife. For a moment Josh stood rooted to the spot, uncertain whether to run or call out a warning to the lady, who'd turned her back to take something from the shelf overhead. At last he heard his voice rising in his throat almost of its own accord, drowning out the sound of the rain: "It's them! It's them two chased us through the woods after the ambush last night! Look out, ma'am . . .!"

The men jerked their heads around in surprise, then reacted more swiftly than Josh could have imagined. The shorter one's hand dropped to the pocket of his coat and he drew out a wicked-looking revolver. At the same instant his partner was rounding the counter to make a dash for the boy in the doorway.

There was a collection of brooms and farm implements against the wall, and with a wild sweep of his arm Josh managed to scatter these in the tall man's path. Following through the movement without a pause, he spun and disappeared back into the hall toward the rear of the house. Behind him he heard a crash and vicious swearing, followed by a gunshot and the thud of a bullet into wood not far from where he stood.

For a frantic moment Josh could not recall where he'd seen another exit from the building. Almost without thinking his hand found the flintlock pistol beside him, and then the memory returned: the kitchen!

He made it down the hall in three steps, caught the door jamb with his free hand, and careened wildly around it, almost falling as another bullet crashed into the pine logs behind him. A second later he was across the room to the outer door.

It was stuck! The rain and humidity had expanded the wood so that it was wedged firmly into the heavy frame. Desperately Josh planted his feet and tugged at the metal latch. He felt it give, but it was already too late. The sound of heavy boots had entered the kitchen behind him.

Turning, the boy dropped to his knees and reached across to cock the ancient pistol with his left hand. The tall man halted when he saw the weapon. Then he took a step backward and smiled.

"You ain't plannin' on shootin' at me with that there pop-gun, are you?" Josh saw that the intruder's hands were empty. It was evidently his partner who'd fired the earlier shots.

"Why, in this weather alls you'll prob'ly get out of that thing's a snap anyway," the man went on calmly, "or maybe a flash in the pan. And if you was to get in a shot an' missed, then you'd be plumb out of luck. I'd have my hands on you 'fore you could even say your prayers." He paused, but Josh said nothing, holding the pistol steady with its muzzle pointed toward the other's midsection.

"Tell you what I'll do," the tall man said, holding his hands away from his body in a conciliatory gesture. "You come acrost a gold locket somewhere along the line what belongs to my partner an' me. It's right important to us, an' we mean to have it back. But 'tain't no reason either one of us has got to get shot or hurt over it." He lowered his arms and reached out with his left hand. "So if you'll just give me that little piece of gold, we'll say fair enough and leave out of here without no more trouble." Still Josh kept silent, watching him. The pistol in his hand did not waver.

"Okay." The man shrugged. "I reckon maybe you got a right to somethin' for your trouble, findin' the locket and holdin' onto it an' everthing. How 'bout I give you a dollar for it to boot, just as sort of a finder's fee?"

When he reached casually into his pocket with his right hand, Josh saw a sudden narrowing of the eyes. The walnut butt of a pistol appeared in the tall man's fist and the boy did not hesitate. Flint struck fire and there was a deafening boom in the small enclosed space, followed by a startled gasp from the wounded man as he fell back against the kitchen counter, still trying to free the revolver from its hiding place.

The smile on his face stretched into an angry grimace, baring his teeth as he finally yanked the weapon free and drew back the hammer. Josh watched helplessly while his antagonist struggled to raise the barrel, staggered, then discharged his pistol harmlessly into the wall beside him. A moment later the tall man slumped forward. His knees gave way, and he collapsed in a heap onto the hard pine floor.

There were shouts at the front of the building. Josh jerked his head up as if awakening suddenly from a dream. He threw down the now-useless flintlock and jumped to his feet, turning to tug frantically again at the rain-swollen door. There was an icy chill between his shoulder blades as he realized the tall man's partner might be behind him at any second. And he had nowhere else to run.

With a mighty heave he swung the door aside at last, launching himself across the narrow porch and taking the stairs beyond it in a single bound. He was a dozen splashing steps into the rain-puddled yard before he recognized the familiar voice behind him:

"Josh! It's all right! You c'n stop runnin'! We got the other one. He's down an' hog-tied up to the front of the store!"

Pulling himself to a halt with difficulty, the boy turned and looked over his shoulder to see Matt Panner's grinning face at the top of the stairs. Mr. Brooks was beside him, and other men could be seen in the background — lean, hard-faced men, each carrying a rifle, pistol, shotgun, or some combination of these.

"Come on in out of the rain, boy." The storekeepers' face was grim, but his voice sounded surprisingly gentle. "The trouble's over now. And you done just fine."

Josh walked the thirty feet back to the store slowly, chill wind-blown drops drenching his bare head and clothing as he climbed the stairs to the shelter of the porch. He took Matt's outstretched hand without speaking, and Mr. Brooks placed an arm on his shoulder to lead him indoors.

"Reckon we just barely made it here in time," the younger boy was saying. "Been goin' the rounds gatherin' up some of the men here for a council of war like, and we was right out front when we heerd all the ruckus inside. Busted in whilst that short feller was lettin' loose with his second shot, an' . . ."

LEE GRAMLING

Josh was not listening. As they came through the door he glanced across the kitchen into the half-open eyes of the man he had killed, and felt the bile rise in his throat. With a sudden twist he tore himself from his companions and dashed back out into the rain. For several minutes he was violently sick.

When he returned, the outlaw's body had been removed and the storekeeper's wife was on her knees scrubbing the floor with lye soap and a thick-bristled brush. Mr. Brooks had just finished bringing in a fresh bucket of water from the barrel on the porch. He set the bucket beside his wife and rose, turning to meet the boy's eyes.

Josh shrugged in embarrassment. "I'm sorry. It was just . . ."

"'Tain't nothin' to be ashamed of, son." The man came closer and laid a hand on the youngster's shoulder. "Anybody for who takin' a human life is a easy thing, ain't much of a man to my way of thinkin'. Don't matter who it was, nor how much he might of needed killin'. There still ain't a awful lot of pleasure in it." He turned and started leading Josh toward the hallway and the sleeping quarters beyond.

"You could do with some dry clothes, I reckon. And it happens the missus done already laid out a couple things from the store she thought might fit when she seen the shape your others was in. Go on in an' get dressed. Then come join us up to the front room. We got us a sort of a town meetin' goin' on, and it 'pears like what happened to you-all on the lake last night is the main topic on the agenda."

19 ☀

Josh changed clothes quickly, noticing as he did that Sara Jane had risen and joined the Brooks' children in another room of the house. The building seemed alive with activity now, doors opening and closing, people coming and going, voices raised in greeting or in partially heard conversations.

When he entered the large front room there were more than a dozen visitors present, most of them armed men.

He took the offered chair, and at Mr. Brooks' invitation repeated the story he'd told over dinner, with occasional questions from the others and added comments from Matt, who was present also. It seemed the younger boy had already described his father's murder for the gathering, together with the taking of their horses and property.

The hundred and fifty dollars Quinn Jordan had forced upon him lay out on the counter in plain view. From time to time one or another of the men would glance secretly at it and then look quickly away. Most of them had never seen so much cash money in one place before. Nor had Josh, for that matter.

Questions were raised about the men in long coats, to which the boy could offer few answers. Clearly they were in league with the river pirates, but beyond that Josh could not even guess at their motives. It appeared their quest for the gold locket was some private matter having nothing to do with the others. He described how it was found beside the creek in north Florida, and how the two men had acted when they saw him looking at it on board the riverboat. When he took it from his pocket to show around, everyone studied it admiringly, then handed it back with puzzled shakes of their heads.

The man taken prisoner had offered no information at all, steadfastly refusing to speak a word even in the face of dire threats of hanging, and worse, by various of the townspeople.

When Josh finished, there was a long and thoughtful silence. The rain had slackened to a soft irregular patter on the roof now, accompanied by the occasional rustling of branches beyond the door and windows.

At last a white-bearded man in greasy overalls leaned forward to spit into a box of sand a few feet away.

"'Pears to me," he said, straightening slowly in his chair, "that them varmints set out to own theirselves a riverboat. Was it only robbery they'd got in mind, 't would of been a sight easier to just leave her or burn her and ride off into the night." He spit again while several of the others nodded agreement.

"If'n that's true," the older man went on, "I 'spect

they ain't near through with all the raidin' and killin' they got planned for this country. Boat like that with the horses they brung aboard an' all means they can go most anywhere they please, strike at anybody or everbody all up an' down the river." He paused to indicate Matt with a jerk of his head.

"Add to that what this young-un here tells us, and I reckon we can figure on a couple other things too. One is they want land, ever how they can get it. My land. Your land. Everybody's land, more'n likely. And two, 'pears like they got enough cash money to buy whatever they can't come by through no other means." The old man paused to let that thought sink in, wiping his tobacco-stained mustache with the back of a hard-knuckled hand. He studied the faces of his comrades, one after the other.

"Now maybe that last is temptin' to some, and each of you boys can do what he likes. But I'm goin' to tell you the way I feel about it, right here an' now." He spit again, sharply and accurately.

"I ain't about to get myself run off no land what I done homesteaded an' slaved to prove up on this past ten year. And I don't mean to be bought off'n it neither. I'll fight for what's mine, and if I die here y'all can bury me here. Either way I ain't a-leavin'. Anybody wants this old cracker's land is goin' to have to pay a price for it, in blood. That's the only way they're goin' to get aholt of it."

When he fell silent no one else spoke for several long minutes. Then one of the men across the room slapped the wood stock of his shotgun and nodded. "By God, Nate," he said, "I'm with you. 'Tain't like me an' mine couldn't use the money if'n it was offered.

Times are hard, and we're barely makin' it. But what's ours is ours. And I'll be damned if I'll let no outland skunk push me off'n it without a fight!"

There was a noisy murmur of assent following this, and Mr. Brooks rapped on the counter with his knuckles for attention.

"All right," he said. "It's agreed we'll fight. And I reckon we'll do it together like we've faced near 'bout ever other trouble since we come here to live." The storekeeper's lips curved into a thin smile. "And because that didn't come as no special big surprise, I already done a small amount of thinkin' on the matter." He paused until he had everyone's attention before continuing:

"I expect them men's goin' to come at us right soon now. 'Cause we're smack-dab in the way if'n they mean to have theirselves a free ride up the river anywheres from Lake George. So here's my plan . . ."

It took only minutes to explain the basic outline, followed by perhaps half an hour of arguing over details and deciding who would be responsible for which tasks. By then it had grown fully dark outside, and the rain had stopped entirely. The sound of frogs and crickets was loud in the dripping night beyond the shuttered windows.

They were still at it when a musket shot boomed suddenly in the distance, bringing a momentary halt to the conversation.

"That'll be Tom Eggers' boy Rollie," Mr. Brooks said calmly. "We sent him up to the point 'fore dark to watch out over the entrance to the river. 'Pears like he seen somethin' just now, and I imagine we can all guess what it was." He rose from his seat on a wooden cracker box and reached out to take his Kentucky rifle from the counter.

"Go on an' get to your places, men. Time for talkin' is over!"

The storm reached the west shore of Lake George on a driving wind, rushing and swirling among the treetops, drenching Ramsay and his companions with its gusting force before clattering noisily down among the dry leaves of the forest. It had been more than an hour since they'd left the creek, following Abby's lead among the dense and darkling woodlands, across endless sand hills overgrown with pine, palmetto and low winter-dead brush.

Rather than let the weather slow their pace, Abby quickened it instead, taking them rapidly over the crest of yet another hill and down its far side, then across a narrow strip of open prairie before turning sharply to cross a forest road into thick woods beyond. Ramsay suspected this southbound trail was the same one they'd followed the day before. If so they must be close to the lake now, and to the spring where the outlaws had their camp.

It was almost pitch black as the trees closed around them, and he had to tread carefully in order to avoid a misstep while holding his eyes level to keep the others in view. Abby advanced another hundred yards before halting suddenly near the crest of a small ridge, listening intently into the windswept shadows before her.

As Ramsay came near, he saw her squeeze water from her bow-string with two fingers and notch an arrow. His own hand moved instinctively to the butt of his Navy Colt.

After a moment Abby straightened and turned to her companions, leaning forward so that her face was only inches from theirs. Still her voice was barely audible above the rain:

"They's somebody's just over that li'l rise ahead. Stirrin' around a mite, not talkin'. Don't seem to be more'n two, maybe only one." She looked at Davies. "You reckon that's near to where you left them hurt men of yours?"

The riverboat captain frowned. Ramsay saw his other pistol had found its way into the big man's fist. "Might be," he whispered. "Everthing looks different here in the dark. But I'd say we come about the right distance."

Abby nodded. "Spring's a little further on, 'nother couple hundred yards maybe. But I don't hear nothin' sounds like no big crowd anywheres close by. Likely them others ain't made it back with the boat yet." She raised her head to glance cautiously around them. "You two wait here whilst I investigate."

In seconds she had disappeared over the crest of the low hill, her bow at the ready, moving catlike through the storm-drenched darkness. Davies and Ramsay stood motionless a few feet apart, each in a half-crouch to shield his weapon from the rain as they awaited her return.

Both were thoroughly soaked by now; the water poured in rivulets from the brims of their hats. Fortunately the weather had been growing warmer of late, and tonight was not especially cold. But the effects of the damp and their current inactivity still had an effect, so that Ramsay found himself clenching his teeth together tightly to stop them from chattering.

After what seemed a long time the young woman was suddenly beside them again, appearing like a ghost from the surrounding darkness.

"Found your man, Cap'n. Tryin' to make it off from here on his hands and knees. He's in a bad way, but game. T'other one died a little over a hour ago." As her companions made ready to follow, she added quietly, "I took a quick look over towards the camp too. Don't appear to be nobody there. Not alive anyways."

They moved quickly. While Abby and the captain paused beside the injured man, Ramsay mounted and rode directly to the outlaws' camp. He was unsure what he expected to find, but anything might be a help in their present situation: food, weapons, ammunition; perhaps some means for transporting the wounded.

The rain had begun to slacken as the storm passed on toward the northwest, and an early moon could be seen peeking occasionally from behind scudding clouds. The visibility was not good, but it was possible to make out shadows and movement for some distance if one watched carefully.

Chance Ramsay was more than careful, riding at a slow walk around the perimeter of the camp with his Colt ready and every sense alert. But he saw and heard nothing. The area near the spring and its run-off appeared to be completely deserted.

A half-dozen white canvas tents had been pitched in a small clearing beside the water, and he paused to study them at a distance for several minutes. Nearby he could see the Carpenters' and the Merriweathers' wagons, parked alongside the two which had been brought here overland by the Budds.

Continuing on without dismounting, he drew rein at the edge of a stand of water oaks some fifty yards beyond the tents. Peering into the shadows underneath them, Chance Ramsay smiled suddenly to himself. Even before he returned to the wagons and leaned forward in his stirrups to inspect their contents, he knew the journey here had turned out far better than expected.

After several more minutes he holstered his pistol and clucked to the mare, turning her head toward a large live oak a short distance west of the spring. Abby and Davies stood talking nearby, and as he drew rein Ramsay could make out the dim shapes of the slain guards beneath the spreading branches, close beside the still form of 'Lias Carpenter's big mastiff. The dead crew member was visible also, a short distance off in the open where he'd crawled with his comrade before finally succumbing to his wounds.

Ramsay dismounted and stepped forward in time to hear Abby saying, ". . . t'other man back there's just liable to make it, if'n we can rig up some kind of a travois from poles an' blankets." She turned to the man in black. "Your Lady'll have to pull double onct we get back an' pick up that Carpenter gent. But I reckon . . ."

"That won't be necessary." The gambler smiled faintly as he turned to point in the direction he had come.

"If you will look in that small grove over there beyond the camp, you will find ten good mules picketed among the trees, together with two oxen and a milk cow belonging to the Carpenters. The last may be too slow to take with us, but the mules should be a great help in tomorrow's flight. I also saw what I believe to be weapons and ammunition in one of the wagons. If you two wouldn't mind going to gather up the animals, I'll have a quick look through the tents and see what else we might . . ."

He broke off suddenly, turning his head toward the southwest. A distant roar could be heard echoing through the forest, accompanied by the faint crackle of what was almost surely small-arms fire. Ramsay looked at his companions.

"Our luck is holding," he said quietly. "The raiders are attacking some other poor devils at the moment, so I'd guess we'll have several hours until there's any danger of their returning. We'd best make the most of it while we can."

Davies listened thoughtfully as the cannon boomed again from the south part of the lake. "Volusia," he said. "I'd bet a dollar on it." The big man glanced at Ramsay.

"Them 'poor devils' down there is some rougher'n you'd expect. Been fightin' Injuns sinct Methuselah was a pup, an' whipped the last bunch only three year back. I wouldn't go to mournin' for 'em just yet. They'll make Mr. Coltrane's boys pay for their fun, and it could turn out to be a right steep price."

"Maybe," Abby said, "an' maybe not. Either way 't won't do us no good to be too close when they come back. They mightn't chase after escaped prisoners half so hard as they would them mules. Let's gather 'em up and take a quick look around, then leave on out with your hurt man whilst we still got time to make some tracks."

Ramsay knew immediately that she was right. Important as the animals would be for the women and wounded, they could not hope to take so many back through the woods without leaving a trail behind them. And if the outlaws followed, they would be mounted also. The best plan was to return with the mules as quickly as possible, then rouse the others and get them started on their way to Volusia at once, tonight.

Assuming it was still safe to go there. At any rate they could put distance behind them, and with luck the pursuers would have to wait for dawn to follow. If their trail could be further disguised . . . . Ramsay thought about this while Davies and the young woman went to collect the animals and he began his hasty search of the camp.

The cannon continued to boom off and on for perhaps another half hour. By the time Ramsay had completed his survey and the mules were gathered on lead ropes nearby, the rain had slowed to a drizzle and the forest around them had grown silent once more.

Abby prepared litters for the wounded from tent poles and canvas while the two men set about rigging a number of crude pack saddles from the same materials. When these were ready they began loading arms and supplies into them from the wagons brought to Florida by Levi Budd and his sons.

The wagons themselves would be useless in the rough scrub country they'd be traveling through. But besides a supply of canned food, their contents included three or four boxes of new Sharps rifles, an assortment of pistols, and substantial quantities of powder and ball.

Ramsay selected only as many weapons as he thought their party could reasonably use, adding ammunition and food until the packs were full without weighing down any one animal too heavily. While they worked, he explained his plan:

"Abby, you go ahead with two of the mules and get the wounded man onto a travois and ready to travel. The captain will lead the other animals in a broad half-circle, muddying the ground and then coming back over his tracks in the opposite direction." He looked at Davies. "Two or three trips would be better, moving gradually outward to conceal the direction of our escape. When you've finished, head straight for the camp on the creek, rouse the others and arm them, then set out for Volusia at once."

"And you?" the riverboat captain finished tightening the draw rope on the last of the packs.

"I'll stay here until the boat returns, then see if I can't add to their difficulties by setting some fires and explosions with what powder is left. If I'm lucky, there'll be enough noise and confusion to cover my escape and delay any chance for a pursuit as well."

"Sounds okay," the larger man said, "far as it goes. But what if they decide to just pull up stakes an' leave here instead?"

Ramsay looked at him curiously. "Then we'd all be safe, I imagine. For the time being."

"For the time bein'." Davies straightened from his task and glanced at his two companions. "But what of tomorrow or the day after? Or the week after that? If they get away with that riverboat tonight, ain't no tellin' when or where we might be able to come up on 'em again, all to one place an' not lookin' for no extra trouble."

The man in black studied the other's face thoughtfully in the pale moonlight. "You have a suggestion?" he asked mildly.

20 ⚜

G<small>IL</small> D<small>AVIES</small> N<small>ODDED</small>, P<small>AUSING</small> to wipe water from his eyes with the back of a sodden coat-sleeve.

"A part of a idea anyhow. It seems to me if we mean to stop those men from doin' what Mr. Merriweather thinks they got planned for this country, we wouldn't find no better time nor place for it than this here. They get off now to keep buyin' up land and hirin' killers, scarin' away decent folks an' murderin' them as won't scare, pretty soon ain't nobody liable to stop 'em.

"This whole peninsula's backwoods frontier, an' not many outside it know or care what goes on. Man comes along with money and a good story, land staked out an' a few hired voters to back him, I reckon he might find hisself a sympathetic ear or two in Tallahassee an' Washington. First thing you know he'd be the law hereabouts, and those agin him is the outlaws an' renegades. After a man's got the power, ain't too many asks questions 'bout how he come to get it."

Ramsay recognized the truth of what the captain said, for it was an old story on the frontier and elsewhere. And he could understand the logic of trying to stop Mason Coltrane and his men at the outset, before they could establish themselves so firmly in this country even constituted authority might have difficulty dislodging them.

What he did not understand was why he, Chance Ramsay, should feel any particular urge to take a personal hand in the matter. He was still a hunted man after all, an outlaw himself in the strictest sense of the word. And if he stayed around these parts much longer, news of the murder warrant and the reward for his capture were sure to reach even this remote location.

Yet there was something within him that compelled him to see this matter through to an ending, regardless of consequences. Some innate sense of justice perhaps, combined with the special liking and respect he'd developed for the Merriweathers and Carpenters in the short time he'd known them, for what they all planned to build on this new frontier. By comparison, his own life so far appeared shallow and inconsequential.

Or perhaps it was simply, as Mrs. Merriweather had suggested, that Chance Ramsay was a fighting man who happened to arrive at a place and time where his skills were needed. . . .

He found himself glancing at Abby Macklin while she finished readying her mules for the ride to camp. When she straightened and met his eyes, it seemed almost as if she knew what was in his mind. She grinned suddenly, and Ramsay shrugged. He turned to Davies.

"What did you have in mind?"

The captain put his hands in his pockets and hunched his shoulders. The rain had almost ceased by now.

"I know these folks up an' down the river here a sight better'n most, I reckon. Ain't many won't fight if give the chance. And they been used to comin' together to help each other sinct the Injun wars. If we was to spread the word an' gather everbody at this place before daybreak . . ." He glanced at Abby as she finished picketing her mules and approached to stand beside them. "How many you reckon that might turn out to be?"

She hesitated only a moment. "A dozen or so from up north of here, maybe a couple dozen more to the south, give or take. That's countin' the ones at Volusia, assumin' they're in any shape to come."

"Some will be," the captain said. "I'd bet on it." He paused and added soberly, "Or if they ain't I expect we won't have near so many bad men to worry about tomorrow."

"What if they've captured the town?" Ramsay asked. "Will the outlaws come back here at all?"

"*If* they took it, which I got my doubts about, I reckon they still meant to use this here as a base, all the goods they left behind. But it might be awhile 'fore they could get back to it. They'd have to leave somebody to hold the town an' protect their passage upriver. Otherwise wouldn't make no sense takin' it in the first place, just to leave on out right away."

The man in black nodded, squatting on his heels and pushing his hat back from his forehead before glancing at his companions. "I agree," he said calmly. "So it looks like the situation is this:

"If the pirates failed to capture Volusia a short while ago, they'll almost surely return here tonight with the *Andrew Jackson*. Then, by your estimation, we should be able to recruit two or three dozen men from the surrounding country in order to attack them first thing in the morning.

"If they took the town, on the other hand, they still might send a party back here with the boat for their supplies. We won't be able to muster as many men in that case, but their numbers will be fewer also. We'd have a good chance of recapturing the vessel and striking a crippling blow against Mason Coltrane regardless."

He looked at Davies. "I believe you're right, Captain. The opportunity is too good to pass up."

"What if they took Volusia but don't come back here tonight?" Abby asked. "They'll be holdin' the riverboat an' the town too, then."

"Two chances out of three aren't bad, and we'll cross that bridge when we come to it. At least the countryside will be aroused, and we can destroy their goods here before we move on. We'd all be better off than we are now, even so."

Chance Ramsay felt an odd exhilaration as their plan came together. Some primitive thirst for battle perhaps, which stirred the blood and sharpened his senses in the process. He found himself as impatient as Davies now to bring their foes to a final confrontation.

"Where do you think we ought to assemble?" he asked, glancing at the young woman beside him before rising and accepting his second gunbelt from the captain. As he buckled it on, the big man took two captured pistols from a mule's pack and shoved them into his own waistband. "Somewhere along that north-south road, I would imagine, so that we can discuss final plans before moving here to the spring."

"Uh-huh." Abby nodded. "Reckon the easiest place to find in the dark'll be where that trail crosses the creek a couple mile south of us, same one our camp's on a ways farther up. T'others could come downstream from there to meet us, too."

"What about our women and wounded?" Davies asked. "Who'll look after them while the rest of us are off fightin'?"

"If we manage this proper they won't need no special lookin' after," she answered calmly. "We'll leave most of the mules with 'em and let 'em get a head start south, even before we gather the men from the countryside. Whoever rides off that way first will know if Volusia's safe to go to, and can circle back to warn 'em if it ain't. That case they can just keep on movin' south an' west towards Fort King." She shrugged.

"Suppose we could spare that Dan Hester to stay with 'em, though truth to tell, you give them women some pistols an' shotguns and I figure they'd do just fine without him. Didn't none of 'em strike me as the sighin' and faintin' type when I talked to 'em earlier."

"All right." The man in black spun the cylinder of his spare pistol and shoved it into its holster before looking at the others. "Captain, you and Abby head back to camp with the mules and your wounded man. From there Abby can ride north, where she knows the people and the trails, and you can start south for Volusia. I'll stay here to keep an eye on things."

Davies cleared his throat. "I'd soon trade off on

that last job," he said, "if you don't mind. Couple matters I'd like to take care of on my own." He indicated the spring with a wave of his hand. "One's got to do with what might happen if them boys come back an' decide to just leave out again onct they find out we been a-visitin'. I had a li'l idea about that. Figure I can rig a pretty good barricade downstream outen them four wagons, usin' the Carpenters' oxen with the river-crossin' tackle they brung along. Any luck, I'll have it done even before they get through tyin' up and start to look around good.

"T'other thing's a more personal matter," the big man went on mildly, interrupting Ramsay's intended protest. "Y'see, one of them dead men out there in the cold an' the wet is mine. He done lived on my boat, et my food, and give me full measure of his time an' his sweat an' his loyalty. I'd soon see he gets a decent buryin', and it's not a job I'd care to ask nobody else to do for me."

Chance Ramsay hestitated only a second before reaching out to grasp the captain's hand.

"All right," he said. "Do what you think best. But don't take any foolish chances. If they get back, set the barricade and then stay out of sight until you hear the rest of us coming. We'll try to make it as close to dawn as possible." He looked around and saw that Abby was already mounted bareback on one of the mules, with a second in tow pulling a travois for the wounded man.

"Let's go. And good luck!"

He gripped the lead rope for the remaining mules in his left hand and watched the young woman lead off, then climbed into the saddle of his Arabian mare.

With a brief parting wave to the captain, he began leading his awkward caravan in single file across the muddy clearing which separated the camp from the small rise to westward and the darker mass of forest beyond.

He guessed their talk and preparations had taken a little over an hour all told, including the distantly heard battle at Volusia. Since Davies estimated it to be some eight or ten miles from here by water, the earliest the men on the boat might return would be another hour from now. Just about long enough to make it back to their camp on the creek but no farther. Afterward they would have to move swiftly.

Urging the mare into a trot, he struggled to turn the mules back over their tracks to make pursuit more difficult. Then he slowed the animals to a walk before climbing the rise to where Abby waited with her human cargo.

Taking one last look over his shoulder, Ramsay could barely make out Gil Davies' hulking form among the other shadows of the camp, bending rhythmically to his lonely task with a shovel recovered from one of the Budds' wagons.

The fight at Volusia had been sharp, bloody, and not at all what those attacking from the riverboat expected. The two men in long coats had orders to wait inside the store until the first shots were fired, then draw their weapons and seize the place before its occupants could put up a resistance. The other townsfolk should have been in their individual homes at this hour, eating supper, visiting, or otherwise relaxing after the day's labor. No one was supposed to have any suspicion that an attack was on its way, much less from what direction or how it might come.

The riverbanks were low and swampy downstream, so that horsemen could not easily be disembarked and find their way into action from north of the settlement. With the element of surprise there should be no need for that anyway. They would come ashore after the landing, spreading out from there to ravage isolated homesteads in the surrounding country.

As it turned out, nothing went according to plan. From the moment the noisy, plodding craft rounded the final bend prior to slowing along the east bank, more than a dozen rifles and shotguns were trained upon her decks and thinly paneled superstructure. When the first armed men made their appearance from behind a crude barricade of bales and cordwood on the port side, they were met by a blinding hail of death from defenders who felt no need to offer either warning or mercy to their ruthless invaders.

The small cannon spoke repeatedly from her sheltered position amidships. But she afforded little more than a noisy distraction against widely dispersed marksmen firing from the dark cover of trees along the water's edge. The stout heart pine of the store's construction withstood the eight-pound balls with only superficial damage.

It was the would-be attackers' great good fortune that the river here was wide and deep enough to allow the *Andrew Jackson* to turn awkwardly and steam back out toward Lake George before she was destroyed entirely. Any stray shot reaching the boilers or firebox could have written a sudden and explosive ending to all of Mason Coltrane's schemes for Florida.

Their crude defensive preparations served the river pirates better than they had expected to need, and after the first withering volley they hugged the deck closely among rough stacks of cordwood and the sprawled bodies of their dead and wounded comrades. Only a few showed enough presence of mind or motivation to lift their heads and return the settlers' fire.

Josh saw it all from a protected depression in the shell mound beside the porch of the general store. It began so suddenly and was over so quickly that had it not been for the cries of the hurt and dying, the pungent lingering odor of black powder accompanied by the screams of a wounded horse as the boat disappeared once more down the river, he might have had difficulty thinking of it as a battle at all.

And yet he had a guilty realization that the experience had left him strangely invigorated, as if his survival amid the death and destruction of this brief half hour had made him more conscious of his own vitality. It was an odd feeling, one he was not sure he cared for — despite the new-found sensation of strength and well-being.

When it was over, the defenders gathered again at the store, excitedly rehashing each detail of the aborted attack. It seemed a long time until Mr. Brooks finally assigned guards and the townspeople began dispersing toward their separate homes. Josh could barely keep his eyes open as he hastily downed a late supper and joined Matt and Sara Jane in their sleeping quarters for a much-needed rest.

❖ ❖ ❖

He was awakened by an urgent knocking and the sound of men's voices at the front of the store. One of the voices was Mr. Brooks'; the other sounded familiar as well.

Several minutes later the bedroom door opened and the storekeeper entered carrying a lantern. When he stepped to one side the man behind him moved quickly to Josh's bed and looked down.

"Son, I don't know when I've seen a more welcome sight! Your sister-in-law has been worried half sick about you and that little girl over there."

"Mr. Ramsay?"

"None other. I understand you've been having your share of adventures since we last met."

"Yes, sir . . . I reckon." Josh rubbed his eyes and swung his feet over the side of the bed. "We had us a couple bad times out there in the woods an' all. But Matt — that's Matt Panner over yonder — he helped us when we needed it." The younger boy was awake now, and Sara Jane was stirring sleepily in her cot nearby. Ramsay turned and extended a hand to Matt.

"Pleased to make your acquaintance. I'm Chance Ramsay, a friend of the Carpenters. We're all very grateful for your help."

"All?" Josh hesitated. "Is 'Lias . . . ?"

"He's alive, and doing as well as could be expected considering the seriousness of his wound. Mrs. Carpenter has been with him, together with the Merriweathers and several others who were able to escape the river pirates."

"Where . . . ?"

"In the forest west of us. They're on their way

here at this moment." The man in black looked again at Matt Panner, who was sitting up cross-legged on his bunk now. "Mr. Brooks tells me that a week ago you lost your father to two of the men responsible for these troubles. I am sorry to hear it." He paused. "The names he mentioned sounded familiar to me, but he was unsure if he remembered them correctly. . . ."

"Jordan." The boy's voice was quiet and utterly cold. "Quinn Jordan was the one's name what shot my pappa down. And it was his brother Luke who watched him do it. I ain't ever goin' to forget those two names, not so long as I live. Some day I'm a mind to meet up with both of 'em one more time."

Ramsay nodded. "I understand your feelings, son. But you might have to stand in line. The Jordan family has some unfinished business with me at present, and I don't expect they'll forget that very soon either." After a moment he turned to the storekeeper.

"I've explained our plan to attack those pirates at daylight, and we could use the help of any local men who'll join us. From what you've told me, our prospects for a final victory may be even better than we'd hoped. How many do you think we can recruit?"

"Ever one that can carry a gun and walk or ride'll be there. I'll see to it personal. We ain't none of us too much for puttin' off no fight what's goin' to come sooner or later. You just set here peaceful for a mite, and I'll spread the word." The bearded man took a lantern from a nail by the door and lit it, putting the other on a table nearby for Ramsay and the children.

"Coffee's on, and I think I hear the missus stirrin' around out in the kitchen. Go ahead an' get yourselves a bite to eat if you're hungry." A minute later he'd disappeared toward the front of the store, taking his long Kentucky rifle with him.

Matt Panner rose from his bed and started to pull on his trousers; Josh got to his feet as well. Ramsay took a step backward to lean casually against the door post with his arms folded, watching them.

"Were you gentlemen planning on going some-place?" he asked quietly.

"I reckon." Matt slung his suspenders over his shoulders and bent to pick up his shoes. "This here's the fight we been waitin' on, the one where we roust them outlaws out of this country entirely — or bury their carcasses where they lie!"

"I see. But you won't be coming with us. Neither of you."

The younger boy spun on his heel and glared up at him. "Who's going to stop me?"

Josh thought he could see a faint smile at the corners of the gambler's lips, the barest hint of a twinkle behind his pale gray eyes. "I expect you're looking at him."

Matt Panner stared at the relaxed form of Chance Ramsay for a long moment. Then he turned abruptly and threw his shoes into a far corner of the room.

"Gol-dern it anyhow! One of these days I'm goin' to be full-growed, and then ain't nobody goin' to tell me where it is I can an' can't go!"

"I appreciate your offer," the man in black said seriously, "and I respect the desire you both have to do your part. But we'll have enough help without you this trip I think. So you'll serve us better by remaining here to greet the others when they arrive.

"Besides . . ." He smiled at Josh. "I believe Mrs.

Carpenter would personally nail my hide to a board if you and your niece were not both here waiting when she reached Volusia!"

21 🌿

Daylight came slowly to the encampment beside the clear waters of the Great Spring, nestled as it was among encircling sand ridges thickly forested with pine, cedar, swamp maple and water oak. A dense white fog clung stubbornly to the low-lying clearing, swallowing up the tents of the outlaws and rising from the broad pool and its run-off in stately silver billows.

By first light only the tall smokestacks of the *Andrew Jackson* could be clearly seen, rising in stark silhouette against the morning sky to provide assurance for the watchers that their quarry had not eluded them. More than two dozen men were positioned now in a wide circle overlooking the camp, waiting with the endless patience of experienced hunters until the coming dawn should offer better visibility for the work ahead.

Chance Ramsay lay concealed among the roots of a huge live oak atop a shell mound near the extreme northeastern flank of the ring of attackers. A few feet away Abby Macklin crouched motionless behind the trunk of the same tree, her bow next to her and the trade rifle ready in her hands. Once, as the day grew brighter, he glanced over his shoulder and she smiled at him.

No sweet, gentle, feminine smile this. Nor one even vaguely hinting at coquetry or flirtation. It was rather the ironic, tooth-baring smile of the warrior: vital, alive, fully attuned to the danger ahead — and savoring it. Such a smile might once have appeared on the lips of the legendary Amazons of Greece, Ramsay thought, or Boudicca of England, or the Valkyries. . . .

He understood well what was behind that smile, for he'd lately become aware of some peculiar relish for combat in his own make-up. Not for the killing, but for the risk itself: the challenge, the danger, the pitting of every ounce of skill and strength against the possibility of his own destruction.

It was a trait he did not view with any particular pride, merely with acceptance. The experience, when it happened, made him feel more completely alive than any other he'd ever known. Perhaps it was a part of the reason he'd been drawn earlier to the milder and more socially acceptable risk-taking of cards and dice.

Now, in the misty dawn of a February morning in this Florida wilderness, he was struck oddly by the coincidence of discovering a kindred spirit in the lovely young woman only a few feet away. . . .

There had been no movement from the outlaws' camp. All had remained still since before first light. Then, as the sun appeared between the eastern trees and the fog began to dissipate, a few men could be seen moving tentatively among the scattered tents and bedrolls in the clearing by the spring's run-off.

They moved slowly, still half asleep, stretching and grumbling occasional low-voiced comments to one another as they built up their fires and fetched water for coffee. It was a strangely listless bunch, after the ambush and unexpected defeat of the night before. Ramsay could imagine what was in their minds, if they allowed themselves to think about it at all: Their leaders had made a serious error in judgment, and they might make others in the future. These were not men to follow an individual or plan where the risk of defeat outweighed any hope of profit.

He'd seen nothing of the Jordan brothers so far, nor of Mason Coltrane either. He recalled Josh's warning, communicated to him shortly before their party left Volusia, of the unusual weapon the boy had seen in the frock-coated man's hands when he shot into Elias. Some kind of repeating rifle it appeared, capable of firing several times in rapid succession. A useful thing to be aware of.

Nor had there been any sign of Gil Davies since the newcomers' arrival. Ramsay could only hope the big riverboat captain had been able to escape detection during the night, and had managed to carry out his plan to block retreat to Lake George by water. It appeared the possibility of flight had occurred to someone at least. The *Andrew Jackson* lay tied up now on the left bank, with her bow pointed downstream away from the spring. Black ribbons of smoke against the lightening sky indicated that her boilers remained active as well.

After a while longer he became conscious of

movement aboard the vessel, still shrouded in thick mist about her upper and lower decks. The peculiar shambling gait of Levi Budd made him easily recognizable as he crossed to spit tobacco juice over the rail, afterward standing to survey his surroundings warily for several long minutes. He spoke over his shoulder and was joined by Jake and Reuben, the former with his long rifle nested comfortably in the crook of his arm. Clyde, the youngest, was not in sight.

It wasn't until Levi turned to look above and behind him that Ramsay saw the others. Quinn Jordan and a lean man in a slouch hat had emerged onto the veranda forward of the cabin area, with enough family resemblance that it seemed certain the second must be Quinn's brother Luke. A moment afterward a tall frock-coated figure could be made out climbing the outer steps to the pilothouse.

There could be no doubt that this last was the man described by the Merriweathers and others as Mason Coltrane. His face was hidden in shadow beneath his tall hat, but Ramsay had the impression of someone younger than he'd imagined earlier. Perhaps it was the lithe, catlike way he moved, mounting the stairs in a few quick strides, pausing almost on tiptoe to glance all around him before bending abruptly to disappear inside the small compartment.

Levi Budd was saying something to the Jordans on the balcony above. Quinn replied curtly and his eyes lifted to sweep the fog-covered landscape with a sudden guarded alertness. Luke turned and stepped to the far rail, leaning out past it to gaze backward along the length of the riverboat toward the spring and the woods beyond.

An instant later Jake Budd raised his rifle to his shoulder, aiming at a point some hundred yards to Ramsay's right. Glancing quickly in that direction, the man in black could barely make out a faint rustling of tall weeds and the retreating crown of a settler's hat. As his eyes swung back to the boat, his pistol was ready in his hand and coming to bear on the rifleman at the rail.

But before he could pull the trigger Abby's weapon erupted over his shoulder with an ear-splitting roar, driving the eldest son violently back against the near bulkhead, his staring eyes blank and lifeless even as his shattered body slumped awkwardly to the deck. The echoes of the young woman's shot were still ringing in Ramsay's ears when he heard Mr. Brooks' deep voice rumble sharply across the clearing:

"Give it up, boys! Drop your weapons and lift your hands up to where we can see 'em! You're boxed in! Ain't none of you got a chanct!"

Total confusion gripped the camp. Men scrambling for weapons and cover froze briefly at the shouted words, so that for an instant it appeared they might do as they were ordered. But then a huge giant of a man with flaming red beard and whiskey-streaked eyes emerged from one of the tents, clutching a double-barreled shotgun in his two hamlike fists.

"The hell you say! Ain't no little weasel-faced sodbuster goin' to tell Red Hanfort what to do! Come on ahead and be damned to you!" He punctuated his last words with two deafening blasts of the shotgun, bringing a scream from one of the settlers hidden in the bushes some twenty yards away. Four rifle balls transfixed the big man almost immediately as he threw down the shotgun and clawed for a pistol at his belt. By the time he'd fallen to his knees the firing on both sides had become general.

When Ramsay looked back at the *Andrew Jackson* Levi and Reuben Budd had disappeared from the lower deck, as had Quinn Jordan from the area above. The only one in sight now was Luke, crouched behind an overturned table on the small veranda with his back to the bulkhead, well protected against fire from the direction of the spring. At that moment he was taking aim with his pistol at a nearby settler who had stood up briefly to ram a charge home in the barrel of his long rifle.

The Navy Colt in Ramsay's fist spoke twice, almost before he had time to grasp the situation. Luke Jordan jerked and swore, flinging the table aside and a second later half-crawling, half-stumbling through the open cabin entrance. He threw a wild shot behind him as he disappeared, hitting nothing.

There seemed to be a brief lull in the fight while men on both sides reloaded and sought fresh targets. Ramsay was scanning the boat's decks and ports for sign of those aboard when a sudden shout from Abby brought his head around sharply. She was pointing in the direction of the outlaws' camp, where a half dozen armed men had risen and begun a headlong dash for the trees to escape the main body of attackers. They were heading directly for the shell mound where he and Abby crouched!

No sooner had she gotten his attention than the young woman brought the rifle to her shoulder and fired. One of the men cried out and lost his weapon, sprawling backward on the ground. Ramsay's first bullet took another in the midsection while Abby ducked behind the tree to recover her bow and arrows. A second shot from the Colt barely missed its target to strike sparks from a rifle in a third man's hands, whining noisily away as the owner jerked and stumbled to his knees.

Ramsay felt the whip of a bullet past his cheek as he fired a third time, and he hugged the ground while more projectiles sprayed dirt and whispered among the leaves nearby. When he raised himself up again others had begun shooting into the fleeing outlaws, and in minutes the charge was over. Three bodies lay motionless on the damp grass and the rest had lost all will to fight. They crouched in the open with their empty hands above their heads, bleeding and calling out for mercy.

As if this were some kind of signal, the remaining defenders in the camp also began throwing down their weapons and raising their arms in surrender. From his vantage point atop the shell mound Ramsay could see only a handful that were able to stand. And half of those appeared to be wounded.

Slowly, cautiously, the settlers began rising from their hiding places to advance into the clearing with their weapons ready. The sudden quiet seemed unreal after the deafening fury of the past few minutes. Ears still rang with the thunderous explosions of shot and powder; the muted cries of the injured seemed to come now from all directions.

It was not until several more minutes had passed that a different sound became noticeable, one that was not identified until a man by the spring happened to look up across the water and shout:

"The boat! She's movin'!"

Ramsay turned and stared. The men on the *Andrew Jackson* had escaped his thoughts completely during the harsh immediacy of the outlaws' charge and its aftermath. With a head of steam up already, it had taken short work to cut the mooring lines and push out into the current under the distraction of the fighting on shore. Now the big paddle wheel was churning the clear waters to a froth as the boat rounded the first bend of the creek on its headlong dash for Lake George.

A sudden movement at the corners of his eyes caught Ramsay's attention and spurred him to action. He'd a fleeting glimpse of Abby descending the shell mound in a long, loping run, holding her bow and arrows before her as she disappeared among the trees to eastward. As he started in pursuit he barely had the presence of mind to switch his revolvers in their holsters so the fully loaded one would come first to his right hand.

He knew what was in the young woman's mind: The narrows where Davies had planned to block the waterway lay some half mile downstream. But the place was considerably closer by land as the run curved sharply back on itself here. If they moved swiftly, they might cut off an escape once the boat and its passengers had reached the barricade.

If there was a barricade; if it proved sufficient to halt the big powered vessel in any event. Even if so it was a rash idea, for there were four or five armed men to be faced when and if the riverboat was forced to stop. Ramsay said a fervent prayer that some others of their party had seen them leave the shell mound and understood well enough to follow. . . .

The woods here were low and marshy, the forest floor littered with newly sprouted black gum, elm and maple amid thick stands of palmetto and treacherous entanglements of briars and wild grape. Over all was a towering canopy of oak, royal palm and cypress. Chance Ramsay advanced more by instinct than by design, catching only occasional glimpses of Abby in the distance and then losing her again to the seemingly impenetrable forest.

Suddenly there was a loud grinding and crunching noise ahead and to his right, much nearer than he'd expected the winding creek to be. With a final burst of effort he thrust his way past the remaining wall of foliage and stumbled out onto a narrow bank only a few feet from the water's edge.

Directly ahead of him, no more than a dozen yards away in midstream, the *Andrew Jackson* had come to a halt with its bow riding up and over the makeshift barrier of wagons where it had apparently been driven while still trying to accelerate. The paddle wheel continued its furious churning as Ramsay watched, relentlessly lifting the bow upward as it pushed the stern ever lower into the shallow waters.

There was a desperate clash of gears as the inexperienced crew realized the danger and tried to back away. But it was already too late. In the next instant the paddles struck bottom and came apart with a violent rending of overburdened wood and metal, strewing wreckage from shore to shore. Minutes later, the steamboat's huge pistons ground to a halt and she settled slowly backward, dead in the water and listing heavily from several deep gashes in her forward hull.

Ramsay tore his eyes from the scene with difficulty to scan the wooded shoreline ahead and to his left. Finally he could make out Abby's slim buckskin-clad figure, crouched in the sparse cover of a clump of hardwood scrub some twenty yards away. An arrow was nocked in her bow, and she held two others ready in her left hand. Her eyes were focused intently on the decks of the motionless riverboat. She seemed unaware of his presence.

He saw the young woman's brow furrow and she began easing the bow higher, drawing back on the string as she did so. Ramsay's eyes flicked immediately to the boat, in time to see Reuben and Levi Budd emerge cautiously from an opening amidships. Both were now armed with double-barreled shotguns.

The Navy Colt was in his fist instantly as the two men stepped to the rail, Levi facing forward and Reuben aft. With his attention drawn first to the wreck and then to Abby, Ramsay realized he had neglected to think about cover for himself until this moment. He stood in full view of his enemies on the sunlit stream bank, with the nearest tree a dozen feet away.

Too late. He saw the younger Budd's eyes widen with recognition and the shotgun in his hands begin to lift. Ramsay fired.

His first shot took Reuben in the chest and the young man staggered backward, still struggling to bring his weapon to bear. A second bullet struck two inches to the right of the first and the shotgun discharged with a deafening roar. As pellets sprayed the water and the reeds near his feet Ramsay felt a tug at his pants leg accompanied by a sharp pain in his lower calf. He tried desperately to place two more bullets beyond Reuben to where Levi was swinging his own weapon around behind his son's slumping body. But neither appeared to reach their target, and an instant later there was a sharp crack from a new direction as the black hat was ripped from his head and a stinging sensation along the length of his scalp heralded the near miss.

Dropping to the ground by instinct, Ramsay rolled over several times before lifting up to fire blindly at the wheelhouse where this latest attack had seemed to come from. There was no effect that he could see, and without pausing he scuttled sideways until he could find partial cover behind a huge oak a short distance from the water's edge.

There were sounds of shooting from other locations now, and spreading wavelets near the distant bow of the *Andrew Jackson* suggested at least one of those on board had decided to abandon ship. Ramsay lifted his head cautiously to gaze back along the lower deck where Levi Budd could be seen kneeling behind his son's body, his shotgun propped at an awkward angle over the dead man's shoulder.

It took a short time to realize that the older man was not moving. His eyes stared straight ahead out of a brown, creased face that had been frozen into some grotesque parody of childlike surprise; a bright stream of blood oozed from one corner of his widely parted lips. Under his right arm the feathered end of an arrow could barely be seen where it joined father and son in final union. The other shaft which transfixed Levi's throat a few inches below both ears was a more obvious cause of death.

Ramsay shifted his body to peek around the bottom of the tree trunk toward Abby's position, and he caught a fleeting glimpse of the young woman loosing her third arrow in the direction of the wheelhouse just as a dark shape loomed behind her. Before he could call out a warning the bark beside his cheek exploded into stinging fragments from another near miss by Coltrane's rifle. He swore viciously as he ducked out of sight, blinking his eyes and rubbing at them furiously with his free hand.

A minute later a harsh voice could be made out above the echoes of gunfire, hailing him from where he'd last seen Abby a few yards away:

"Ramsay! Mr. Chance Ramsay!" The voice sounded familiar, though he couldn't recall where he'd heard it last. "C'mon and show yourself, Mr. high-and-mighty! And just be real sure ain't neither of them fancy hosspistols in your hands when you do it!"

He hesitated. The source of the voice was beginning to come back to him now.

"If you ain't out there in the open in another ten seconds . . ." Clyde Budd's words seemed to be growing shriller. ". . . I'm goin' to open up this li'l halfbreed she-tiger's throat from ear to ear, an' then drag her carcass over there and throw it down at your feet!"

22 🕸

Ramsay closed his eyes and took a deep breath, then struggled to a standing position behind the water oak using his free hand to steady himself. Clyde might be bluffing, but the youngest son of Levi Budd sounded all too willing to carry out his threat if given the opportunity. And it was a risk the former gambler dared not take.

He holstered the Colt with his right hand and stepped into the open.

Clyde was standing some twenty feet away, his muscular legs straddling the young woman's back as she knelt on the ground before him. The thick fingers of his left hand were entwined in her long black hair, pulling it roughly backward to expose her slender throat to the heavy Bowie knife which his right pressed close beneath her chin.

He was hatless, and his unkempt hair hung in dripping tendrils from his recent swim in the creek. His eyes seemed to burn with unnatural fury as they flicked from Ramsay to his dead relatives on the boat and back again. Slowly his lips curved into a cruel and wicked grin.

"Not so much left of the Budd clan now, is there? You done seen to that real fine, you an' this li'l she-bitch here." Abby jerked and twisted abruptly, trying to get her teeth on the hand with the knife. But Clyde simply pulled down harder on her hair, bringing forth a gasp of pain as he pressed the blade more tightly to her throat. Ramsay saw a faint line of red appear against the tawny smoothness.

"You settle down now, hear? Fightin' won't do neither of us no good right at the moment. I got to finish my business with this gent real quick an' get off into the woods, 'fore them others has a chanct to come along. Maybe I'll take you with me and we'll have us a li'l go-round later on. If I decide to keep you till then, that is."

A slight movement to his right caught Ramsay's eye, and he became aware that Mason Coltrane had stepped out onto the upper deck of the *Andrew Jackson*. His rifle was in his hands, but he made no immediate move to bring it to his shoulder. There was a curious, amused smile on his face as he watched what was occurring on the bank below him.

"All right," the youngest Budd went on sharply. "Walk on over here an' drop them gunbelts to the ground real slow an' easy. Then back off a ways till I can get my hands on 'em." He threw Abby to the ground with a sudden movement, placing a knee in the small of her back to free his left hand while keeping the knife close against her throat with his right.

"Mind you do it careful, 'cause I ain't so sure I wouldn't rather drain this murderin' heifer's blood out on the ground right here as try an' take her with me!"

Ramsay moved forward haltingly, his teeth clenched against the searing pain that lanced through his injured leg at every step. He was hoping desperately for some chance distraction, some random event however minor, which might draw the knife away from the girl's throat for that single split second it would take him to draw and fire.

He knew he would try it anyway, with or without a clear opening. This man had no intention of letting Abby live once he was finished with her, and Ramsay had a feeling she would prefer a quick death, if it came to that, to the alternative. Perhaps, if he could make his move fast enough . . .

There would be only one chance. Each of his pistols was down to a single load now, and the second must be for Mason Coltrane on the *Andrew Jackson*. One bullet to disable Clyde Budd, another to draw the frock-coated man's fire, and with luck Abby might manage to break free and disappear among the trees while Coltrane was shooting at Ramsay.

His own survival had no part in his thinking. The odds against it were so great that his gambler's mind discounted them entirely. What mattered were Abby's chances for life and what he could do in the next few moments to improve them.

He went over his actions mentally as he halted before the couple on the ground, taking care to keep his face expressionless and avoid any accidental glance toward the riverboat. Yet when his eyes met the young woman's he thought he could detect some secret understanding there, almost as if she were able to see into his mind.

"All right," Clyde said. "That's far enough. Now you just stay put an' unbuckle that first belt there, usin' your left hand." Ramsay nodded and began to comply, but then he swayed on his feet and let his eyes start to close as if weakness had overcome him.

It was a desperate gamble, but in that brief instant of her captor's indecision regarding his foe's impending collapse, Abby moved like greased lightning. Jerking her head to one side away from the lethal blade, she grasped the outlaw's wrist with her right hand and reached behind to cruelly pinch the tender flesh of his thigh with her left.

Clyde's mouth opened to bellow a curse, but Ramsay's Colt was blossoming flame before the words could escape his lips. The young man's head jerked back and there was a brief glimpse of a small round hole over the bridge of his nose, just before the man in black swung around to bring his left-hand pistol to bear on his second enemy aboard the boat.

He saw the sparks and flash of Mason Coltrane's weapon and felt a heavy pressure in his chest as he drew back the hammer, but managed to keep his feet and with an effort took deliberate aim at the vee of white above the other's embroidered satin waistcoat. As the Colt bucked in his fist he seemed to see the pirate leader stagger through a gathering haze of orange and crimson. He fell to his knees.

Abby . . .

He tried to will himself to turn and see if these final moments had given the young woman time to get away. But his neck would not move and his vision seemed hopelessly clouded. He could feel the bright new day slipping slowly, irresistibly from him. . . .

❖   ❖   ❖

For a long while there were no days or nights, only slowly shifting intervals of sleep, delirium and agonizing weakness. It was a perilous time for Chance Ramsay, though he could recall little of his near brush with death once the crisis was past and he finally became aware of his surroundings at the store in Volusia, almost a week after his injury. Yet he'd the distinct impression not very many during this time — least of all himself — would have given favorable odds for his recovery.

There was Abby, of course. If she harbored any doubts about his return to health, she betrayed no hint of them. It seemed she'd hardly left his side since the moment of his shooting, dressing his wounds, arranging for his transport to the settlement, and taking full charge of his rehabilitation from that time forward.

Hers was the first face Ramsay had recognized upon his return to consciousness, and it had become the last he saw now before sleep each night. There was a comforting familiarity about her presence, one he found himself growing more and more attached to as his periods of consciousness grew longer and they were able to carry on occasional conversations.

It was several more long weeks before he could manage even the simplest of tasks without help. Yet his strength was returning, gradually. And at last he was able to achieve the major victory of sitting up in bed and feeding himself. After another few days he was strong enough to rise and move about for short periods, and to entertain occasional visitors.

There had been many earlier visitors as it turned

out, whom Mrs. Brooks and Abby had been obliged to turn away. Everyone in the surrounding neighborhood seemed to find some excuse to drop by the store at one time or another, to express their thanks and pay their respects. Even total strangers had come calling, hoping to shake the hand of the man responsible for Mason Coltrane's demise.

The Carpenters were in daily attendance too, while remaining in Volusia until 'Lias could recover from his own wound. And Matt Panner, who'd be living with the Brooks family until he was old enough to manage his homestead by himself. It was through conversations with these, as well as from Abby and Mr. Brooks, that Ramsay eventually learned details of the outcome of the battle at the Great Spring.

Coltrane had died where he fell, the victim of the gambler's final shot. Luke Jordan had met his end shortly before, in an exchange of gunfire with Gil Davies on the opposite side of the boat. With the earlier deaths of the Budd clan and the rounding up of survivors for swift trials with usually fatal outcomes, it seemed the outlaw invasion of Florida had been thoroughly shattered. Only Quinn Jordan had managed to avoid justice at the hands of the aroused populace, apparently escaping into the river at some point during the confusion of battle.

The days passed slowly, but pleasantly enough while Ramsay gained strength and something of his former vigor in the company of new-found friends. By the time he was well enough to spend long mornings in a rocking chair on the wide front porch of the general store, the defeat of the river pirates was already becoming ancient history. It was mid-March now, and there were crops to be put in, cattle to be hunted out of the brush and branded, buildings to be repaired — all the pressing daily requirements of frontier life, which seldom left time for reflecting on past gains or losses. Everywhere the colors and smells and fresh growth of spring spoke of hope and new beginnings.

The conversations between Chance and Abby seemed to grow more intimate by degrees, and they shared much of themselves during those soft spring mornings and long lazy twilights, talking of their vastly different upbringings, their private pleasures and sorrows, their hopes for the future. . . .

And yet when it came to this last, the man found himself speaking most often in carefully worded generalities. It was not that he wished to keep his dreams from this young woman for whom he felt an ever-growing fondness. Quite the contrary. But there was something Ramsay still could not — would not — bring himself to discuss with her. Something that promised to make all those dreams as empty as any short-lived wind off the river.

He knew the time must come, very soon now if his recovery continued at its present rate, when he must leave this place behind. And Abigail Macklin with it. Ramsay had not forgotten for a moment the price on his head and the warrant for his arrest. He could see no way out of his predicament but to keep on running. Despite Quinn Jordan's part in the outlaw attack, the warrant was still a legal document. And few bounty hunters would care what kind of man paid the reward, as long as it was paid.

There were times he was tempted to tell her what was troubling him, tempted even to remain in this country and damn the consequences. But he knew it could not be.

The worst perhaps was the day some of the settlers who'd taken part in the fight at the Great Spring arrived with a half dozen fine horses in tow, insisting that Ramsay accept them as a reward for his services and his share in the division of the outlaws' captured goods. When he started to refuse, Abby, who was seated next to him, leaned forward and whispered excitedly in his ear. It was an idea he'd not thought of before, but one that seemed so suited to his own temperament and his half-formed hopes for the future that Chance Ramsay smiled in spite of himself, nodding and accepting the offered animals without further argument.

Her suggestion was impossible, of course. But the horses would make fine remounts for a traveling man, and a movable asset that could be turned to ready cash whenever the need arose. Once the men had gone Abby wanted to discuss her ideas further. But he shook his head and lapsed into a moody silence. He knew his apparent indifference might make her angry. But what could he do?

A short time later the young woman left the settlement for a visit to her cabin in the wilderness, the first such trip since Ramsay had been wounded. It was almost a week before she returned, and when she did there was little talk between them. She seemed to be avoiding him.

The following morning, shortly before noon, Ramsay was roused from his half-slumber in the rocker on the porch by two long blasts of a steamboat whistle. Minutes later the *Andrew Jackson* hove into view around the wide bend in the river from the north.

He'd known that Gil Davies had managed to re-float the vessel and repair it, that he'd even made one trip upstream to Lake Monroe already. But this was the first time Ramsay was up and about to see her. She looked fine, he thought. Fresh paint glistened from her rebuilt paddle wheel and superstructure, giving little evidence of earlier damage.

As he sat watching with more than casual interest, the boat slowed and moved out of the current, reversing gears to ease deftly in beside the landing a hundred yards below him. Today was also the day the Carpenters would be boarding her to complete the final leg of their journey to Enterprise and the lake country beyond.

Soon Ramsay could make out the bulky figure of the captain himself, pausing briefly to give orders for unloading cargo before crossing the short gangway and climbing the rise to the store. There was someone with him, a tall, thin mustachioed man whom the watcher did not recognize at first, until the tin star on his chest caught the morning sun as he mounted the steps.

"Sheriff Braden, isn't it?" Ramsay turned in his chair after greeting Davies, and extended a hand with more show of welcome than he felt at the moment. "I am pleased to see you have recovered from your wounds."

"Likewise, sir. And my thanks to you for makin' the recovery possible." Braden glanced at the captain and smiled faintly. "I've been hearin' a deal about you on this trip upriver. Seems you're quite the hero hereabouts, over an' above anything you might of done for me."

Davies shrugged. "I've only told him the facts, which are pert' well known all the way from Jacksonville to Mellonville by now." He crossed to take a seat on a wood box near the store's entrance before continuing.

"Which reminds me. The Merriweathers sends their regards. They got some land staked out west of Lake Monroe what they started clearin' for plantin'. Put up a li'l one-room cabin too, for use as a house and store till they can manage somethin' bigger." He indicated the riverboat with a nod of his head. "Got their first consignment of goods on board the *Andy* now."

Ramsay looked at him questioningly. "Their own things that they started the journey with . . . ?"

"Well, I couldn't manage to get it all unloaded before drivin' them wagons into the river. But I done what I could. And I reckon the most important thing was that li'l old strongbox I found underneath the chiffonier right close to the back tailgate." He smiled. "Not that I wouldn't of give them folks credit for startin' up if I could. But what with the repairs to the *Andy* an' all, it come in right handy that they was able to pay cash for whatever they wanted. An' with the full load of cargo an' passengers I got this trip, I reckon when I get back to Jacksonville I ought to be just about broke even and ready to make a profit the next time around."

Ramsay nodded. Then he looked at Braden. It was not in his mind to postpone the inevitable, nor avoid the difficult questions which might affect his future. Not any longer.

"I assume you had some reason for making this trip upriver, Sheriff?"

"Uh-huh. On my way to pick up a prisoner."

"A prisoner?"

"Man they say caused a li'l ruckus a while back, chasin' after some young-un with a pistol. His partner got kilt in the process. Both was wanted for a couple murders up in my district, and the sheriff down to Mellonville agreed to keep him penned up till I could come fetch him."

Ramsay was watching him narrowly. "No one else? Just that one man?"

Braden frowned and pushed his hat back from his head to scratch a graying temple. "Not as I can figure. They was them Budd fellers what shot the hell outen my posse an' me, but I hear tell they got theirselves plumb out of reach of the law whilst you-all was doin' some tidyin' up hereabouts." He met Ramsay's eyes. "Anybody else you can think of?"

The gambler smiled for the first time since the visitors' arrival. He felt as if a heavy weight was being lifted from his shoulders. "No, Sheriff. Not if you can't."

The older man nodded, hooking his thumbs in his belt and leaning against the porch rail to study a nest of mockingbirds on a moss-draped limb a dozen yards away.

"Y'know," he said after a moment, "worst thing about this here sheriffin' job is all the dad-blamed paperwork comes with it. Got so bad here lately I can't hardly keep track of nothin' no more. And most of it don't amount to a hill of beans in the long run." He fished a torn and weathered half-broadside from his shirt pocket.

"You take this here for example. Some folks name of Jordan up to the Savannah River claims they're offerin' a thousand dollars RE-ward for the capture of some stranger on a Arabian horse. Why, even assumin' anybody was fool enough to look for that gent this side the Mississippi, they'd purely play hell collectin' their money if they found him. I heard that Jordan family was took for ever cent they owned by some Yankee sharper a couple months ago. And what's more, I just got word they's a warrant out for one of them Jordan boys now, from the Florida law. Fellow name of Quinn." He paused, shrugging slightly.

"So it turns out this paper ain't worth the ink was used to print it, and I got to waste my time lettin' folks all up an' down the country here know about it." He punctuated his last remark by tearing the poster into thin strips and holding them out for the breeze off the river to blow away.

"Nossir, ain't never seen no paper tells a tenth of what a man can look at an' see with his own eyes. And that's the honest truth!"

A minute later Matt Panner was standing in the doorway, with Josh Carpenter close behind him.

"Miz Brooks said to ask y'all to come in an' join us for dinner. We're gettin' ready to dish it up now."

23

Extra leaves had been added to the oak table so that it almost filled the kitchen to overflowing. Enough places had been set for Sara Jane and the other children to join the adults in honor of the Carpenters' departure, and a festive dinner of fried chicken, biscuits, fresh greens and sweet potato pie awaited them, with all the fixings.

'Lias met the latest guests outside the door with warm handshakes, and led them to their places. Davies clapped a big paw on his shoulder as he moved past him to his chair.

"You're lookin' right pert, boy. Wouldn't of give two cents for your chances when we first brung you out from that pirates' camp. But I reckon they's somethin' to be said for good food an' good nursin'." He winked at Mary and grinned. "'Specially from a good-lookin' woman."

'Lias smiled and covered his wife's hand with his own as he took his place beside her. "It's a blessin', Captain. Ain't nothin' like a fine wife to give a man somethin' more'n just his own selfish pride to stay alive for."

"Where's Abby?" Ramsay asked, uncomfortably aware that at the question all eyes suddenly turned his way.

"She'll be along directly." Mrs. Brooks took a piece of chicken and passed the plate to Mary on her left, exchanging a glance with the other woman before breaking open a biscuit and starting to butter it. "They was somethin' she'd a mind to tend to 'fore comin' to table, what she allowed she didn't want no extra help with."

Ramsay looked at her curiously, but the storekeeper's wife was avoiding his eyes.

After they'd all been served, Mr. Brooks seemed to take a long time arranging his napkin before preparing to offer the blessing. When he finally opened his mouth to speak, he glanced up from the table and hesitated, then quickly pushed his chair back and stood up. There was a moment of silence while the others turned to follow his gaze, and a general scraping of chairs afterward as the men in the room rose to greet the new arrival.

Abigail Macklin stood framed in the doorway, a startling vision of beauty and elegance in crisp white dress and petticoats, demure lace bodice, satin sash, and rows of small decorative ribbons which matched those at her throat and in the long black hair cascading gracefully over her slender shoulders. She smiled shyly as Chance Ramsay recovered from his surprise and hurried to take her arm.

"What you think?" she whispered as he led her to her place and drew back the chair. "Am I fittin' to be seen alongside some of them riverboat ladies now? Ones like you used to squire around?" Ramsay could feel the eyes of everyone watching as he seated the young woman and took his place beside her. He pointedly ignored them, turning instead to gaze into his companion's delicately blushing face.

"More than fitting," he said seriously. "I cannot imagine a one of my acquaintance who would not be positively green with envy." As he took up his napkin to replace it in his lap, he added softly, "But then I'd never any doubt of that, from the first day we met."

After Mr. Brooks completed his interrupted blessing, the company fell to with ready appetites. As was customary, serious conversation around the table was postponed in favor of the more important business of doing justice to their hostess's excellent meal.

But at last, when the dinner was over and coffee was being passed around, 'Lias Carpenter put down his spoon and looked across the table at the visiting lawman. "They's still one thing puzzles me, Sheriff, 'bout this entire business. And it strikes me you just might be the gent to clear it up." He took a sip of coffee before glancing at Josh.

"We never was able to figure out why them couple of outlaws went to chasin' after these young-uns in the woods that night the boat was attacked. Joshua an' me talked it over some, but alls we could speculate was it had somethin' to do with this gold locket the boy found up near the Georgia line." He paused while Josh took the object from his pocket and held it out it to the lawman.

"That's what the taller one said they was after, just before he drawed iron and got hisself kilt. But we can't imagine how his kind would come to know any fine-lookin' lady like that, much less have a gold locket with her paintin' inside. . . ."

'Lias let his voice trail off as he watched Braden open the locket and stare down at the picture with a pained expression on his face. After a long moment the sheriff pressed the two halves together and laid the object gently on the table in front of him, shutting his eyes and reaching up to pinch the bridge of his nose with a rough, callused hand.

"I knowed about it," he said, "all along. But still it ain't the same as peekin' in there and seein' her lookin' back at you, just like she was, without never . . ." He shook his head. "Let me have a minute here."

When he looked up again his eyes were red, but his voice was steady and deliberate.

"That's Marth Carter's locket, and it's her picture inside. Her folks wasn't rich, but they'd a mite of money and she was their only daughter. Had that li'l picture painted by some travelin' artist on the occasion of her eighteenth birthday, a year before she married Jed. Everbody in Ware County knowed about it. She an' her husband never did get tired of showin' it off." He paused, glancing slowly around the table.

"When them murderers come an' kilt the two of 'em, they took everthing they could find what 'peared to be made out of silver or gold. This here was just one more li'l somethin' they expected to sell for a dollar or two. Only they never realized how easy a thing it'd be for folks to recognize." Braden turned to Ramsay.

"You 'call that woman whose house you brung me to up yonder, that Miz Lucy Steed? Well, she an' her husband see all kinds passin' through the country thereabouts, an' don't hardly let any of 'em go away hungry or thirsty. They both seen the locket, and they could describe real good the men what had it with 'em. Don't rightly know how that managed to come up in the conversation whilst I was stayin' there, but you know she's a woman who likes her talk.

"Anyway I got a feelin' them two might of wanted to kill the Steeds right away after what they seen, if they'd had the chanct. But another bunch of travelers come along about then and they got skittish. Left out real quick afterwards." The Sheriff took a swallow of coffee and shrugged.

"Now the rest of it I'm guessin' mostly, together with what Cap'n Davies here's told me and what I heard from you folks. I expect maybe they stayed in the neighborhood a day or two, still lookin' for a chanct to do away with the Steeds. And in the process they spent a night up by that creek where you found the locket. Either they lost it there, or what's more likely, got shut of it a-purpose. 'Cause with it gone an' nobody alive to say they had it, twouldn't be no evidence a-tall to link 'em up with the killin's.

"But then come the ambush them Budds pulled on my posse an' me — nervous theirselves from thinkin' we knowed somethin' we didn't — and Mr. Steed was gone off someplace an' Mr. Ramsay there at the house with me. And all of a sudden it looked like the safest thing to do was just light out for the south and hope for the best. At least that locket wasn't no part of their lives no more. Or so they thought."

He waved a hand toward Josh, who didn't look up. "Can you imagine what come into their minds when they seen this young-un here with it on the boat? Same kid was earlier starin' up at them and Mr. Coltrane so terrible suspicious-like? They was just sure it was some kind of a omen, that the boy knowed everthing about 'em and everthing they'd done. In their minds the locket proved it." The older man leaned back in his chair.

"Maybe they wasn't exactly thinkin' with all the brains God give 'em right then. It's kind of like the Good Book says: The guilty flee where no man pursueth. But onct they'd got it into their heads, they couldn't manage to shake the idea that if they let this young-un go, their own fates was sealed." He paused again, then added mildly:

"And in a way, I reckon they was right."

There was a long silence after the sheriff finished speaking. The story of the young Georgia couple's murder, already known to most of them, had cast a somber pall over the after-dinner conversation, and it appeared no one had much else they felt like saying.

Ramsay glanced across the table at Josh Carpenter, who was sitting perfectly still with his head lowered, staring unseeing at the empty plate before him. The gambler frowned thoughtfully. He'd shared some conversations with the youngster during his convalescence, idle talk of guns and hunting and his former life on the riverboats mostly. But the subject of the lady in the locket had come up a time or two also.

Perhaps it was because Chance Ramsay struck Josh as a "man of the world"; or perhaps it was just easier to share one's private thoughts with a stranger. In any event, he'd become aware of the boy's fascination with the woman in the painting, and had a pretty good idea the kind of dreams a thirteen-year-old might build from that. It had seemed harmless enough at the time. He could recall having similar fantasies over magazine illustrations at Josh's age. But now, in the light of Martha Carter's gruesome death . . .

"Well," Sheriff Braden said at last, shaking his head and reaching out to take up the locket. "I reckon I best hold onto this for evidence for the time bein'. Likely return it to Marth's folks by and by." He rose from the table, slipping the golden object into his pocket as he made his way to the door. As if this were some kind of signal, the others got up and started drifting out of the room as well. Mrs. Brooks shooed Mary off to finish her preparations for boarding the riverboat, while Abby stayed to help with the dishes.

Josh kept his seat until all but the two women had departed. Then he got up and slowly made his way into the adjoining hallway. Chance Ramsay was waiting, leaning casually against the wall which separated them from the store proper.

"She was a very beautiful woman," the man said quietly. "That lady in the locket. Mrs. Martha Carter."

Josh looked at him curiously, then started to turn away without answering.

"I've an idea she is someone we might both have taken a great deal of pleasure in knowing." At these words, uttered calmly, almost callously, the boy halted and glanced back. Ramsay thought he detected a trace of resentment in his look. A not unexpected reaction.

"Only . . ." he went on after a long moment. "We didn't. Neither of us." He moved closer, interrupting the intended protest with a gentle hand on the youngster's shoulder. "Think about it, Josh. However fine a person Martha Carter may have been in real life, and I'm sure she was, we did not know that person. We only knew her painted image."

Josh hesitated, started to speak, then turned away and rubbed roughly at his eyes with the back of a clenched fist. "But . . . But she was so, so . . ."

"Real? To you, in your dreams, I'm certain she was. It is a curious thing about the male creature, son, that he is capable of loving an image, a dream of a woman, even when he has no experience with the real thing." Ramsay paused, glancing past his young companion into the kitchen, where Abigail Macklin stood with her back to them, drying her hands on a linen dish towel. His grip on Josh's shoulder tightened, and he smiled warmly.

"But some day you will meet a real woman. The right woman. And when that happens, you will not have the slightest difficulty recognizing the difference."

While the Carpenters returned to the store for a final short visit after seeing to the loading of their wagon aboard the *Andrew Jackson*, Ramsay made his way slowly down to the landing with Abby at his side. Though he could feel his strength increase with each passing day, he was still very weak, and he didn't like others to see the effort it took him to travel even this short distance.

Besides, it was the first opportunity the two had had to be alone since his earlier conversation with the sheriff. And they had much to talk over.

"So that's it," Abby said quietly, once he'd explained his lingering worries about his fugitive status and the welcome news from Braden this morning. "An' here all along I thought it was somethin' else entire. I mean, whenever the subject of you stakin' out a place of your own come up, and you kept actin' skittish like a new-borned colt, I'd a idea maybe you was longin' for them fancy riverboats again, an' all the high-toned society you used to run with . . ."

Her voice trailed off and she stopped suddenly, turning her face away from him and twisting her hands in the folds of her white cotton dress. "I mean, that's the reason why I . . . I . . ." As he halted next to her, Ramsay was sure the redness at her throat had nothing to do with the afternoon sun.

"I know. And I'm more flattered than any man has a right to be. But I meant what I said back there at dinner. Even in your buckskins, the most elegant Southern belle would seem plain by comparison."

Her flush grew deeper, and she still did not look at him. "You think maybe . . . that idea I had onct upon a time 'bout raisin' horses in this Florida wilderness . . ."

"Sounds better every time I hear it." He placed a hand gently around her waist. "With your help."

"Them horses is doin' real fine out to the pasture yonder." She leaned back so that her head was against his cheek. "'Pears this country agrees with 'em."

"Uh-huh." Ramsay was silent a moment, enjoying the fresh scent of her hair. "Perhaps I could talk young Master Panner into loaning his two Morgans when it's time to breed Lady. The combination should make for some outstanding foals." He fell silent again, then laid his free hand on Abby's arm and turned her toward him. "As for us . . ."

"Well, isn't this a fetchin' picture?"

The voice came from the direction of a solitary

live oak some twenty yards away. With a start, the man and woman turned quickly to seek out the speaker. As they did, Quinn Jordan stepped into view from behind the massive trunk.

He was coatless now, and his elegant clothing showed signs of much harsh wear. But his weapons appeared well enough maintained. The Sharps carbine was slung barrel downward behind his right arm, and the Dragoon Colt was thrust into his belt where it would come ready to hand.

Jordan seemed in no particular hurry to bring either of these to bear at the moment, and the reason was obvious enough: Neither the man nor the woman before him was armed. Quite apart from Mrs. Brooks' rule about weapons at the dinner table, Ramsay had taken to leaving off the heavy pistol belts of late since they tended to disturb his bandages and pull ominously against the freshly knitted chest wound. He'd enough trouble getting about at present anyhow, without the added weight.

He cursed himself for not thinking to carry some sort of hide-out at least, on this rare excursion out-of-doors.

Abby, who seldom went abroad without at least a Bowie knife in her leather belt, was equally helpless at the moment. Weapons and lace had not seemed to make a particularly ladylike combination.

With a glance over his shoulder in the vain hope of seeing someone watching or approaching from the store, Ramsay thrust the young woman away from him and gauged the distance to the man beside the live oak. Too far. Even had he been in peak condition, he doubted he could have crossed the open space between them before bullets from one or both weapons ripped him apart. Now, with his injury . . .

Quinn Jordan was smiling. He seemed to know what was in Ramsay's mind, and he was enjoying his enemy's discomfort.

"I told you you was a dead man, up in Georgia near three months ago. Just didn't expect it'd take this long to run you to ground." He shifted his gaze to Abby briefly. "But it looks like it might of been worth the wait. Now I got the chance of bagging two for one."

"Leave her out of it, Jordan," Ramsay said quickly, "for God's sake. It's me you want. She's nothing to you."

"Didn't appear that way back up to our camp on the Great Spring. I remember this li'l she-tiger real good. Fights like a man, shoots like a man. An' them as mixes in men's business got to expect to pay the piper, soon or late." He bowed mockingly and touched his hat to Abby with his left hand. "Beggin' your pardon, ma'am, but ain't no ribbons nor lace in all the world goin' to change that."

As Jordan straightened from his bow, Ramsay realized he'd no options left. He must make a try for the man, unarmed and weak as he was, in hopes that Abby might somehow use the distraction to get herself temporarily out of the line of fire. With Braden and the others due to appear from the store at any moment, Quinn couldn't remain here long. A few seconds of blazing agony was all that would be required.

The man by the tree was smiling again, wickedly, viciously. "You're thinkin' I'll take my first shot at you, don't you Ramsay? An' if you was heeled I sure enough would. But you ain't no danger to me now, and I think it'll hurt you just a little bit worse to see this here she-cat get hers first, before I attend to you." He turned his eyes toward Abby, and his hand started to drop to the carbine at his side.

"You ready, girl?"

24 🖐

A SUDDEN EXPLOSION FROM THE FOREST a hundred yards away distracted Ramsay, and he almost missed seeing the bullet take Jordan in the midsection and spin him around, throwing him hard up against the tree trunk before he slumped to the earth, still clutching feebly at the carbine by his side. In another instant Abby was standing over him. A slippered foot pressed down on the long gun while she bent to snatch up the pistol and turn it against their assailant. But there was no need. Quinn Jordan was already dead.

By the time Ramsay reached her side he could see the slight form of Matt Panner emerging from the trees, his long musket in his hands. The youngster's stride was slow and deliberate as he approached them across the grassy clearing; and he never once took his eyes from the man on the ground.

"Is he . . . ?" the boy asked quietly, halting a dozen feet away.

"Done for," Abby said. "Shot clean through the brisket."

"Good." Matt Panner took a step closer, gazed coldly down at Jordan's lifeless body for a moment, then turned away.

"I seen him come skulkin' past the house a li'l while ago," he said. "Recognized him right off. When I'd fetched my shootin' iron, I just trailed him along real careful until I could get in a clean shot. Knew I'd only have the one chanct, an' I meant to make it count."

"You did that, son." Ramsay laid a hand on the boy's shoulder. "You saved both our lives. And we're grateful."

"I'm pleased it turned out that way, sir." As Matt looked up, the man beside him saw that his eyes were red and beginning to fill with tears. "But it wouldn't of made me no difference whether you-all was here or you wasn't. I'd got it to do. I . . . I made a promise on my pappa's grave."

The others from the store had arrived now, drawn by the sound of the shot. While Ramsay nodded his understanding, Mrs. Brooks gathered the boy into her arms.

"There, honey," she whispered as Matt began sobbing quietly against her bosom. "There, now. You done what you'd got to do, and you done it like a man. All on your own. But we're family now, an' we'll stand together from here on out. You don't got to be alone ever again."

A short while later, 'Lias, Mary, Sara Jane and Josh descended the bank to the landing. Davies and the sheriff had already boarded the riverboat, after saying their good-byes a few minutes earlier.

There appeared to be little need for lengthy conversation as everyone shook hands and wished each other well. Sara Jane gave Ramsay a quick hug and ran to join Josh and 'Lias at the gangway, while Mary seemed to hang back and hesitate a moment, before extending a hand and looking up to meet the gambler's eyes.

"You keep well, Mr. Ramsay," she said simply. "And thanks. For everthing." She glanced at Abby, then added more cheerfully, "We'll be lookin' for you-all to come callin', now. The minute you make it down south there to our part of the country. Good neighbors is hard to come by and it'll be a pleasure havin' you both livin' close."

As she turned and stepped aboard, two black clouds huffed from the riverboat's tall smokestacks, and deck-hands hurried to take in the lines before pushing off from land. A minute later a clash of gears started the big paddlewheel churning to drive the *Andrew Jackson* slowly upstream into the interior of Florida.

When they'd waved the travelers out of sight around the first bend, Chance Ramsay glanced at the young woman beside him and placed an arm about her slim waist, smiling in pleasant if unaccustomed contentment.

For he was certain that this was not . . .

THE END

Historical Notes

ALLIGATOR — Earlier name of present-day Lake City.

COVERED WAGONS — Some settlers did indeed use the famed Conestoga wagons to move their goods and families into Florida during the 1800s. But for many these big Pennsylvania-made cargo carriers were not only cumbersome, they were expensive. A few green willow branches and a good-sized piece of canvas were all it took for the average family to turn almost any farm vehicle into a very serviceable "covered wagon."

DINNER — The major meal of the day was customarily eaten between noon and two o'clock in the South. The evening meal was "supper," a light repast consisting of cold meat and leftovers, or perhaps nothing more substantial than buttermilk and cornbread. Breakfast for most settlers was whatever food might remain from the night before — if any.

ENTERPRISE — This town on the north shore of Lake Monroe near present-day DeBary was founded in 1841 by Major Cornelius Taylor, a cousin of future president Zachary Taylor. In the 1870s and 1880s it would become a major steamboat landing and resort for Northern tourists.

THE "FAST DRAW" — Western legend has it that Cullen Baker of Texas was the first to invent and use the "fast draw" during the 1860s. But even if he did develop the special technique of drawing from the hip, he surely was not the first to realize that getting one's weapons into play quickly offered a substantial advantage. It was something any man who faced other armed men in personal combat would have thought about; and a few could be expected to study and practice the skill as diligently as they might dealing seconds from a cold deck.

HOMESTEADING — On August 4, 1842, the U.S. Congress passed the Armed Occupation Act as one means of defending territory vacated by the Indians during the just-concluded Second Seminole War. The Act made available 160 acres of free land in Florida to any homesteader who owned a gun and would promise to defend and "prove up on" his property within five years. Land offices were established in Pensacola, St. Augustine and Newnansville (near present-day Alachua). Over the next decade some 1,600 families took advantage of this opportunity for a new life in Florida.

JACKSONVILLE — Known as the "Cow Ford" until 1824, its population was around 1,500 at the time of this story — the third largest city in Florida after Key West and Pensacola. The downtown business district would be almost completely destroyed by fire a few years later, in 1854.

"THE LATE MR. CALHOUN" — John C. Calhoun of South Carolina, called the "Cast-Iron Man" by admirers and detractors alike, was the most vocal and articulate advocate of individual states' rights during the decades preceding the War Between the States. Until his death in 1850, he never deviated from his belief in the legal right of those commonwealths which had voluntarily entered the Union in 1776 to voluntarily leave it again at the will of their constituents.

MARION COUNTY — Established in 1844; at the time of this story it extended from Orange Lake south to the Hillsboro River.

NAVY COLT — .36 caliber, Model 1851 (but actually placed on the market in 1849). Favored by many early gunfighters, including Wild Bill Hickock. With a 7 1/2-inch rifled barrel, it was accurate and powerful enough to be used for hunting. Colt sold an attachable stock which could turn the weapon into a sort of short-barreled carbine; but this was not popular for a number of reasons.

OKLAWAHA RIVER — In order to have some remote idea of how this scenic spring-fed waterway appeared before the Cross-Florida Barge Canal and the U.S. Corps of Engineers had their devastating impact, it is now necessary to view it south of State Road 40 near Silver Springs. Until the 1960s it was crystal clear and the swiftest-moving river in Florida, with a current estimated in excess of 7 miles per hour.

ORANGE COUNTY — At the time of this story it extended south along Florida's east coast from Matanzas Inlet to Cape Canaveral, and inland as far west as Lake Apopka. Until 1845 it had been known as Mosquito County, named after Mosquito Inlet near present-day New Smyrna Beach. The latter was renamed Ponce de Leon Inlet by tourist-conscious public officials during the 1920s.

PALMER REPEATING RIFLE — Based on an original design by Walter Hunt of New York, this early forerunner of the famed Winchester repeater was first produced in 1850. Its complex reloading mechanism and the requirement for specially made cartridges rendered it unacceptable for military use, and its ownership was generally limited to a few wealthy sportsmen. But in the hands of one who knew how to use it, it could offer a substantial advantage in firepower over other long guns of the day.

PILATKA — Near the site of "Spalding's Lower Store" in British times and an earlier Indian settlement, the town became a major military supply base during the Second Seminole War (1836-42). At the time of this story it was just beginning to recover from an economic depression following the army's withdrawal. Many buildings remained abandoned and vacant. Some twenty-five years later the spelling was officially changed to "Palatka."

SOUTHERN ABOLITIONISTS — Many Southerners spoke out openly against the institution of slavery during Colonial times;

LEE GRAMLING

and it was Southerners who established the African nation of Liberia as a haven for freed slaves. George Washington made provision in his will for his slaves to be released upon his death. Thomas Jefferson, a far more vocal advocate of abolition in his lifetime, never could bring himself to follow suit. With the invention of the cotton gin and the resulting profits to be made from "King Cotton," compounded by growing friction between the distinctive Northern and Southern cultures, things began to change. By the 1850s it had become dangerous in the extreme for a citizen of the South to openly espouse the cause of abolition. And yet some did, right up until the first shots were fired at Fort Sumter, and afterward.

ST. JOHNS RIVER — One of the few North American rivers which flows north. Called *Welaka* by the Timucuan Indians, *Rio de Corrientes* by the early Spanish explorers, the *River of May* by Jean Ribault, and *Rio de San Mateo* by Pedro Menéndez de Aviles, it came to be known as *Rio de San Juan* in the early 1600s after a mission near its mouth of the same name. The British kept this designation after 1763, first as the *St. Juan's*, then the *St. John's*; the apostrophe was dropped in the 1800s. Early settlers liked to tell visitors from the North that the river went "all the way to Hell and blazes." (Lake Helen Blazes, west of present-day Melbourne, is close to its headwaters.)

STEAMBOAT TRAVEL — Almost as soon as Florida became a U.S. territory, steamboats began plying its major waterways, including the St. Johns, Apalachicola and Suwannee rivers. Water had been the preferred means of travel through this thickly forested, swamp-infested wilderness since prehistoric times. But prior to the War Between the States, transportation south of Jacksonville was haphazard at best. The boats periodically carried passengers and goods as far upriver as Lake Monroe — but only when a captain might see some clear hope of profit in the venture. Regularly scheduled passenger service waited for a later age.

VOLUSIA — First platted and recorded as a town in 1834, this settlement on the east bank of the St. Johns south of Lake

George is in fact much older. It was the site of "Spalding's Upper Store" visited by William Bartram in 1774, and had been a well-known river crossing for more than two centuries before that — recorded on maps by both Spanish and French explorers (as Volucia and Velutia respectively) in the 16th century. The huge live oak which still stands near the river served as a landmark for the natives from earliest times. Volusia's residents did indeed re-pel an attack by a raiding party of Indians in 1849.

If you enjoyed reading this book, here are some other fiction titles from Pineapple Press. For a complete catalogue or to place an order, write to Pineapple Press, P.O. Drawer 16008, Southside Station, Sarasota, FL 34239, or call (800) PINEAPL.

Cracker Westerns:

Guns of the Palmetto Plains by Rick Tonyan. As the Civil War explodes over Florida, Tree Hooker dodges Union soldiers and Florida outlaws to drive cattle to feed the starving Confederacy.

Riders of the Suwannee by Lee Gramling. Tate Barkley returns to 1870s Florida just in time to come to the aid of a young widow and her children as they fight to save their homestead from outlaws.

Trail from St. Augustine by Lee Gramling. A young trapper, a crusty ex-sailor, and an indentured servant girl fleeing a cruel master join forces to cross the Florida wilderness in search of buried treasure and a new life.

Other Florida Fiction:

Forever Island and *Allapattah* by Patrick Smith. *Forever Island* has been called the classic novel of the Everglades. *Allapattah* is the story of a young Seminole in despair in the white man's world.

The River is Home and *Angel City* by Patrick Smith. *The River is Home* tells of a Louisiana family's struggle to cope with changes in their rural environment. *Angel City* is a powerful and moving exposé of migrant workers in Florida in the 1970s.

A Land Remembered by Patrick Smith. Three generations of the MacIveys, a Florida family battling the hardships of the frontier to rise from a dirt-poor cracker life to the wealth and standing of real estate tycoons.